SUNSET PARK

By Dana Mansfield

Martin Sisters Publishing

Published by

Ivy House Books, a division of Martin Sisters Publishing, LLC

www. martinsisterspublishing. com

Copyright © 2012 Dana Mansfield

ISBN: 978-1-937273-78-1
Fiction
Printed in the United States of America
Martin Sisters Publishing, LLC

DEDICATION

This book is dedicated to my grandma, the late Elsie Timmons.

ACKNOWLEDGEMENTS

Randee Baron, Frank & Sandi Baron, Dr. Stephen Coyne, Dr. Radha Rao and the staff of the June E. Nylen Cancer Center, Danna Burgess, Stephanie Strain, Betsy Reynolds, Robert McLey, Polly Meissner, Jodie Larson, my early readers Michelle, Becky, Stephanie, Brianne & Twyla, and Allie F. Thank you to my 2010-2011 school year periods 4, 5, and 7, my 2011-2012 school year blocks 1B, 2B, 3A, 4A, and 4B, my 2012-2013 school year blocks 1B, 2A, 3A, 3B, and 4B and my colleagues at West High School. Go Wolverines!

An especially heartfelt thank you to CD & DD for your presence and unknowing support and a big thank you to all my Twitter friends :) .

An imprint of Martin Sisters Publishing, LLC

Chapter One

April 2003

Laurie sat on the rooftop stone patio in the slowly melting light of the early April Monday. The unusually cold and snowy winter that Memphis had experienced finally surrendered and spring, bit by bit, took hold with crisp mornings and promising afternoons. Newness abounded with blades of green emerging in the neighborhood of Sunset Park and soft, fuzzy buds of sleepy trees waking. Robins returned for sunrise services and even Laurie felt the slightest sense of optimism, more than she felt in a very long time. The long, horrible winter was almost over and she hoped that the new season that lay ahead brought better days.

She drained her now chilled cup of tea and sank further back in the weathered Adirondack chair. Exhaustion bore into her bones from the long day cooking in the café's kitchen; the double shifts beginning to take their toll. That moment, as the sun made its final descent and the sky moved from pale blue to pale orange, was her favorite. It gave her strength knowing she made it through another day and hope that she could face the next. Despite itching to head out on her nightly run, Laurie wasn't ready yet to give up the flawless view, relishing in the awesome transition Mother Nature conducted. Laurie took a deep breath of crisp air as the mixed aroma of fresh baked bread and coffee wafted up from the café below. *Perfection.*

The optimism that eluded her for the last two years bubbled a touch within Laurie and she could not wait to share this new discovery with Ben, who also felt burdened by the downward spiral they'd been riding helplessly on. He was due back soon, they would talk, and then she would make her run despite the exhaustion. Although off from his job at the furniture factory, he slipped out early that morning with only a brief nod in her direction as he descended the stairs in the café's kitchen. Laurie felt something was bothering him but they rarely ventured into those deep conversations they once shared so freely. She was guilty of closing off also and the optimistic feeling of just a few moments ago was shoved aside by her ever-present worry and insecurity.

A cardinal landed effortlessly on the wrought iron railing that ran around the patio Laurie shared with the other apartments situated over the café where she worked. Sunset Park Café was owned by her best friend Jamie, who was also Ben's cousin. For ten years, she shared one of the studio apartments with Ben while Jamie shared the larger apartment with her fiancé, Marcus; those two having only cohabitated for the last year despite being a couple since high school. A third studio sat empty, used mainly for storage. The living areas, only accessible by the staircase in the café's kitchen, gave the whole building a very homey feeling and it was home for Laurie. Twelve years earlier, she became The Old Man's foster daughter.

Laurie shivered as a slight breeze kicked up, reminding her that maybe winter was not amused about being replaced. Still, she sat waiting for Ben. It was peaceful on the patio and above all, that's all Laurie wanted – peace. Too many rocky seasons of change and sorrow and fights left her soul tired. All she wanted was a few weeks of just serenity; nothing to worry about, nothing to anticipate. But it was April and as the clichéd saying goes, it is the cruelest month. "Laurie?" a voice behind her called out. She didn't jump as usual, recognizing the controlled Southern drawl of Ben. Her heart warmed and stomach fluttered at the sound of his voice that typically brought her a sense of safety; however, when she looked at his somber face, her soul began to ice. "We need to talk."

Chapter Two

The Players

The circle of friends consisted of a half-dozen individuals. Ben, Teddy, and Marcus were still as close as brothers while at one time, Jamie, Laurie, and Mei Zheng were just like sisters. The entire group went back as far as their diaper days in Sunset Park, a borderline rough neighborhood near the Mississippi River in Memphis. High school arrived and the hormonally charged cat fights between Mei and Jamie strained the group. Mei, volatile on a good day, alienated herself over a decision she forced their sophomore year and since that day, she drifted in and out of the circle. Laurie, the kindest heart of the group next to Ben, always tried to continue the friendship with Mei, both in school and after, despite Mei's repulsive treatment of Laurie. However, Jamie chose to be cautious of the woman. She heard and believed too many of the rumors that sped through Sunset Park.

Blue collar. A touch rough. Loyal. A Phoenix. All were perfect describers of the circle's home neighborhood. At the center was St. Anthony's Catholic Church, the place of worship for most of the neighborhood throughout its existence. Teddy Kelly, one of the circle, was the current priest.

The neighborhood radiated out in a grid from the church beginning with the actual Sunset Park, a calming green space in the often boisterous quarter. The residential areas comprised the next ring of the neighborhood and finally the business district. The Mississippi provided the neighborhood's western border with the Sunset Park Furniture factory to the north and Sunset Park Cannery to the south. The eastern boundary was the worst sore spot of the neighborhood. Blighted row houses greeted visitors on their way into Sunset Park, giving those new to the area a somewhat erroneous opinion of what lay ahead. Thus, after thirty years of decline, gentrification set in beginning with those row houses along with several other rundown domiciles within the neighborhood proper. Times were changing for the best in the area that was bound and determined to buck the violent trends of the past. Sunset Park's history was rich in both good times and bad; the circle was very representative of this.

Chapter Three

April 2008

Jamie Polniacek paced nervously behind the counter of the café. Officially, she was closed for the day, a few hours earlier than normal, but she was still waiting for one individual to arrive at the café and that person was late. It wasn't a customer she waited for; it was her cousin. He called though; that's the way he typically was. Considerate, caring, hard-working, a bit rough around the edges just like the neighborhood. That was her cousin Ben and it was the first time in five years that he was returning home. When he left, it was ugly. Jamie and her soon-to-be-husband Marcus Bailey witnessed most of the fight and it shook them both to the core; so much that it took four years to even discuss setting a wedding date. If Ben and Laurie couldn't make it, then who could?

Two members of Jamie's childhood circle of friends and family were damaged. The damage was only emotional in those first few moments after the fight. Ben left in anger, leaving for Panama City Beach that night, while Laurie, so shocked she couldn't speak, ran down the stairs and into the alley behind the café. Although she always ran in the evenings to de-stress from the café, that night she chose to run instead of talking about what happened. It was a life changing decision and not for the good. Her bad habit of running through the alleys of Sunset Park to get to the running trail next to the Mississippi caught up with her and her assailant held her for four days before dumping her behind the café, bleeding nearly to death from multiple stab wounds. In the end, Laurie's damaged mind, body, and heart retreated inwards and upstairs to the apartment that she no longer shared with Ben. The wall that Laurie added to the walls already encompassing her was so thick that not even a trebuchet could demolish it.

The death of that relationship became the white elephant of the neighborhood and eventually splintered it, changing friends to strangers and enemies. Although most did not stand up and verbally take sides in the matter, it was evident in their actions afterwards that everyone chose Ben's side. Laurie never complained, though. Those who were no longer her friends pathetically felt that she deserved what she got from her attacker. They believed that it was karma for messing up the seemingly perfect relationship even though both Laurie and Ben were at fault and it was Ben that did the walking. Jamie was mortified that even some of their own family actually believed it all. What was worse, a thousand times worse, was that Laurie believed it also.

"Fuck!" Jamie threw down in frustration the damp towel she used to wipe the counter. Reliving the demise of her cousin and her best friend always frustrated her. It was a relief when they all made it through their childhood and adolescence in one piece even though they were all scarred in some way. But honestly, who wasn't scarred from that time of great changes both physically and personally? Yet for Laurie and Ben, they were each other's redeemer. Together they moved past what would have impeded others and when friendship moved into something more, it was as if fate was smiling down on them, finally giving them a break.

But behind that seemingly perfect façade, the nightmares began to eat at Ben and Laurie. The bond weakened and then, with a spectacularly one-sided fight, it was all over. Ben packed up his beat-up truck and left for the Gulf and Laurie went on that ill-fated run. The uncharacteristic silence from Ben towards Jamie in those days and weeks after was unsettling and she eventually stopped begging him to talk about it all. Instead, she moved on and tried to resume the previous relationship with her cousin, minus any mention of Laurie. Jamie had to for her own sanity and to focus on taking care of her best friend.

It hurt Jamie's heart, both to see Laurie whither in the small apartment and to hear from Marcus and Teddy about her cousin's own demise in Panama City Beach. There were certain things Ben wouldn't share with Jamie. He didn't bring up his fall into alcoholism at first; Teddy and Marcus were the ones to tell her about it. She was angry but then saddened to hear about the drinking but eventually, he cleaned himself up and appeared to move on and away from that fateful April night, leaving only Laurie trapped in those nightmarish days and weeks.

Another April was upon them now but this one would see Marcus and Jamie married after a multiyear engagement. Many questioned her choice of wedding date but after so many horrible Aprils, she was bound and determined to redeem the month. Besides, it was getting close for Jamie who wanted to have the ring of gold before the middle of June. Marriage before baby was still her motto even if the marriage was only a few weeks old at birth. Finally, after seven plus years of engagement, Marcus and Jamie set a date the previous April. The pregnancy came as a complete shocker a few months later.

For the first time in a long time, most of the circle would be back together, except for Laurie, as Ben was coming into town to do the honors of walking Jamie down the aisle. When she called to ask him, there was no hesitation in his voice. Of course, the wedding would be a safe zone for Ben and everyone else. Even though Laurie was her best friend and rightly should be her maid of honor, she would not be in attendance at the nuptials. That would have required Laurie to leave her apartment and that was just something Laurie no longer could do. Three years had passed since the last time she crossed the threshold and even then, it wasn't under her own power.

Jamie didn't even attempt to talk Laurie into going; she knew it would be a futile effort trying to get her out of the apartment even for the wedding. She used up all her energies on that front four years earlier, using her colorful verbal arsenal to come short of excommunicating her. That was just something even Jamie could not do to her best friend. It was too close to what Ben did and she didn't want to even entertain any thoughts on what Laurie might do if Jamie went down that same path. And as Marcus pointed out during the most heated days of that argument, Jamie was legally bound to take care of Laurie now.

And besides, Jamie wanted her wedding to be a happy event after so many years of darkness and with the presence of Laurie, there was a rather large chance that the wedding might not be everything Jamie wanted it to be. Despite the fact that it was Ben that did the walking, too many people blamed Laurie for the breakup. They even went so far as to blame her for her own abduction and what happened during those four days. Those that blamed her included other Sunset Parkians, who knew Ben and Laurie all their life, along with members of Laurie's own estranged family. The blamers were not silent on the matter either. If Laurie made in appearance, hurtful words would be said and Jamie was just having none of that if she could help it. She knew that with Ben's involvement in the wedding there would be some commentary but much less if both Ben and Laurie were in attendance together.

Jamie sat down at a table next to the front window and put her feet up. The pregnancy was not planned and the morning sickness rough. Marcus wanted her to stop working in the café after an early scare but even Doc Jr., the son of their childhood doctor, said it was okay for her to return to work. Marcus tried to pull the 'I can handle it all' routine but Jamie knew better. The café, even one as small as Sunset Park Café, needed four full-time employees. Jamie, along with one of Marcus's younger sisters, manned the front while Marcus and his younger brother Louis took care of the kitchen. Many of the recipes they served went back to when The Old Man ran the place. In addition, both Laurie, when she still worked in the café's kitchen, and Jamie added their own items to the comfortable menu. Everything ran like a finally-tuned machine; the only missing piece was Laurie. Sunset Park Café was Jamie's pride and joy, soon to be vying for that spot with the tater tot she was incubating.

Jamie heard the tinkling bell of the café's service door in the kitchen and another member of the circle came through the swinging doors that divided the kitchen from the dining room. Very tall, athletic, blonde and blue eyed, Teddy Kelly was quite the looker. He was also very much taken as the black button down shirt with white notch at the neck indicated. Teddy broke many a girl's heart when he announced his intention of becoming a priest. He could easily have chosen any path from entertainment to business but his calling came early when they were all still in junior high.

"Ben here yet?" Teddy asked and gave Jamie a peck on the cheek.

"No, but he called and said he would be about an hour late. Ran into some traffic coming through Birmingham," she explained. "You haven't missed him."

"Good, I'm going to change," he said and disappeared into the men's restroom at the back of the dining room. Although a dedicated cleric, there were times when he chose to kick back with his longtime friends. Teddy returned looking very much non priest-like in a pair of ripped jeans and faded Sunset Park High t-shirt.

"So, how are your nerves?" he asked.

"Nervy," she replied and they laughed. Jamie spilled her guts to Teddy a few days earlier about how nervous she was with Ben coming into town for the wedding considering everything that happened with Laurie.

"And how's Laurie been today?" he asked.

"Her usual self; no mention of Ben at all. Marcus is with her now." She shrugged her shoulders. At a certain point of time, that's all one could do. Marcus came through the swinging doors at that moment with a tray of glasses and a pitcher of the café's famous iced tea. Teddy did the honors of pouring three glasses.

"How's Laurie?" Jamie asked after a long drink.

"Quiet," he replied after a moment of thought.

"Did she eat?"

"No," he replied with a sigh. "She picked. Again."

"Fuck," she muttered under her breath. Jamie chewed her bottom lip. She didn't know if this new issue, Laurie's lack of appetite, had something to do with Ben's involvement in the wedding or if it was another reaction to the attack that happened five years earlier. The kidnapping and what happened during those four days exacerbated many of Laurie's issues and she was a therapist's dream. That therapist happened to be Marcus. Although he left private practice from burnout six months earlier, he continued to work with Laurie as she refused to see anyone else. He was the second person, behind Jamie, to acknowledge that Laurie was often an exercise in futility but still he tried out of a family-like love, mainly to make sure she wasn't a threat to herself. Again. Teddy was the only one that believed she wasn't a lost cause. It would have been his belief even if he wasn't a priest; that's the way Teddy was. The man believed in hope.

Jamie's thoughts of Laurie were distracted by a familiar sound. From down the street she could see, and hear, Ben's beat up but trusty white Ford chugging its way towards the café. She hadn't seen him since he walked out on Laurie, the café and Laurie taking up all her time, but they spoke and texted nearly every day once past those initial weeks after the breakup. A handful of times Marcus and Teddy visited Ben in Panama City Beach but Jamie was always too busy with the café to head to Florida. Or so she told herself.

She stood and was surprised at how fast her heart was beating and her palms were all sweaty. Marcus put a reassuring hand on her back and whispered into her ear. "It'll be okay."

"I hope so," she whispered back.

"CJ!" Ben hollered when he hopped out of the truck. CJ, short for Cousin Jamie, was his nickname for her and called her that since they were little. They embraced, a bit awkwardly due to the baby bump.

"It's so good to see you," she said as she held him in a tight hug. "Five years is too long, Ben, too long. Don't fucking do that again." Jamie felt her emotions starting to go wacky so she quickly broke the embrace and held him at arm's length to get a good look at him. Beneath his attire of jean jacket, black t-shirt, worn jeans, and black work boots, he was compact and muscular. A high school wrestler, he had landed a job in construction in Panama City Beach and the physical side of that vocation had done him good. Ben hadn't shaved in a day or two and it just added to his rugged handsomeness. He looked very much like he did on that April night five years ago, even keeping the shaved head to distinguish himself from his abusive father whom Ben looked eerily, and sadly, like. The only true difference she saw in her cousin was in his deep brown eyes. They used to sparkle and hint at his good nature and heart but now, they were dull and pained, just like Laurie's blue eyes.

"And look at the mini CJ!" he exclaimed as his hands hovered above Jamie's bump. Unlike most strangers, he did not seem to think it was okay to just start feeling her up without permission.

"Hey, Marcus," Ben said after the stereotypical man hug and back pound. "Finally making an honest woman out of her, I see."

"Honestly," Marcus said with his hands up innocently. "It was her idea. She just told me when and where to be for this shindig." They all laughed in good humor though.

"Stretch," Ben said and moved on to Teddy. Stretch was another nickname as Teddy towered over everyone. Of course, Teddy countered the nickname with his own.

"Shorty," he laughed and they repeated the bromance actions.

Just as they settled in at the table with a new round of iced tea, Marcus's cell phone chirped. His face fell when he read the text.

"Go ahead and go," Jamie said wearily. "How much bail money this time?"

"It's not my turn," he replied and stood. "It's Louis's turn. He just needs a ride to the jail to spring Cassie. I'll see you later," he said and gave Jamie a quick kiss and then fist bumped Ben. "We'll catch up later."

"Looking forward to it," Ben replied, then waited until Marcus was out of earshot before asking his question. "Sassy Cassie still giving him fits?"

"Yes," Jamie said and shook her head. "I still can't believe how different Callie and Cassie are considering they're twins. Marcus hoped Cassie would stay clean until the wedding but she's been picked up twice now for shoplifting, probably wanting to sell the goods for drug money just like before. I assume it's the same this time."

"He deserves a medal for taking care of that spitfire," Teddy noted.

"That he does," Jamie agreed and looked out the window. The back of Ben's truck was visible and for a moment, she wasn't sure she was actually seeing what she was seeing. "Ben," she finally said, looking at him through suspicious eyes. "You have too much baggage in the back of your truck for just a few days." She paused and contemplated. "Are you moving back here?" Ben's first response was to sigh and not make eye contact with Jamie.

"Construction has slowed, CJ," he explained. "The economy, you know?" Jamie was torn on how to react. She was glad that Ben was back and for more than just the wedding weekend but there was Laurie to think about. Then she mentally kicked herself;

Laurie never left her apartment. It really didn't matter that Ben would be living in the same city again.

"So do you have a job lined up here yet?" Teddy asked. A broad grin spread across his face and Jamie could tell that his excitement at having Ben back equaled hers.

"No. I just found out I was laid off two days ago. Figured I'd put some feelers out at the wedding, maybe swing by the headquarters of the gentrification company and see if they need any help in the neighborhood."

"You're a jack-of-all-trades, Ben, that'll help," replied Jamie. He was talented in many hands-on tasks.

"You know I'm up for any honest work," he said and turned to Teddy. "If you need any help around St. Anthony's, let me know." Of the five others in the circle, not counting Teddy since he was a priest, Ben was the one with the most faith. He was quietly devout much like his mother had been. His father, on the other hand, had been a brimstone breathing atheist.

Later, as the sun set and Teddy was called away to the neighborhood hospital, Ben and Jamie moved to the patio on the second floor of the building. The space held a rooftop greenhouse that both Jamie and Marcus enjoyed growing some of their ingredients for the café's offerings. An awkward inner city oak tree stretched up from the alley and offered shade for much of the patio; a godsend during the humid Southern summers.

It was a peaceful evening punctuated by the hypnotic drone of crickets. It had been a warm April day and the night was comfortable, serene. Jamie enjoyed every minute of her time with Ben so far, knowing that starting with the next day the nuptials would take most of her time. She would probably see less and less of Ben but she was okay with this; after all, he was moving back to town and she could see him a lot more often. Call and he'd be there. That's the way he always was – an honest friend willing to do anything if help was needed. To put it succinctly, Ben was just a darn good guy. Well, for the most part. She called once for him to return to Memphis and her pleas went unanswered. It was their own white elephant; one that Jamie didn't have the energy to address at that moment.

There was actually a lot nagging her about him that built up over the last five years. Maybe it was their long, long history that included her dad (Ben's uncle) gaining custody of him when they were fourteen or the more recent history – Laurie – but all of a sudden Jamie found herself wanting to know more about the ugly stuff. Not just what he was thinking five years ago but how he lived with himself down in Panama City. Jamie understood that Laurie was only partly to blame but she just needed to know more in regards to Ben and his reasons. She also wanted to know how much he knew about how far Laurie fell in the last five years. She knew he didn't know about the suicide attempt; Laurie made them all promise not to tell him. Jamie was actually glad about this; it took Ben a lot of strength to climb on the wagon and she didn't want him to fall off.

She sighed. The whole Laurie-Ben issue took a lot of energy which she didn't have much of lately with the café, the wedding, and the baby. Jamie also didn't want to ruin a perfectly good reunion evening and she sighed again.

"Okay, CJ, spill it," Ben said and refilled her glass from the iced tea pitcher. "You're sighing as if the weight of the world is dragging you down."

"No," she said after a few moments. "Just…thoughts."

"Thoughts you want to share?"

"No, not yet," she replied honestly. Now that he was back, there would be a time when she would share those thoughts; she was too tired at the moment.

They chitchatted for a little while longer until her eyes started to droop. Even though the café would be closed the next four days, there was still a ton to do and she needed to start early. She also needed to be hospitable; after all, she was Southern. Maybe a little too liberal with the f-bomb to be a Belle, but she still knew her manners. "Do you need a couch for the night?"

"I was going to ask Stretch if I could bunk in the rectory but he left before I had a chance so…" He let his voice trail off and Jamie noticed him flick his eyes very briefly towards the windows of Laurie's apartment. "I do, but…" Jamie knew where he was going and she was honest.

"Don't worry about it. She doesn't leave her apartment and you'll be in ours." It was the first almost mention of Laurie.

Chapter Four

Delicate Predicament

The wedding was exactly what Jamie wanted – simple but fun. It was even good to have the circle together again, except for Laurie. She was there in spirit, to Jamie at least. She wasn't sure how Laurie did it, she guessed that Callie had been Laurie's partner-in-crime, but in her bouquet of white roses she found a small note of heartfelt sentiments from Laurie.

The only part of the festivities that angered Jamie was those individuals who spoke badly of Laurie. Jamie knew this would happen but it was still tough for her to hear on her wedding day. They weren't just making light of Laurie; they were darn right rude and disgusting. The worst was, of course, Mei. Jamie felt obligated to invite Mei despite their cold relationship.

It was Mei who voiced her wish that Laurie had been successful the night she tried to kill herself. *You'd think someone who used to work in a kitchen would know how to use a knife properly* was her comment to those she held court with, all of whom laughed. Jamie was so taken back by that comment that instead of her usual colorful remarks involving a few four letter words, all she could do was turn on her heel and hide out for a few minutes in the bathroom as she dried her tears. Jamie rarely cried and the awful comment really hit her hard. But Marcus talked her out of the bathroom after Teddy took off his priest's collar for a few minutes and chewed Mei out. Mei took his suggestion and left the reception.

Ben was, as Jamie knew he would be, perfect throughout the wedding days. He completed a bunch of errands for her, stuffed several tulle bags with bird seed, and been quite the handsome man in his suit and tie as he walked her down the aisle. However, the next day things turned scary.

Although she didn't overdo it at the wedding, Jamie did not feel well when she woke up the next day and by noon, she was having sporadic contractions. After a trip to the ER, Doc Jr. was able to stop the labor but put her on bed rest for the next eight weeks. It was a quick and somber conclusion that having only three individuals working the café was a recipe for financial disaster. They had saved up to allow the café to be closed for the wedding but there was no way they could survive losing any business for their lack of hands.

Marcus paced as Jamie went over the café's spreadsheets on her laptop as she began day one of fifty-six of bed rest. They knew that eventually they would have to address Jamie being out of the café for maternity leave, at least for two or three weeks, but that was supposed to be eight weeks away and a much shorter time period than what they were facing now. They had less than twenty-four hours to find a solution.

"I know it's a long shot," Jamie started, not even knowing why she was proposing what she was about to propose. "But we could ask Cassie if she could help."

"No," Marcus said quickly. "She's not to step foot in this place." Marcus rarely allowed his anger to show but Sassy Cassie always managed to bring it out. When Louis paid her bail, it wasn't for shoplifting, it was for prostitution and Marcus finally put his foot down. As the oldest man in the Bailey family, he decided it was time for them all to show the youngest some tough love. Sassy Cassie was on her own now until she realized how much help she needed. They tried several interventions before but none of them ever worked. Cassie needed to hit rock bottom.

"I'm out of suggestions," Jamie said in frustration. Although Mrs. Bailey sometimes helped out with pouring coffee, she wasn't up to full-time work in the café. They needed someone full-time but really couldn't afford to pay someone for full-time work. "Maybe our only hope is Laurie," she joked.

"That's not even funny," Marcus replied dryly. Jamie knew that within the last year all of Laurie's issues had grown worse and the only reason why Marcus broke therapist-client confidentiality is that he felt that it might only be a matter of time before Laurie would need the next level of care – institutionalization – and Jamie held power of attorney over Laurie. It would need to be her decision to put Laurie away in the loony bin. Deep down Jamie already knew her best friend was on this path; it wasn't a matter of 'if' anymore, it was a matter of 'when,' unless a miracle came along. And that's why when she realized that Ben was moving back to town that 'when' date could be closer than anyone realized. She had no idea what his prolonged presence back in Sunset Park would eventually do to Laurie. At first she didn't think it would matter but as fragile as Laurie was, no one knew for sure how she would handle the news.

Ben.

Jamie groaned and held her head in her hands. Marcus was at her side in an instant and was nearly to the second one in 911 on his cell phone before she snatched it from him and stopped him from making an ass out of himself.

"I'm fine," she said.

"You didn't sound okay," he replied impatiently.

"I just realized that I have a solution to the problem."

"And it caused you to groan like you were back in labor? What kind of solution is this? It can't be…" Jamie reached out and clamped her hand down on her new husband's mouth.

"Will you be quiet for just a minute, Marcus?" Jamie closed her eyes and took several deep breaths; she needed to lower her stress level or she would end up back in the hospital. "Ben was not very successful with finding any leads for employment at the wedding and the construction company doing the gentrification work has no openings yet. I know if we ask him, he'd help us out in a heartbeat."

"I know he's a good guy but I'm sure he'd like to get paid and we can't really afford a livable paycheck right now." Jamie already had an answer for that.

"We let him keep any tips he gets and he could clear out the other apartment and live there." Marcus rubbed his face and appeared deep in thought.

"From a business standpoint, I see it as a good solution."

"But?" Jamie asked, knowing her husband.

"I think we need to let Laurie make the decision, don't you? It's one thing if Ben is here for an hour or two every couple of days visiting but to live under the same roof? I think for her own…"

"Sanity?" Jamie piped in and immediately felt sorry for saying it. "God that was awful," she chided herself. "Her own family rejected her and we're the only ones left and I go and basically call her crazy." A surge of tears welled up in her. "I can't believe I said that, Marcus. My god, after everything she's been through and I'm making light of how that's left her mentally."

Marcus sat next to her and gave her a hug.

"She has issues; she'd admit it, Jamie, and those issues aren't without merit. But we also have to think of those issues with this decision. That's why I thought she should make it."

"Do you think she's capable of making that decision?" she asked slowly. "I mean for her own good? She's not going to put her own feelings ahead of us. That's one of the reasons why Ben left her. She never thinks of herself."

Marcus sighed. "You have a good point."

"I always do, honey."

Chapter Five

Like Sisters

Jamie waited until the next day to sneak next door to talk to Laurie. Marcus wanted to try and convince Laurie into coming to their apartment since Jamie was on bed rest but Jamie knew that would never fly. She was allowed to walk to the bathroom so she figured that she would just use the bathroom in Laurie's apartment. It was just a technicality.

Marcus and Jamie stayed up late the night before discussing the situation and decided there was no choice but to ask Ben for help regardless of what Laurie said. As a business, they needed to survive the next eight weeks. They decided to just tell Laurie and hope for the best.

"Laurie?" Jamie called after knocking gently on the door. If Jamie didn't announce herself first, Laurie wouldn't come to the door to even see who it was. That's how scared she was of the outside world. "Laurie? It's Jamie. I'd like to come in and talk to you." She waited at the door hoping the baby wouldn't take offense. Finally, she heard the unlocking of the five deadbolts that kept the outside world where it belonged. The door opened a couple inches, the chain still securing the door. Laurie was nothing more than a profile in the low light from the apartment. "May I come in?"

"You should be lying down," Laurie replied in a nervous whisper. "Marcus told me what happened."

"I will but I need to talk to you. It's important." Laurie finally opened the door just enough to let Jamie in. Once inside, Laurie quickly relocked the door with shaking hands. For several moments she checked and rechecked the locks until Jamie put a gentle hand on her best friend's arm to silently stop the maddening loop.

"Sorry," Laurie needlessly said. Jamie wanted to argue that Laurie needed to learn to stop being sorry for everything but she flogged that dead horse too many times in the past. So had Ben; it was another reason why he left.

Jamie headed farther into the small apartment. It truly wasn't much more than a glorified studio – a main room with small kitchenette, a sleeping alcove, and a bathroom. The studio sat in the back of the building and the barred windows, along with a small door, overlooked the rooftop patio. However, Laurie covered up those windows with heavy drapes, although Jamie knew that on occasion, Laurie might actually open the door in the darkness of night and slip out onto the patio to sit with Teddy. It was a contradiction in how Laurie now lived but Marcus could never get her to tell him why she did it and why only with Teddy. *I just need to*, that's all she would say. When Jamie asked Teddy about it, he would remain mum also.

A single floor lamp lit the space and even then, it did a poor job of illumination. Jamie could remember how the apartment looked before the fight. Small but homey and both Ben and Laurie put their own spin to the décor. Now, those touches were hidden in shadows, to keep those memories in the dark. Laurie also kept herself in the dark when anyone was in the apartment. She wanted no one to see the scars, to see how the attack left her, both physically and mentally.

"Can I get you some water?" Laurie asked. Her voice, damaged from one of the knife wounds, was rarely above a loud whisper. Anything louder than that caused her pain. There was also a light slur to her voice after a blood clot caused a stroke a week after the attack. Insult to injury, that's what that was.

"I'm okay," Jamie replied and made herself comfortable on the large and very comfortable couch. She put her feet up on the coffee table. Laurie limped closer; her right foot dragging just slightly behind her. She took a seat in a straight back chair just outside of the circle of light from the floor lamp. Jamie could see her right arm and hand tucked against her abdomen while her left one began to fiddle with the hem of her sweatshirt. Her long, dark brown hair was loose and Jamie realized that with all the hubbub around the baby scare, she forgot to come over and braid Laurie's hair as usual. With only one good hand, Laurie was unable to do it herself.

"Why don't you come over here and I'll do your hair?" Jamie suggested.

"You're supposed to be resting," Laurie replied quietly.

"Bed rest," she countered, "and besides, it's braiding hair, not too stressful." Laurie still seemed hesitant but this was just the way Laurie was and it was that way that Ben found fault in. "Get your brush and I'll tell you about the wedding and reception." This prospect appeared to pique her best friend's interest. Slowly, Laurie stood and retrieved her hairbrush.

When Laurie stepped into the light, she did her best to try and face herself away from Jamie even after five years but Jamie never saw the scars; she only saw her fragile best friend.

"Sit here," she said with a light voice and patted the spot next to her on the couch. Laurie complied and as Jamie brushed and then braided the dark brown hair that smelled of peaches from Laurie's shampoo, she described the ceremony and reception at the Sunset Park Ballroom. Of course, Jamie left out all the ugly comments Mei and the others made about Laurie. "There, all done," she said. Laurie used her good hand to pull the long, thick braid over her shoulder.

"Thank you," Laurie said and picked up the remote for her DVD player. Jamie recognized the DVD that Callie, Cassie's twin sister, put together of the wedding ceremony and reception specifically for Laurie. "You were a beautiful bride."

"Despite looking like a beach ball," Jamie laughed and she saw a small smile on Laurie's face. They continued watching the video as Laurie asked questions or made comments. It was nice talking, just the two of them. It reminded Jamie of some of the better times.

Jamie enjoyed seeing Laurie's smile grow as she continued to watch but then it faded quickly. When Jamie looked at the screen, she saw herself dancing with Ben. Laurie's face became sad and Jamie noticed her quickly wipe away an escaped tear. She quickly turned the TV off and turned her face away from Jamie. It seemed like the perfect opening. Jamie took Laurie's hand in hers.

"Ben is moving back to Memphis and because I won't be able to work down in the café for a couple months, we're going to have Ben help us. He'll also be staying in the spare apartment." There, she said it.

"Okay," replied Laurie in a voice that relayed nothing about how she was feeling.

"We don't have a choice," Jamie explained. "We can't afford to hire someone full time."

"Okay," Laurie said again.

"I wanted you to know," Jamie found herself saying a bit lamely.

"Okay," Laurie said one final time.

Chapter Six

A Coward's Truth

"And that's all she said?" Marcus asked as he put a bed tray in front of his wife. "Okay?"

"Yes. Three times. And then I had to pee. When I came out of the bathroom she had retreated into the sleeping nook and pulled the curtains." Jamie frowned at her turkey sandwich Marcus brought her. She was hungry but not hungry for a sandwich and really, all she wanted was a big bowl of pasta with lots of gooey cheese instead of the more reasonable sandwich.

"I'll see if I can get her to talk later when I bring her dinner." He sat across from Jamie on the bed with his own turkey sandwich. "You'll get your pasta for dinner," he said with a grin. "And Louis is making your favorite coconut cream pie."

"I can't wait," she said and decided the turkey sandwich wasn't so bad in anticipation of pie. "Did you call Ben?"

"Yes and just as we figured, he said he'd help us. Teddy's got him doing some handiwork at the church and so Ben will be by a little later to move in."

"Good," she replied and felt several pounds of tension leave her shoulders. She ate a few more bites of her sandwich, then realized that her new husband was awfully quiet. Looking up, she could tell something was on his mind. "Coconut cream pie...What's going on? What did you do?" Marcus looked up, a very guilty look on his face.

"You've got to promise me not to get upset; I don't want to have to haul you back to the hospital."

"Well," she said in exasperation. "When you start out saying that, I'm going to get fucking upset."

"I know," he said and moved closer to her so he could rub her shoulders.

"Marcus, what the fuck is going on?"

"When I called Ben, he said he'd help us..."

"You've already told me that," she singsonged.

"Let me finish, sweetie," he instructed in a slightly patronizing voice. "But please take a few deep breaths first." Jamie went to object but Marcus planted a kiss on her to stop her. "Deep breaths," he said again. Jamie knew Marcus very well and whatever was on his mind was serious. She took seven deep breaths and then braced herself. "When Ben said he would help us, he asked me to do him a favor."

"And that favor is?"

"To break a secret," he replied in a grave voice.

"Why did he ask you to break a secret?"

"He needs you to know this... information but he wasn't sure if he could tell you."

Jamie frowned. Other than the issues surrounding his silence after Laurie's abduction, they never kept secrets from each other as far as she knew. Apparently, that was no longer the case.

"Does it have to do with why he refused to fucking talk to me after what happened to Laurie?"

"No, not at all. That's still something that's locked up deep inside of him," Marcus said in his therapist voice.

"Just tell me what it is then," she said. All of a sudden she was very tired and didn't want to play the game anymore.

"Well, there are two things actually but we've always lumped them together and really one of them you kind of already…"

"Marcus, please," she said, her patience gone.

"You know that Ben started drinking while in Florida and that after nine months he sobered up."

"Right, just a brief blip." Marcus cringed when she said that. "It wasn't a brief blip?"

"No. He was only sober for about three months before he started in again."

"For how long?"

"Three years. He went into rehab the day after you asked him to walk you down the aisle."

"Three years?" Her anger flared. "Fucking coward," she spat. "He's been a fucking coward these last five years." There was no need for him to lie to her about his sobriety. The last five years were trying her patience with him.

"That's exactly how he described himself, Jamie. He flat out called himself a coward for not being able to tell you sooner and then asking me to tell you now."

"Why did he lie to me?"

"Ben knew you had your hands full between the café and Laurie. He didn't want to add to your stress," Marcus explained and continued massaging her shoulders.

Jamie's anger quickly died but was replaced with sadness.

"Three years," she said. "He must have been hurting."

"He was. The guilt he felt about everything related to Laurie was immense. Still is."

"Bastard," Jamie muttered. She picked up her cell phone and began a text to Ben. *You could have told…* That's as far as she got before Marcus took her phone.

"I'm not done," he said and it was his turn to take a deep breath. "It wasn't just alcohol he abused, Jamie." She closed her eyes and waited for the other shoe to fall. "He was also a heroin addict."

Her anger flared again. She couldn't believe the stupidity of her cousin.

"He should have fucking told me," she growled.

"I know. You guys have never kept secrets from each other but he just didn't want to make matters worse." Marcus kissed the top of Jamie's head and brushed back her wild and red Irish (from her mom's side) curls. "How are you feeling?"

"Baby-wise fine," she said. "I'm very pissed at Ben, though."

"He knew you would be and he said you could yell at him all you want but not until after the baby comes."

"And I will," she said but then took her phone back. "Let me just text him one thing."

You could have told me but I understand why you didn't. Once this tater tot is popped, watch out, fucker! She wasn't sure if she was actually kidding about that.

Chapter Seven

Back Home

By midnight, Ben settled into the small apartment that overlooked the front street. It was a mirror image of the apartment he shared with Laurie for so long but it lacked the warmth of that previous dwelling. The walls were in need of a paint job and he spent a good half hour using a Shop-Vac on the scuffed wood floors getting all the dust up. The furniture was sparse – a bed in the sleeping alcove, The Old Man's lumpy couch, a card table with a couple chairs and a dresser. It wasn't much but it already felt more like a home than the furnished rat trap he rented in the bad part of Panama City Beach. When you drank and shot up most of your earnings, you couldn't afford the best surroundings.

The furniture he did once own, he left in Laurie's apartment and when he packed that night five years ago, he took only his clothes and two footlockers of items – some photos, family mementos, and copies of his favorite books. That's all he had for possessions but he was never one for collecting things. For Ben, life was more about the people and not the stuff.

Unfortunately, he ended up treating the people he cared about the most worst. It was time now to make amends. When Jamie asked for his help, of course he said yes; he couldn't turn her down, especially in their current desperate time of need. It was also his way of making up for the fact that he lied about his drinking and drug abuse to her. He knew from the text message she sent him that she took the truth roughly and he wasn't looking forward to the day she confronted him about it. He could deal with that later. For now, he found himself in a perfect solution. An honest job, a roof over his head, a little pocket money. For the most part, that's all he needed at that moment.

He sat on the side of the bed and tried to rub the stress of the last few days from his face. A variety of emotions ripped through him in the four days since pulling up in front of the café and he did not expect them to dissolve easily. There was fear at seeing Jamie for the first time in five years, worry about what people might say at the wedding and a ton of Laurie anxiety in general. When he saw how beautiful his cousin looked before he walked her down the aisle, he felt nothing but joy and happiness. A different fear and worry hit him when Marcus took Jamie to the hospital and then relief when she came back home. Nervous excitement followed the phone call from Marcus where he was offered the job in the café and a place to live. Fear returned again as he wondered how Jamie would take the news of his extended drinking and drug abuse and that fear was relieved a bit after Marcus told her. And now he felt a slight surge of optimism. Just a small amount but it was enough for him to look forward to the coming days.

He slipped off his long sleeve t-shirt and caught site of the crooks of his arms. It was just over a year since the last time he shot up but the scars were still there. Maybe not as visible as Ben believed; he often covered them at his most pathetic moments. The yearning for a hit was bad enough but seeing the scars often weakened him to the point of wondering where he could score just enough to make the pain go away.

Shame exploded within Ben. To differentiate himself from his drunken father, Ben added heroin to his arsenal. The crash from the brief euphoria deepened the guilt he tried to eradicate and he would begin the vicious cycle all over again. Ben wished he never took the needle when presented to him; the cravings for heroin were ten times worse than the craving for Jack Daniels.

"Stop it," he told himself aloud. The year sober taught him to stop the fall downwards before he lost it completely and he focused on what was important at that moment. Ben pulled off his boots, then stripped to his boxers. Five in the morning would come quickly but he was far from tired. Leaning back on the bed, his thoughts immediately went to Laurie. How could they not? She was entwined so deep into his soul that death would be the only way to separate them.

With his first stretch of sobriety, alcohol being his only drug at that time, he finally accepted what a huge mistake he made in walking out on her but what he could never forgive himself for was not coming back when he was begged by the two most important women in his life. Bits and pieces of those messages haunted him whether he was sober or drunk. No matter how much he drank, and later injected, he could never get away from those words. *Missing, abducted, knife wounds, stroke, life support, coma, raped...* Over and over they haunted him. He was numb; unable to do the right thing after leaving her. And then Ben did the one thing he promised himself he would never do – he went into a bar and took a drink. It was a split second decision that turned him right into his father, minus the physical abuse.

Ben languished in the bottle before realizing that drinking wasn't solving his problems and he went to his first AA meeting but stayed sober for only three months. It was April; one year after the breakup and Laurie's nightmare began. There was no thought other than trying to forget everything and back to the bottle he went and eventually, the needle when it was offered. For three years he used and abused but even at that he failed and after Jamie asked him to walk her down the aisle, he turned to his old sponsor for help. Ben did ninety days in treatment and it was during rehab that he realized his only hope for long term sobriety was to face his darkest fear – Laurie. Another April came and he was back in Memphis and Sunset Park. Hopefully, he would find the strength he needed and make amends. If he couldn't, deep down he knew that his next round with heroin would be his last. Only once did he come close to overdosing and that offer of complete absolution of his pain had been very tempting.

The streetlights cast a pale beam on the wall behind Ben. He wondered if Laurie was lying in the old brass bed just a few inches away from his own head on the other side. Quietly, he sat up and put his ear to the wall and listened. Nothing. It was silly for him to even try to hear what was going on next door but that's how bad he was hurting inside for his huge mistake.

Ben settled back into bed and with horrific whispers of past regrets bouncing around his head, he fell into a fitful sleep.

Chapter Eight

First Day Jitters

Ben's first day in the café was going great despite how nervous he was to see so many people who knew his background. Not the drinking and drug part but the Laurie part. The café was busy after being closed for four days and some of the older clientele wanted details on the wedding and then details about why Jamie wasn't there.

Jamie's biggest supporters were a group of ladies who had bonded over the years as policemen's wives. One of those individuals was Marcus's own mother. Marcus's father had been the local beat cop. It was Officer David Bailey who arrested Ben's father the night he murdered Ben's mother and he was also the arresting officer when Laurie's father tried to burn their house down with Laurie locked in the attic. And it was Marcus's father who found Laurie in the alley five years earlier, bleeding out. It was just three years ago, weeks away from his retirement, that Officer Bailey was gunned down while assisting with a drug bust in the next neighborhood over. That's when Marcus's mother joined the group that met daily in the café; she needed the distraction from her pain.

The clientele of Sunset Park Café reflected the old neighborhood, a combination of kind souls who had seen many, many days, and the new neighborhood, an ever increasing population of the next generation coming back to Sunset Park to be part of the revitalization of their childhood home. The coffee, both regular and fancy, was a hit along with the simple food and desserts. Good food, good conversation, a great combination.

Jamie and Laurie both began working for The Old Man during high school and although he was as crotchety as they came, he took a liking to both of them and after graduation, sent Jamie to culinary school and trained Laurie himself in his kitchen. The current menu combined both The Old Man's food along with additions by Laurie and Jamie. A black and white picture of The Old Man stood next to the cash register.

When he left the café to Jamie, there were two provisions that The Old Man demanded in his will. The first was that Jamie had to rename the place. 'Old Man's' didn't go with Jamie's delicate features and wild Irish curls. The second was that Jamie watch over Laurie. This stipulation always stymied Marcus a bit. Nothing could separate Jamie and Laurie; she didn't need it spelled out in a legal document that she look after her best friend. The only thing he could think of was that The Old Man had seen the horrific conditions Laurie grew up in and after being abandoned by her family, he wanted to make sure that there was always someone there to take care of her. What was ironic is that eventually Jamie would actually become legally responsible for Laurie. Did The Old Man have some sort of premonition that Ben would one day leave her and she would need someone to care for her?

But Jamie always took care of Laurie and had for as long as they were friends going back to the toddler years. The core of the circle – Jamie, Ben, himself, Teddy, Laurie, Mei – had known each other since they were all wearing diapers and the first clear memory Marcus had of Jamie's devotion to Laurie was set on their first day of kindergarten.

The six of them were sent on their way to Sunset Park Elementary as a group, five of them wearing brand spanking new outfits, while Laurie, however, wore a faded dress that had seen better days in the previous decade along with dingy white sneakers. This would not do for Jamie and after pulling Laurie back into her house, Jamie dressed her in one of her other new outfits and shoes. Off they went to start their education. Later that night, Sunset Park heard how upset Laurie's father was at the wardrobe change and the next day, the group saw on Laurie what her father's anger looked like. Where Ben's dad was just a son of a bitch when he drank, Laurie's father was an evil man twenty-four hours a day. He didn't need a drink to hurt his family.

The noon rush came and went on Ben's first day and Ben, Louis and Callie were eating their own lunch in the kitchen as Marcus fixed Laurie's plate. He tried to make it as healthy as possible and said a silent prayer that she would eat. Her only source of food was what they brought up from the cafe, other than the pizza Teddy would bring her, and the fact that she resorted to picking at her food the last couple weeks worried him greatly. Her once athletic runner's body was nothing more than a brittle shell now and she couldn't last much longer if she didn't start eating more. Marcus would give her another week before saying anything and if she still didn't increase her intake, he would be forced to have Jamie use her power of attorney.

"Keep an eye on the front?" he asked Ben as he picked up the tray.

"Sure, Marcus," his friend replied and Marcus ascended the stairs in the kitchen. After unlocking the five deadbolts Laurie asked him to install, he entered the stale air of the apartment. Feeding Laurie had become routine but that's what she needed in her skewed mind.

As usual, the light above the small table near the kitchenette was on. It was the only thing providing light during lunch. Out of the corner of his eye he saw Laurie standing near the bathroom door. He relocked the door, set down the tray and then sat down himself. A long time ago when he would rush from his office to bring Laurie's lunch, she asked if he would stay while she ate and he agreed as long as they could talk. Laurie eventually acquiesced and her meal times became their sessions. He built her session into his daily schedule when he still saw clients. Sometimes their sessions were productive but most weren't but at least they allowed Marcus to observe her. Even after he switched careers, he kept the same schedule with her.

Once he was settled with a cup of coffee and piece of spice cake he brought for himself, Laurie approached. Her gait was clumsier than usual and she moved slower, using furniture to assist. When she sat, he could see exhaustion in her thin, pale face. Laurie looked at the chicken salad and fresh croissant Marcus brought her for lunch. She made no attempt to eat. Her dark brown hair was contained in a single thick braid that hung down her back. It was Jamie who braided Laurie's hair every day; the style worn since before that first day in kindergarten. Marcus could tell she was nervous as her left hand pulled the braid over her shoulder and began to fiddle with the end of it.

Laurie's cheeks seemed more sunken than usual. The temperature in the apartment was warm as the heat of the April days began to increase but Laurie wore a heavy sweatshirt. Marcus was beginning to think he shouldn't wait a week for her eating to return to an acceptable level.

"How are you doing today?" he finally asked and sipped at his straight coffee. Although they could rival Starbucks in the fancy coffee department, he preferred old fashioned black. The clock over the sink ticktocked the time away without an answer from Laurie. She picked up her fork in her left hand and clumsily spread some of the chicken salad on the split croissant. Unlike Jamie, Marcus didn't try to do everything for Laurie and when he could, added some occupational therapy to her meals like giving her the components of a sandwich but not putting it together for her.

Although the stroke weakened her right side, her dominant arm was left nearly useless and partially frozen from her attacker's knife, causing her to relearn many of her tasks with her left hand.

"How is Jamie doing?" Laurie said slowly and low, stalling.

"She's already going stir crazy," he laughed lightly. For a moment, he almost saw a small smile on Laurie's face. "Now, I've answered a question for you. It's your turn. How are you doing today?" She finished assembling her sandwich and took a small bite.

"Tired," she finally said after a sip of iced tea. The answer was unenlightening. It was also a typical answer when Laurie's anxiety level was up.

"So you're not sleeping," he ventured but received nothing in return as she ate. Her bites were slow and she chewed thoughtfully. Halfway through her sandwich, she put it down and wiped her mouth. That can't be all she was going to eat. He brought her a small bowl of raw vegetables to crunch on, a mixed fruit bowl, and piece of spice cake.

"Is...is everything working out downstairs?" she asked louder than she should have and her left hand went to her throat. Marcus replaced *everything* with *Ben* in his mind. It was the first time in their sessions that she even came close to mentioning him.

"Yes," he replied and went with the opening. "Ben is doing a great job. I'm glad that the situation is working out for all of us." Laurie nibbled on a carrot stick and yes, he did think of a rabbit as she did so. He snapped out of it and continued on. "How do you feel with Ben living next door and working downstairs?"

"There was no choice; you guys needed the help," she replied and stared at her food. Her voice was rough after raising it too far. Marcus asked no more questions as she picked at the fruit for a few minutes and finally just pushed the tray away. "I'm done."

"Laurie," Marcus began gently. "I'm worried about you and your lack of eating."

"I just haven't been hungry."

"Have you been worried about Ben coming back to town?" He didn't expect an answer, he rarely did, but Laurie shocked him.

"Not worried," she replied reluctantly. "Nervous."

"Your nerves are eating you up from the inside," he noted and not for the first time. "What can I do to help ease those nerves? Do you want me to ask Ben to leave?"

"No," Laurie replied in a quick and frantic voice. "You can't do that. You need the help; Ben needs the job and a place to live." As her voice rose in volume, it cracked and sounded terribly painful.

Marcus regretted even bringing the suggestion up as Laurie's anxiety level skyrocketed.

"Please promise me you won't ask him to leave?" Her words were becoming more slurred and she clumsily stood up from her chair. "Please," she pleaded emotionally.

"Calm down, Laurie," he said, keeping his voice even. "I promise I won't ask Ben to leave. He can stay as long as he needs to and as long as we need him." His words were having no effect and he recognized the beginnings of a severe panic attack. Laurie looked at him with frightened eyes and her breathing was so ragged that it sounded like her breaths were catching in her throat. He knew he needed to stop the attack. Quickly, he guided her down onto the couch and retrieved the locked box from the refrigerator. Only Jamie and Marcus had the combination and it had actually been a few months since the last time Laurie had such a severe panic attack that he needed to use a sedative on her. He filled the syringe and made sure the box was locked again.

He spoke quietly as she began to calm down a few moments after he administered the drug.

"Don't worry; Ben will be fine. We won't ask him to leave."

Chapter Nine

Mothering

They say it takes a village to raise a child; to sustain Laurie it took a café, a priest, and an orange and white tabby cat. Each employee of the café had both a café job and a Laurie job and because everyone was family, or felt like family, no one complained. And besides, who would, considering the circumstances?

Jamie started out the day by bringing up breakfast to Laurie in between the early and late morning rush and then returned about an hour and a half later to braid Laurie's hair and help her with any other personal needs. They would chat for a little while until it was time for Jamie to go back downstairs to help prep for lunch. During this time, Laurie would read the news on the internet or whatever book Teddy brought her. Marcus delivered her lunch and they spent that time in a session. Afterwards, Laurie would rest and Jamie often woke her up for dinner. Laurie wasn't the best sleeper so this afternoon stretch often comprised a majority of her sleep. Marcus once offered to have a sleeping aid prescribed for her but she declined.

The evenings were for Teddy unless he was called away on church business. He never arrived wearing his uniform and Jamie knew they never spoke of religion. Teddy visited Laurie as her long-time friend and not as a cleric. They talked about the books he brought her or watched a big Hollywood movie on DVD or just talked. Jamie didn't know exactly what they spoke about; when she asked Laurie once all she said is that they talked like friends. She often wondered if that talk was about Ben. Although Ben and Marcus were close and Ben and Jamie even closer, Teddy was definitely Ben's best friend. His reaction to Ben's leaving was one of utter shock; the two shared so much but Ben never, ever hinted at his wanting to leave Laurie.

And so they each played a role in providing for Laurie with Louis and Callie filling in for Marcus and Jamie in the café when they were with Laurie and the wheel moved smoothly for the most part. The only time a wrench jerked the wheel to a stop was on Laurie's bad days. Those were the days where the only thing everyone could do was hope for the best. Typically, they were isolated days, maybe a couple a month, but occasionally there would be a string of three or four where Jamie wondered if she needed to have Laurie hauled off to the mental hospital. She would hole herself up in the sleeping nook, refuse any food other than her steady supply of tea (hot during the cold months, iced during the hot months), and only associated with Clementine, the orange and white tabby cat that she and Ben found in the alley the Thanksgiving before Ben left. Sometimes Laurie would allow Jamie or Teddy to sit with her during these very gray days but sometimes she just wanted to be by herself and if that was the case, Jamie just made sure to check on her throughout the day to see that she hadn't harmed herself. Several months had passed since the last stretch of gray days and Jamie hoped that the reappearance of Ben didn't spiral Laurie downward.

The Laurie machine underwent some modification with Jamie's bed rest; Louis brought Laurie the meals Jamie used to and Callie took care of Laurie's hair. But there was one aspect of Laurie's care that no one could take over for Jamie and that was the deeply engrained emotional support Jamie provided Laurie. When Marcus broke the news to her that he sedated Laurie, she once again rebuked her bed rest to venture across the hall. Laurie felt more vulnerable by the sedative and Jamie always made it a point to sit with her until it wore off. Laurie needed Jamie's kind words and actions that provided a sense of safety for her. It was a job that Ben used to do until he threw her away.

She let herself in with the keys that Marcus 'accidentally' left behind. Laurie was in her bed somewhere between consciousness and sleep. To appease Doc Jr., Jamie laid on the bed next to Laurie.

"Hi," she said quietly and wiped several stray hairs from her friend's face. Laurie's eyes were very droopy.

"Hi, Jamie" she replied, her slur very noticeable from the sedative. "Don't make Ben leave," she continued.

"No, of course not," Jamie reassured. "Marcus is sorry for even bringing it up."

"Ben needs you," she said as her eyes finally dropped shut. Those words were so true and Laurie had no idea how much so.

When Jamie first found out she was pregnant the shock threw her into a week of denial. *No, I'm not going to have a baby* she would say over and over as she dove even further into the café and taking care of Laurie. She convinced herself that the morning (and afternoon and evening) sickness was just nerves and she refused to talk about any of it with Marcus. They spoke of having children, before Laurie's issues, but once what little energy was left over after the café was taken by Laurie, children were just not even close to Jamie's horizon.

The denial was the cause of that early pregnancy scare but as soon as she heard the baby's heartbeat in the hospital, the denial melted away. Her female plumbing had always been unreliable so for her to miss a period or three wasn't unheard of and she and

Marcus grew lackadaisical in the birth control department. Jamie honestly thought she was unable to have children, taking after her own mother who struggled to have another child after Jamie (and failed). She was at the end of her first trimester the day she heard the heartbeat and Jamie was completely transformed into a waiting mommy.

The first thing she did when she was released from the hospital was cancel the order for her wedding dress; there was no way she would fit into the form-fitting gown and although Marcus suggested moving the wedding day up by a few months, Jamie refused. She was going to redeem the month of April with her wedding and didn't care how big she was when she exchanged vows. Of course, they needed to change the ceremony venue but it was an easy fix to a frowned upon situation.

After leaving the Sunset Park Ballroom she stopped by to see Teddy at St. Anthony's. He was quite amused with her and agreed to preside over the ceremony at the ballroom instead of the church. She knew he would marry her, pregnant or not, and Marcus in the church but Jamie was more worried about the old bitties that made up a lot of her clientele. Yes, for the sake of business, she chose to have the ceremony at the ballroom instead of dealing with the still-eating-fish-every-Friday crowd looking down their nose at her in the beautiful St. Anthony's. The next stop she made was, of course, Laurie's apartment. Despite everything, Laurie was still Jamie's best friend and on the good days, it was if the last few years hadn't happened. The day Jamie told Laurie about the baby was one of those days and for the briefest moment, the sparkle returned to Laurie's blue eyes.

"You're going to be a mama," she said and gave her a one-armed hug. "You'll be the best mother ever." Jamie laughed at this.

"How do you know?" she countered and the sparkle faded quickly.

"Because you've been such a good mother to me," Laurie said quietly to her feet. Jamie bawled in Marcus's arms that night when she told him what Laurie said.

"It's true, sweetie," he said and dried her tears. "Over these last few years, you've mothered and nurtured her through so much."

Today, Jamie stayed the entire afternoon with Laurie. She seemed almost more vulnerable than the other handful of times she needed the sedative and that's why Jamie stayed until Teddy arrived.

"It's been a while since she's had such a bad panic attack," Teddy said while Laurie was in the bathroom. "Do you think it has something to do with Ben?"

"The panic attack was about Ben," she replied. "Marcus asked her if we should have him leave to help with her own anxiety and off she went. It wasn't about him being here; it was about Ben being put out."

"Of course," noted Teddy. He took a deep sigh and let it out in a touch of frustration. The bathroom door opened and Laurie slowly exited. She stopped after noticing both Jamie and Teddy looking at her. As usual, her eyes dropped to the floor and she looked terribly uncomfortable. Jamie took it as the perfect moment to leave.

Chapter Ten

Mei Zheng

Ben enjoyed working in the café. He always was a people person and the individuals that came and went for food, coffee, and conversation kept him busy taking orders, serving and also talking. Many of the customers, especially the older ones, he remembered from growing up in the neighborhood and it was nice to reminisce about the better times. He noticed that no one brought up Laurie and for this, he was thankful.

But then Mei Zheng appeared a week after Ben started. It was just past two and the start of the afternoon lull. Marcus was upstairs with Laurie, and Louis and Callie were in the kitchen completing prep work for the supper offerings. Ben had just walked a group of retired teachers, including his third grade teacher who was his favorite, out the door and was busy doing a once-over on the black-and-white tiled floor with a broom when Mei lazily walked through the front door.

He'd known Mei just as long as the others but he long considered her an outsider of the group for her past behavior that few were privy to. Jamie tolerated her in small doses and for the most part she steered clear of the circle anymore, unless she wanted something. She was the last person on Earth Ben wanted to see. It had been a few months since he last saw her in Panama City Beach and he was successful at staying off her radar at the wedding but he couldn't exactly ignore her as she settled herself at the counter.

"Hello, Ben," she purred and slid her designer sunglasses up onto her head. Egotistical, drop dead gorgeous, and dangerous. Those were the words that Ben used to describe the woman who once tried to shed herself of Sunset Park, only to realize that beyond the brick and wrought iron fences, she was nobody. For her, being the head snake was her place and the only place to be that was in the neighborhood of her youth where she knew the ins and outs and everyone's business. She used that business to get what she wanted. Yes, Mei Zheng was a dangerous femme fatale who downed plenty of men, and innocent women, along the way. However, for Ben, Mei was just plain dangerous and he was dreading the day he would see her again.

"Mei," he replied with a nod of his head. He bent down to sweep the small pile of coffee grounds, sesame seeds, and other crumbs into the dustpan and he inadvertently caught a glance at the tanned legs that stretched forever. The weather was warm enough for early summer attire and she was wearing well a short skirt and tight tee. Mei knew how to use her feminine wiles and Ben was embarrassed to admit that he fell for those wiles as a stupid teenager and as an even stupider drunk.

"I'm in the mood for something coffee-ish. What would you suggest?" Mei flicked her shiny black hair over her shoulder.

"For you, Mei," he said as he poured the dark liquid into one of the café's white mugs. "Just a plain cup of bitter black coffee. Decaf," he added and set the mug in front of her. But Mei was ready, she played this game with him before, and out of her voluminous bag she pulled out a shiny steel flask.

"Would you like a drink, Ben?" she asked in an innocent tone that was completely fake. Her smile could have soured milk in under a minute as she added a hefty dose of amber liquid to her coffee.

"Low blow, Mei," he said.

"Is that a request?" She cocked her left eyebrow and then inched the flask towards him. He looked at it for a long damn minute before excusing himself and calling his new sponsor.

But Mei wasn't done with Ben yet and as he took out the last two garbage bags for the night, she emerged from the shadows by the dumpster. He clenched his jaw and vowed to himself not to let her get to him. It would be hard, though, as Mei knew exactly what buttons to push.

"What do you want, Mei?" he asked after tossing the two bags. He was about four feet from her and he could smell Jack on her breath as she spoke.

"You know what I want," she said, her voice completely in control. Mei was a drinking professional, having kept her wits about her even when Ben was too wasted to even stand. Those were some of his lowest moments in Panama City, especially when Mei got exactly what she wanted.

"No," he answered the unspoken question. "I told you a year ago that it wasn't going to happen again. I don't do any of that anymore."

"Are you saying I took advantage of you, Ben?" Again with the innocent voice. She had been inching forward and was close enough to stroke the side of his face with her perfectly polished black fingernail. "I'm not stupid, Ben. You could easily have stopped if you wanted to. And remember, you weren't shitfaced every time you fucked me." Ben didn't need reminding about that. "What say we go back to my place and relive some of those moments? Better yet…" An evil grin spread across Mei's ruby red lips and she glanced to the rooftop patio. "We could go upstairs." Her hand made its way south and Ben looked away from her. Yes, he could go there, he was a man after all, but not anymore.

"Just leave, Mei," he said in a strained voice and took a step back. Mei gave him a satisfied smile and he looked away again. A mixture of emotions boiled within him. Embarrassment, anger, worthlessness. They were all there. Mei laughed and Ben returned his weary gaze to her.

"You are so pathetic," she said. "You have been ever since you chose her over me seventeen years ago." She spat out *her* with a terrible venom. "I can only guess what your ulterior motives are for staying in Memphis but let me give you a few things to chew on. Laurie is fucked in the head. What was left of her mind from her childhood was damaged after you walked out on her and then when she was raped. She's only left that apartment once in the last four years. Do you want to know why? Because she tried to off herself. Took a chef's knife to her wrists and forearms but Jamie found her just in time. That's how messed up she is. You'd be better to forget about her, Ben. You've walked away from her once before and I would suggest for your own sanity you do that again." Instead of a flask, Mei pulled out a bottle of Jack Daniels. She shoved the bottle into Ben's chest. "Screw your one year sobriety; you'll thank me later." And with that, she strode off down the alley, her heels clicking on the cobblestone.

Chapter Eleven

An Unanswered Question

Teddy and Laurie were sitting on the patio when they heard Mei's unmistakable voice float up from the alley. When he went to the wrought iron railing to investigate, he saw that it was Ben Mei was addressing. Teddy turned to shepherd Laurie inside as he was pretty certain she didn't need to witness the two. It was too late as Laurie already made it to the edge of the patio.

"It's getting pretty chilly out here," he whispered so as not to draw the attention of Mei and Ben. He also wanted to dissuade Laurie from eavesdropping but Laurie shushed him with her hand. She crouched down at the edge of the patio and he took a few steps back in case the two in the alley looked up. The speech from Mei was blunt and when she mentioned the suicide attempt, Laurie's hand covered her mouth. She looked terribly ashamed and Teddy knew that was not a good thing. He crouched down next to her. "Let's go inside," he tried again but she shook her head. Her focus was very much on Ben in the alley. They both watched as he stumbled over to a stack of crates and sat down.

"He started drinking," Laurie whispered with a very pained look on her face. She looked at Teddy and he felt guilty about not telling her.

"He's been sober for a year," he said and she returned her gaze down to the alley. Ben looked hard at the bottle of whiskey.

"Don't do it," Teddy heard Laurie say. Ben grasped the top of the bottle and with an angry twist, opened it. She inched forward, accidently kicking a broken piece of brick. It fell quietly until it hit the hood of Ben's truck which was parked in one of the few spaces in the alley.

They both froze as Ben looked around. His eyes lifted upwards and for a few moments, he locked gazes with Laurie. Her wobbly crouch gave out and she landed hard on her bottom.

"Are you okay?" Teddy asked. She looked at him and appeared speechless. He was afraid she might panic and wanted to get her back into her apartment. Was she in shock from his drinking? From him having slept with Mei? All he knew was that the best place for her at that moment was where she felt safe. "Let's get you inside," he suggested and she nodded. Carefully, she rose to her feet with his help. When they turned to head back to the apartment, she froze. There, standing in the door by the greenhouse, was Ben.

"Ben," Teddy automatically said.

"Hi, Teddy." It was odd to call each other by their given names instead of their nicknames. The shock of his appearance on the patio seemed to stun them both. Ben never looked at Teddy as his gaze was on Laurie.

Quickly, she backed into a shadow and Ben took a few tentative steps forward which caused Laurie to shrink farther into the shadows. She couldn't go much further; the building next door was four stories and she'd be backed against the wall. Ben took another step and she held up her left hand as a shield.

"Please, don't come any closer," she said in her damaged voice. For him to hear her, she spoke louder than she should have. Ben respectfully took two steps back. She inched around the edge of the darkness until she was within a few feet of the door that led into her apartment. There was a large yellow circle of light outside the door and it was like she was afraid to enter it. Teddy knew the scars she now wore from the attack kept her in the darkness.

"Laurie…" Ben said in a shaky voice. "Can we talk?" Teddy quickly wondered what Laurie's answer was going to be but before she gave it, they were interrupted by Marcus.

"Ben? Are you out here?" Marcus's question distracted both Teddy and Ben long enough for Laurie to slip into her door.

Chapter Twelve

Warmth

Laurie could not sleep that night and ran the encounter with Ben over and over in her mind. Hearing him say her name sent shivers up and down her spine. It had been so long since she heard his voice. It was low and tentative but also warm, so warm. It always had been and she could always rely on it to calm her. *Can we talk?* It was a request, not an order like the last time they were on the patio together.

Time had been good to him and she felt a familiar tenderness in her soul. His touch, his voice, the depth of his deep brown eyes. None of those memories faded over the years. There were some insignificant memories she lost due to the stroke but none of her Ben memories, not the good or the bad. They were all there for her to relive over and over and wonder what she could have done differently to keep him from leaving.

The only thing she was shocked at from the speech Mei gave was when her deepest and darkest secret came out into the open. Ben looked utterly shocked when he found out that she tried to kill herself and the same shame that boiled within her was tough to handle but she focused her attention on what she learned about

Ben. Hearing that he and Mei had a sexual relationship hurt her but, to be honest, it was his right to move on to Mei after her. Even hearing that he began drinking didn't shock her. She always felt there might be a moment of weakness for him and apparently that moment happened while he was in Panama City.

Her heart ached for Ben. Laurie knew that for him to take that first drink, after vowing never to drink for fear of becoming like his father, he must have been in terrible pain and feeling weak. Guilt rose within her when she realized that she was probably the cause of his drinking. Tears began to fall but she quickly wiped them away. She was tired of crying.

The memories of the good times with Ben started advancing in her mind like a slide show. There were the fun times together, dinners with Marcus and Jamie and larger Sunset Park events. The quiet times though were the ones she relived the most. Those were her favorite. Those moments were the ones she missed with an aching soul. Laurie felt the safest when it was just the two of them.

And then Ben walked away and the good memories slowly dissolved.

Can we talk? The fear that racked her at that moment was a new fear and it rattled her almost as much as her dread of the outside world. Ben wanted to talk to her but did she want to talk to him? She did not know.

Chapter Thirteen

Talking Points

Ben sat until sunrise on the patio; his mind unable to calm down enough for sleep. Part of him hoped that Laurie would come back out while the other part of him knew that wasn't going to happen. When he saw Laurie from the alley he knew he shouldn't have gone up to the patio; he hadn't yet formulated a plan for their talk and instead of listening to his head, he listened to his heart. He so desperately wanted to speak to her and he acted prematurely. This wasn't the first time he'd done this and Ben hoped that he hadn't ruined any chance of talking with her.

Once the café opened, he let his work distract him from the encounter. When the afternoon lull came, his thoughts zoomed back in on Laurie. She acted so frightened on the patio when he tried to approach. He didn't know if it was him causing the fear or if it was related to the kidnapping. More than likely it was both and it just reinforced his realization that talking with Laurie was going to be an uphill battle, that is, if she allowed him to talk to her at all. There was no way he was going to force her into the conversation he so desperately wanted and needed.

Teddy came in through the back door of the café in his priest of the street outfit (traditional priest on top, ripped jeans and Chuck Taylors on the bottom) and helped himself to a cup of coffee. Marcus sent Louis upstairs with a snack for Jamie and settled himself across from Ben at the stainless steel worktable while Teddy leaned against the nearest counter. Ben, who was slicing a boat load of apples for several apple kuchens that Mrs. Bailey was buying for a social at the church, looked from Teddy to Marcus and then resumed slicing.

"What gives?" he said, knowing his two good friends. In the middle of the table Marcus set the bottle of whiskey that Mei gave Ben the night before. In the confusion of the encounter with Laurie last night, he forgot that he left it in the kitchen.

"It's open," Teddy noted. "Did you take a drink?"

"No, but I wanted to," he said honestly. If it hadn't been for the loud noise and him seeing Laurie, he would have probably finished the bottle off. "Mei gave it to me," he explained. "Please dump it."

"Is she going to be a problem considering your most recent history with her?" Teddy asked after discarding the liquor down the sink and returning to the worktable. Ben had never mentioned to Teddy about sleeping with Mei.

"You heard the conversation in the alley too?"

"Mei's voice tends to carry."

Ben sighed, realizing that Laurie must have heard it also.

"She'll probably be no more of a problem than she usually is," replied Ben.

"That's not exactly a good thing. I think we have enough to handle around here without her continuing a bunch of shit. Now, tell me what I walked into the middle of last night." Marcus poured two cups of coffee and set one of the cups in front of Ben. He finished slicing the last apple, sprinkled the slices with lemon juice, and put them in the walk-in refrigerator. Sitting back down and trying to stall, he took several sips of coffee hoping the dark liquid would help clear some of the spider webs from his brain.

"Stretch was there also, why don't you ask him?" Ben stalled some more.

"I'm asking you, Ben," Marcus said with little humor in his voice.

"I ran into Laurie on the patio," he said simply and stirred two spoons of sugar into his cup.

"And?"

"And I asked her if we could talk. You came along and she disappeared into the apartment before giving me an answer." Ben looked at Marcus; he seemed to be troubled. "What's wrong?"

"I don't know if anything's really wrong. I'm just wondering if it's too soon for you to try and engage Laurie in discussion."

"Are you saying I should wait?"

"Yes," he said slowly. "Laurie's still going through a period of adjustment with you being in the same atmosphere as her on an extended basis and now she knows that you want to talk. Also, I want you to understand why you want to talk to her. Go into this with a clear goal in mind. Prepare for only having one shot at this if you even have that chance. Ben, it's up to Laurie to decide if you get to talk to her."

"I know that, Marcus. I'm not going to force her."

"I'm serious, Ben, you've got to know where this is going, what's the goal, what are your expectations. When you've got it figured out, please, let me know first or even Teddy. Dealing with Laurie now is not the same as dealing with her five years ago."

"I will," he replied, and then asked a question of his two close friends. "How is Laurie doing? I've picked up things here and there but..." He paused a moment to think over what he was trying to say. "Mei said Laurie tried to kill herself. I had no idea; I can't believe neither one of you didn't tell me."

"Laurie asked us to keep quiet," Teddy said. "We promised her we wouldn't say anything to you and besides, you had plenty of your own problems to deal with. You didn't need one more."

"What happened?" he asked. Marcus and Teddy looked at each other and both shrugged their shoulders.

"She took her chef's knife to her forearms," Teddy explained. "It was Easter three years ago." Ben took a deep breath and let it out slowly.

"Is Laurie still in that bad of shape?" he asked Marcus, not sure if he really wanted to know the answer.

"I'm her therapist," Marcus started. "My hands are tied in what I can tell you."

"Understood, but what can you tell me? It may help me figure out what I need to say or how to approach her."

"The only thing I'll tell you is that Laurie is fragile, both physically and mentally." He stood and walked over to one of the cabinets near the pantry. Ben noticed during his days working with him that Marcus often looked into it several times throughout the day but he just assumed he was checking supplies. Marcus motioned Ben over and he opened the cabinet. Inside was a large monitor with four views of Laurie's apartment. Currently, Laurie was sitting on the couch in the semi-darkened room. In her lap was Clementine the tabby cat.

"Does she know you can watch her?" Ben asked with a touch of somber surprise.

"It was her idea, Ben, after the suicide attempt. She asked me to install the cameras and I complied after talking with Jamie. We thought it was a good idea. She doesn't trust anyone, not even herself anymore." Ben blinked several times as he watched Laurie. His heart ached for her and his level of guilt rapidly increased.

"I caused this," he said quietly.

"Don't flatter yourself, Ben," Marcus said, a bit in jest. "You are only a small part of what ails Laurie." Marcus paused for a moment and his next words dug into Ben quite a bit. "Think back five years ago. Didn't you leave her because of some of her problems?" Ben found himself wanting to snark back at Marcus but he couldn't. Marcus was right. "Issues were there before you walked out on her and in response to your actions and… and the kidnapping, rape, knife wounds, stroke, everything, they spiraled at an alarming rate."

"Is there any hope for her?" Ben asked as he sat back down at the table. His body and soul felt so heavy.

"Do you want the therapist's answer or the friend's answer?"

"I think that was an answer in itself."

"Maybe, maybe not. I do believe she is better than three years ago. I don't see some of the signs I saw back then in the weeks leading up to the suicide attempt."

"But you're also watching her twenty-four seven," noted Ben.

"It was her idea."

"But would you have installed those cameras if you didn't think it was necessary?" It was Ben's turn to play devil's advocate. Marcus let out a big sigh.

"Jamie, Teddy, and I are her only family; we love her. We want to see her better. The cameras," he motioned to the cabinet. "The cameras give us a safety net; gives us, and Laurie, the time that she needs to get better. It's been three years since she cut herself. I'd like to believe that if she still wanted to end it all, she wouldn't be waiting." He paused. "And I'm saying that as her friend. As her therapist, take my advice, Ben, and work on what you want to tell her. Figure out why you want to talk to her and also, figure out what your role is going to be in Laurie's life. You two go way too far back and if you're planning to stay in Sunset Park, you need to decide who you are going to be to Laurie. Both of you are part of our family and I think for everyone's sake, especially Laurie's, figure it all out now. I'm going to check on Jamie."

Ben watched Marcus take the steps two at a time as tension began to tighten his temples.

"Marcus is right," Teddy said and Ben sat back down on his stool.

"I know," he replied. "It's just…" He wasn't sure how to say how he was feeling.

"Be honest with me, Shorty. You didn't think you were just going to walk back into Laurie's life as if nothing happened, did you?"

"God, no," Ben said quickly. "I may have killed a few million brain cells these last five years but I'm not that stupid."

"I didn't think you were that stupid either." Teddy refilled their coffee cups. "So... you're back for good and you want to talk to Laurie. You obviously had a reason for doing so before Marcus gave you homework. May I ask why you want to talk to her?"

"Isn't it obvious? I need to apologize to her," he said.

"Okay, so you apologize. Then what?" The question took Ben by surprise.

"I don't know," he replied with complete honesty.

Chapter Fourteen

Unsettled

The afternoon left Ben feeling very unsettled and for the first time since returning to Sunset Park, he wondered if he made a mistake. The tasks Marcus saddled him with weighed heavily on him. Yes, he wanted to go into the talk with a plan; he always knew that but in his mind that plan was something simple. Maybe too simple as all he knew was that he wanted to talk to her. What Marcus wanted him to do didn't sound so simple and although Ben had only run away from his troubles once, five years ago, he was disappointed to feel that same urge to run now. But he couldn't; he refused to do that to Laurie again. She knew he wanted to talk to her and if he took off now, what would she think? He didn't want to add to the problems.

In the evenings, after his work was completed, Ben would sit on the patio and think. He chose his position carefully, staying far away from Laurie's door and sitting on the other side of the greenhouse that separated the two sides of the patio. Other than the darkened café he sat in when it rained, the patio was the only other place he could truly think about what he needed to accomplish.

Ben kept a notebook and pen with him and on occasion would scribble down a few words.

Time passed and he wasn't any closer to figuring anything out. In fact, he was more confused than ever. Neither Teddy nor Marcus asked how he was coming and Ben didn't offer up anything. Everyone settled into a comfortable routine except for Jamie. She still had five weeks to go and was completely going stir crazy. "So you want to talk to her," Jamie said two weeks after Ben's encounter with Laurie. He had brought up her lunch and she asked him to stay a few minutes.

"Yes," he said and settled himself at the end of the bed.

"How are you coming with your plan?"

"Does Marcus tell you everything?"

"You know I make him," she jeered. "Except for what goes on during his sessions with Laurie. I let him decide what he can and cannot tell me."

Jamie started eating her lunch while Ben absentmindedly picked up the baby name book that was lying on the bed. He laughed when he saw nearly the entire book was highlighted. "Problems figuring out a name?"

"It's one of the hardest decisions I've ever had to make," she exclaimed. "Naming a kid is so fucking important and the last thing I want to do is start him or her off on his or her way on the wrong foot."

"Don't stress about it now, CJ. Why don't you just wait until you meet the little one? Then decide."

"I suppose you're right," she sighed and took several bites of the Caesar salad Marcus made for her. The only concession to eating the salad was the small wedge of flourless chocolate cake Ben snuck up to her. She was always more of a burgers and fries kind of girl but for the café, the fare was on the lighter side. Still filling, but there wasn't a deep fat fryer to be had in the place. Their fries were baked. "So, Mei's tempting you."

"I guess that's what you could call it," he replied and frowned. He didn't want to think about her at all. She was dangerous for him and he wasn't sure if he could resist her and her temptations the next time she appeared. Mei knew how to manipulate Ben when he was weak, which felt like all the time these days. Every day for the last two weeks, Mei made an appearance in the café during the afternoon lull. He had no choice but to wait on her.

"She's trouble waiting to happen, Ben. Don't let her get to you. When she shows up again, just go into the kitchen and let Louis or Marcus serve her." Jamie paused a moment. "Let Louis serve her. I'd rather Marcus stay away from her also."

"Did she always hang around the café so much?"

"Sometimes. It just depends on what current angle Mei's working. Laurie would allow her to visit right after the kidnapping despite us saying it wasn't a good idea but she still allowed it. After Laurie's suicide attempt…" Jamie stopped with a shocked expression on her face.

"I know about it now," he said. "Mei told me and the guys filled me in."

"Laurie begged us not to tell you."

"I know." It took him a while to get over that but in the end, he realized that it was good that they kept their promise to Laurie. If Ben had found out about it, he probably would have overdosed the first chance he had.

"Marcus and I decided that if Mei tries to see Laurie again, we're going to head her off at the pass. She tries to come off as all concerned but everyone knows better. Honestly, Ben, I think a lot of that bitch's problems have to do with the fact that she has just never gotten over the fact that you chose Laurie."

"I often think that's the case also. The last thing Laurie needs is Mei back in her life," Ben said. He worried that she might flaunt their sexual history from Panama City Beach in front of Laurie just to hurt her. He made a mental note to be on the lookout for Mei in case he needed to stop her from slipping upstairs. He would not allow Mei to get anywhere near Laurie. In addition to the less than favorable history he shared with Mei, she was also more dangerous than anyone realized.

Chapter Fifteen

Afternoon Tea, Part 1

Three days later, a development happened. After Marcus came down from taking Laurie her breakfast, he gave Ben some startling news. "She wants to see you this afternoon."

"Excuse me?" Ben asked as he set the tray laden with several bowls of oatmeal down hard on the worktable.

"It's something we've been talking about for a few days. I think she's willing to eventually have the talk with you but as I'm sure you remember, she doesn't trust very easily."

"And I certainly destroyed any trust I had with her."

"Yes, you did. To be honest, Ben, you'll never have a chance to clear your conscience if she doesn't feel comfortable around you. I make no promises, though. Take these baby steps and see where they lead. Teddy will be there, though."

Later that afternoon, when Teddy arrived, Marcus sent them up to Laurie's room with her afternoon tea and a plate of sugar cookies, her favorite. Ben was unbelievably nervous and let Teddy lead the way. Marcus gave Teddy the keys and said that if the chain was still pulled after unlocking the door that meant Laurie changed her mind.

"Laurie, it's Teddy and Ben," Teddy said after knocking. They waited a moment before Teddy began unlocking the deadbolts. Ben held his breath as his best friend unlocked the last one and slowly opened the door. The chain was off and they entered the apartment that Ben had called home for ten years. It was a surreal moment but he focused and quickly threw all five deadbolts, his job since entering the apartment last. Turning around, he made a quick sweep of the semi-darkness but didn't see Laurie. The curtains were pulled in the sleeping nook and he assumed that Laurie was behind them.

With tentative steps he moved into the center of the apartment and set down the tray that held Laurie's tea and cookies. Looking around, he noticed that very few things seemed to have changed since he packed his bags. The kitchen table was the same 1940's table with mismatched chairs and the couch still looked inviting. He remembered the lazy Sundays he and Laurie would spend napping in each other's arms on the couch. The memory made him smile.

The differences, though, were very noticeable and sobering. The glow the apartment had was gone and heavy drapes barred the May light from shining through the west facing windows. The old mint green Frigidaire was no longer covered with neat rows of snapshots. In fact, there were no pictures anywhere. Sadness now filled the interior of the studio apartment, chasing away all of Ben's happy memories. He deserved to have those memories taken; it was his fault, after all. In their place were the difficult memories of the fights that plagued them the last two years of their relationship. What started out as simple discussions by Ben in trying to help Laurie with her fears ended up in one-sided arguments. Laurie just sat there, looked down at the floor, and rarely stuck up for herself. This only angered him more and eventually, he walked.

"I'll go see if she's ready," Teddy said and moved towards the sleeping nook.

Ben sat on the couch; its feel hadn't changed in five years but so much about Ben and Laurie had.

He felt something against his leg and he looked down to see Clementine. Bending over, he petted the cat who began to purr loudly. When he patted his thigh, she jumped up and rubbed her chin against his. Although five years had passed, she seemed to remember him and for some reason, this eased some of Ben's tensions.

"Do you really remember me, Clemie?" he asked the purring feline. She purred even harder and then curled up in his lap. He softly chuckled and continued to stroke her.

Out of the corner of his eye he saw the crisp white curtains move that cordoned off the sleeping alcove from the rest of the apartment. The light wasn't the best but he could see Laurie's shadowy figure emerge from the nook and take a few hesitant steps forward before she stopped. Ben went to stand but Laurie halted him.

"No, don't," she said in a loud whisper. "Clemie's comfortable." The voice was only a figment of what he remembered. Although Laurie was always a quiet woman around groups of people, they would spend countless hours talking, just the two of them, on the patio or the couch or as they walked through the neighborhood. They shared so much during those first eight years. Her voice had been soft and kind; now it was painful. Jamie warned him about her voice, explaining the damage from one of the knife wounds. But even through the roughness, he recognized Laurie's sweetness.

She slowly walked towards the couch, her right arm bent at the elbow and tucked against her stomach. Her right foot dragged a bit and her gait was unsteady. During their encounter on the patio, she had been so far into the shadows he couldn't see her very well. Now, he could see the effects of the horrific experience she went through, at least the physical effects. Jamie explained to Ben, in preparation for him seeing Laurie more, that she had come a long way since those first few months but Doc felt that she plateaud. Where she was now physically was probably the best she would ever be. Laurie was damaged.

The floor lamp illuminated most of the couch area and Laurie seemed to debate whether or not to step into the light. Ben knew exactly why. Again, he could thank Jamie for preparing him. Laurie's assailant, when he finished four days of brutally raping and beating her, attacked her with a knife, stabbing her nineteen times. Two of the wounds were to her face and neck. Jamie told Ben to expect to see two big scars that left Laurie terribly self-conscious. His cousin described them in detail so he wouldn't be shocked. The first scar started above her right brow and travelled across her face and down her left cheek while the second one started in the middle of her right cheek and then sunk straight down onto her neck before crossing her throat to the left. Jamie explained that Laurie's jugular had been nicked and her vocal chords damaged. It was Marcus's father who plugged the neck wound with his own fingers, effectively saving Laurie's life. The surgery on her vocal cords was risky but without it, she would have lost the ability to speak. It was Jamie's decision when it came to the surgery and decided that some voice was better than none.

Teddy put a reassuring hand on Laurie's shoulder. "You're doing fine," he said and motioned towards the couch. She nodded her head and when Laurie did step into the light, Ben focused on her blue eyes and not the scars. He grew up with those beautiful eyes that had been filled with various levels of pain, sorrow, and fear so many times. Now, the amount of pain, sorrow, and fear he saw in them unsettled him even further but he did not let it show on his face as Laurie sat down. She was so nervous he could see her trembling and he had to stop himself from rushing into his talk, thinking it would calm her. Instead, he smiled at her although, except for a brief moment, she never made eye contact with him.

"Hi, Laurie," he said gently as Teddy took a seat opposite them. She stiffened a bit and for a moment, Ben thought she might bolt.

The silence was overpowering and he felt his stomach clench with nerves. Laurie didn't run and instead settled back against the couch. He took her in for the first time in five years. She still wore her long hair in a single thick braid which she pulled over her left shoulder. He was surprised to see she still wore the small locket he gave her for her twenty-first birthday. Were their pictures still inside? The University of Tennessee sweatshirt she wore, which he recognized, was frayed more at the cuffs and hem and it hung on her thin frame. Ben now understood Marcus's concern with her eating; he hadn't seen her this thin since they were in elementary school and he learned the only food she ate in those days was their measly school lunch.

As Jamie said, the scars were shocking, especially the one zigzagging across her pale face. The other one was a somber reminder of how close Laurie came to dying. Ben felt nauseous at this thought. If she died, he would have drunk himself to his own death. But she hadn't and now he hoped he would have the chance to right his wrong.

"Please don't stare." Ben was so engrossed in seeing her clearly for the first time in five years that he didn't realize he was staring. She made the request without raising her gaze from the floor.

"I'm sorry," he apologized truthfully. Had he ruined his chances already after less than five minutes?

"The scars," she said. "I'm sorry about the scars and if they make you uncomfortable." It was just like old times with Laurie needlessly apologizing. In those last few months before the breakup, this habit angered him greatly. Ben had not been patient with her at all. But now was not then.

"Don't worry about it," he said. "They don't bother me." And they didn't; he didn't feel the need to turn away. They both wore physical scars from their childhood; it was second nature to look beyond them.

They sat in the stillness for a few moments. He felt like he should say something but he wanted Laurie to take the lead. She needed this reunion of sorts; he was afraid he might say something stupid to upset her. Ben looked at Teddy but he was very noncommittal. Finally, he couldn't take it anymore and asked a very non-threatening question.

"Would you like some tea?"

"Yes, please," she answered and he busied himself with pouring the pale amber liquid after Clementine jumped from his lap.

"Still two cubes?" She nodded in the affirmative and he carefully dropped two sugar cubes into the steaming liquid. The teacup and plate were antique with pale blue and pink flowers. He put two cookies alongside the cup and then stupidly handed it to her. Ben faltered and stuttered. How was she to hold the plate and drink the tea with only one good hand?

"It's okay," she said and took the plate with her left hand and placed it in her lap. There was enough mobility in her right arm and hand to hold the plate steady. She had adapted and it was his turn now to learn how to adapt. Laurie stirred her tea and took several sips. "Thank you for the tea and cookies." She nibbled on one before asking her next question. "Do you like working in the café?" she asked quickly, almost like she wanted to end the awkwardness that settled heavily in the space again.

"Yes," he replied in relief. "I like talking with the customers. Marcus is even letting me help with some of the cooking if I want during the slower portions of the day."

"You were a good cook."

"You were always better, though. It was just a hobby for me. You were the lucky one to train under The Old Man."

Laurie, whose gaze had yet to rise, smiled a little and he thought her sunken cheeks blushed a bit.

"And every day I have a piece of your pound cake." Again, he thought he saw a smile and a blush. "I missed it while I was gone." Any smile Laurie may have had on her face dissolved and he knew he stuck his foot in his mouth. Ben could have kicked himself as she put the plate on the coffee table, struggled to her feet, and as quickly as her limitations allowed, retreated into the sleeping nook.

Chapter Sixteen

Uncertain

It was late. The red numerals on the alarm clock read 2:37 in the morning but Laurie was wide awake. It really wasn't too odd to find her up in the wee hours of the morning, especially the last few weeks as a terrible ache settled in her body along with a permanent chill. As she lay on her bed, she relived those brief minutes with Ben over and over in her mind. She didn't know why she retreated to the alcove when she did. It wasn't because he alluded to the last five years; that was something that would eventually happen and she knew it. *Why did I back away*? It was a question she ran over and over in her mind.

As soon as she pulled the curtains, guilt washed through her and she wished to redo the last minute. She even parted the curtains slightly to call him back as he walked towards the door but her voice caught in her throat. Laurie wanted him back, wanted to talk to him, but if the offer was made at that moment, she would decline. She had to figure out what made her retreat first so that when she asked him back, it didn't happen again.

Laurie sat up in bed and put her ear to the wall. Was he asleep just a few inches away from her? Try as she might, she heard nothing but Clementine's quiet snoring from the end of the bed. With a sigh, she lay back down and closed her eyes. Not to sleep, her joints too achy for that to happen, but to bring up the image of Ben in her mind. Much closer than when she saw him in the alley, he looked almost the same as five years earlier but maybe a touch more ragged and stubbled. Laurie guessed that his drinking was behind his worn out look.

The first time Ben smiled at her that afternoon, some of the ice that he left in her heart melted. His smile always was a kind one and she couldn't count the number of times just his smile made her feel so much better and safe. That number could best be described as infinite. Laurie surprised herself by strongly wanting to reach out and touch his stubbly cheek; almost as if she couldn't believe he was actually there. The last five years were so surreal to her and she wondered if his reappearance was an apparition.

But she didn't need the physical touch; she recognized the scent of his soap and the comforting warmth he exuded. In retrospect, she figured out perhaps why she hid out in the nook – it was missing the feel of his arms around her, smelling his scent, hearing his words of comfort. She wanted those back so bad but then the pain came back; the pain of his words from that night. *I can't deal with you anymore. I don't even know if I can love you anymore.* When he turned his back on her and walked, it was like a knife to the heart. Quite ironic as four days later she would be fighting for her life from an actual knife wound to her heart.

Laurie's trust of Ben, something that she felt from a very early age, died that night and it would take a lot for it to be revived now.

Chapter Seventeen

Afternoon Tea, Part 2

An uneventful week passed before Laurie asked for Ben again; this time without needing Teddy as a chaperone. Marcus reminded him to think before he said anything. Ben was starting to lose patience and that was truly the last thing he needed to do. Nearly done with his talking plan, the only thing left was the hardest – what role was he going to play in Laurie's life? Sunset Park was his home; he had no plans to leave again and Marcus and Jamie said he could stay in the apartment for as long as he wanted and continue to work in the café even after Jamie came off of maternity leave. Having Ben around in the café would lessen the stress with a baby. So, the question of his every minute became who was he going to be to Laurie and once he figured that out, would Laurie be okay with it?

She was already sitting on the couch when he entered the apartment with her tea and an afternoon snack of berries and cream. He locked all five deadbolts and took his spot on the couch. Maybe it was the lighting, which really wasn't any different than the previous week, but she didn't appear well. Her cheeks were sunken more than usual and she was shaking. She had switched out the Tennessee sweatshirt for a cardigan that was way too big. Ben was sweating as the temperature in the apartment was downright hot and he wanted to suggest that maybe she open a window but he doubted that would go over well.

"Hi, Laurie," he said and smiled but she didn't return the greeting or smile. It set him on edge a bit but he focused on the task of fixing her tea. Clementine jumped onto the couch and he absentmindedly petted her as Laurie stared at the bowl he gave her but didn't touch it. She pulled her sweater tighter around her body. "Are you feeling okay?" he asked. Marcus hadn't said anything about her being sick.

"I'm fine," she said. *I'm fine* in Laurie speak usually meant that she wasn't but wasn't feeling so poorly that she needed to see a doctor. And if she did, would she leave the apartment at that time? "You painted next door."

"How'd you know?"

"I could smell the fumes," she explained.

"I hope they didn't bother you. I had all the windows open and set up a couple fans."

"What color?"

"A light gray, nothing too fancy." Laurie looked around the apartment.

"It's been a long time since these walls were painted," she noted.

"It has. I think it took us longer to pick out this color than to actually paint the place." He was certain that he heard a tiny chuckle from Laurie and Ben decided to take a small step towards what he hoped was progress. "If you'd like, I could repaint the walls for you." Ben held his breath waiting for Laurie's reaction. He prepared himself for her retreat but she stayed sitting.

"That would be asking too much of you," she said quietly.

"No, it's not. Take some time to think about it; there's no rush." Laurie again tried to wrap the sweater tighter around herself to combat the visible shaking that was happening. He wanted to ask her again if she was feeling okay but didn't want to harp. Ben was a harper extraordinaire, one of his many faults. "Would you like a blanket?" Ben asked instead. She nodded and he found the old trunk where the linens were kept, just exactly where they were during his time with Laurie. He pulled out the old quilt that his grandma made him when he was still a tiny tot. Laurie always loved it and when he moved out, he left it for her. Ben approached Laurie to drape it around her shoulders, something he would have done without thought five years ago, but then thought better of it. Instead, he sat back down on the couch and handed it her.

"Thank you," she said and clumsily wrapped it around her shoulders.

Chapter Eighteen

Doc

The next day Marcus announced that Laurie was indeed sick.

"She's running a fever; it's 102°. I'm wondering if this is something that's been brewing for a few weeks and that's why she hasn't had much of an appetite." Marcus rubbed his weary face. He was stressed and Ben tried to do as much as possible around the café. Jamie was growing more uncomfortable every day and adding worry about Laurie to the picture wasn't helping Marcus. "She's not complaining of any symptoms, though."

"Would she?" Ben asked out of experience.

"Good point."

"So what do we do?" Ben asked as he came back into the kitchen with several breakfast orders. "Does she actually go to see a doctor?"

"No," Marcus replied, giving him a look to suggest Ben was off his rocker. "I'll call Doc and see if he could swing by."

"Doc? He's still practicing?" Ben said and chuckled at the memory of the portly doctor who always put on a crabby face that often melted with the tears of immunization. It was wrong to think of him only as their childhood doctor as all of those of Ben's generation continued to see him past their eighteenth birthday. He was the doctor of record of Sunset Park.

"He's semi-retired. Doc Jr. took over the practice and Doc Sr. will actually make house calls for those patients who are too sick to get into the office. And Laurie. He'll come see Laurie."

Later that morning the clusterfuck that would describe the next couple of weeks began. Jamie's water broke in the middle of the lunch rush. There was a flurry of activity getting Jamie and Marcus out the door and the silence that fell over the café afterwards was almost anticlimactic. The café cleared out pretty quickly as the customers wanted to get on with their Memorial Day celebrations. Louis, Callie, and Ben were on their own. Doable, especially with a simplified holiday menu.

Ben was refilling sugar containers at the counter when Doc entered the café. The last time he saw his childhood-turned-adult doctor was about a year before he left Memphis. Ben was ignoring a rough chest cold he thought was nothing but turned out to be walking pneumonia. Doc chided Ben for ignoring his health and then gave Laurie props for being the one to talk Ben into seeing the doctor. She had bent over backwards caring for him over the next two weeks as Doc ordered him to bed. Ben frowned at himself. When Laurie needed him five years ago, he had ignored her.

"Benji!" The loud doctor yelled as he saw Ben at the counter. He hated being called Benji but Doc had called him that probably from the moment he pulled him out of his mother's uterus (the entire circle had been delivered by Doc and his son, Doc Jr., was now delivering the new generation of Sunset Parkians, including Jamie's baby). Doc was the only person Ben never corrected regarding his name. "I see you came to your senses and got your ass back to Memphis."

Ben was left speechless and all of a sudden he felt like he was ten years old and getting yelled at by Doc the time he had set Ben's broken arm. Ben had told Doc that he jumped off of Marcus's garage trying to fly on a dare. *And if Marcus bet that you couldn't dig to China in his backyard, you'd have spent the entire summer tossin' dirt, wouldn't you?* Of course he wouldn't have but Ben needed an excuse for the broken arm. He couldn't tell Doc that it was his own father who had broken it when Ben accidently shattered a dinner plate. Ben's father often punished in the eye for an eye realm.

"Hi, Doc," Ben finally stammered and Doc looked at him through squinty eyes.

"Are you clean and sober?"

"Yes, sir."

"Let me see your chips." Ben pulled his one year sobriety chip from AA from the pocket of his jeans and handed it to Doc. The towering man with a wild shock of white hair tossed it in the air a couple times as if thinking, then pulled something out of his own trouser pocket and tossed it at Ben. When Ben looked at what it was, he was shocked to hell. In his hand he held a sobriety chip with the number 19 on it.

"I had no idea," Ben said.

"They do call it Alcoholics Anonymous, Benji," Doc drawled. Doc was Southern through and through but without all the prejudices. "I went to my first meetin' the day your son of a bitch daddy killed your mama and I found out he had been beatin' the shit out of you. I never took a drink while I was workin' but I certainly didn't want to end up like your father."

They exchanged chips. "Ben." That was the first time Ben ever heard Doc call him by his preferred name. "Remember where you came from and how strong you were to survive that. You made a mistake and it brought you down. Don't let it happen again, for both your sake and Laurie's. Now, let's go figure out what's wrong with our little darlin'," he boasted as if he was on his way out to the barn to figure out why the John Deere wouldn't fire up.

"Oh… wait…" Ben stammered as he shook himself out of his reverie caused by Doc's surprising confession. "I don't go in her apartment unless she asks for me."

"Now, Benji. Jamie and Marcus are a might preoccupied right now. I'm deemin' you Marcus's substitute. I'll talk to Laurie if she complains; I'm sure she'll understand considerin' the circumstances." Doc boomed and headed into the kitchen.

Ben reluctantly followed Doc into the kitchen and picked up the keys to Laurie's door from the hook by the cabinet that held the monitor. Marcus kept them there if he knew someone else needed to help Laurie if he was out of the café. Doc must have known about the cameras because he opened the door and took a look. At first, Laurie appeared to be sleeping on the couch but Clementine jumped up next to her and she reached out to pet the cat.

"Laurie, it's Ben," he said at the door after knocking. "I have Doc with me." The door opened after he unlocked the deadbolts and they entered. Laurie must have been expecting Doc as the chain was not drawn across the opening. The heat in the apartment was oppressive as the temperature soared above 90° for the first time in that pre-summer period. He expected Doc to make a comment. Although he was a proud Southerner, he detested the heat and humidity and was known to spout off to anyone within earshot about his hatred of such. Doc, though, said nothing. Instead, he made himself comfortable on the coffee table. Ben stayed a respectable distance away but Laurie still gave him a quick, worried glance.

"Jamie's gonna be a mama soon, Laurie," Doc said as he held Laurie's wrist and checked her pulse. "She and Marcus are at the hospital now. I'm the one that asked Ben to come up here. Okay, darlin'?" Laurie nodded her head in understanding. He pulled his stethoscope from his doctor's bag and after the usual requests to breathe and such, hung it around his neck. "I've been told you're not eatin'."

"I've just not been hungry," she said in her soft and pained voice, her gaze down. Doc shook down the old fashioned mercury thermometer and slipped it under Laurie's tongue.

"How long have you not been feelin' spiffy, darlin'?"

"A while," she said after he removed the thermometer. Doc was about the only person in the neighborhood that a person didn't lie to, along with Teddy, and Ben was actually glad of this. Doc would get down to what was ailing Laurie. He held the thermometer up to the light and whistled.

"103.6°," he announced. He then felt her abdomen and then her neck. He didn't seem to find anything and then asked her a dozen and half questions that all seemed to go nowhere. "Well, we'll get you all fixed up but you're gonna need to do your part, darlin'."

"I'm not going to the hospital," Laurie said in a panic and a loud voice that surprised Ben. Her hand went to her throat and a look of pain crossed her face.

"Now, darlin', that's not what I'm sayin', at least not right now," he said gently and began searching for something in his doctor's bag. "I'm gonna take some blood, see if that'll tell me anythin'. In the meantime, what you're gonna do is get some rest and make sure you're drinkin' plenty of fluids. I'll have Louis start some chicken soup and I'm sure we can get some ice cream and puddin' into your food rotation. You're skin and bones, Laurie!" Doc boomed in jest. "We gotta get some meat on them bones!"

Doc prepared to take some blood. He asked Laurie to pull up the sleeve of her sweatshirt and that was when Ben saw the scar. It ran from her wrist all the way up the inside of her forearm and into the crook of her elbow. A surge of emotion ran through him and he forced himself to look away. Sweat ran down his face and he felt so shaky that he stumbled into one of the kitchen chairs.

"You alright there, Benji?" Doc asked. *No*, Ben thought to himself. His heart was racing and his stomach felt like it was about ready to turn itself inside out. What had gotten into him? "Benji?"

"S... sorry," he finally got out. "Just a little hot, I guess." It wasn't that but it would do as an excuse.

"Laurie, Benji's done got a point. It is dreadfully warm in here and one of the things you're gonna need to do is crack a window. Fresh air will do you some good, darlin'."

"I don't know," Laurie hesitated.

"It'll be fine. Those are some strong bars that Marcus put on those windows for you. Nothin's gonna get you, I promise." Doc was rubbing Laurie's arm reassuringly. "How 'bout just until I get back with some medicine?" She was looking at the bank of windows with such fear, almost as if her worst nightmare was on the other side. In reality, it was. "Just one window for an hour or so. When I come back you can decide if you want it closed."

"Okay," Laurie finally said in a very small voice. Ben took Doc's nod and went to the window that was furthest from Laurie, thinking that would make her more comfortable. He parted the curtains and the bright May sun filtered in. After the darkness of the last few minutes, the brightness caused Ben to blink a few times. He gave the window some muscle to get it to lift and he realized that it probably hadn't been opened in five years. Although it was the hottest part of the day, even the warm breeze felt good in the hot apartment. The open window intrigued Clementine as she hopped into the window sill and started rubbing against the screen.

"Like I said, Laurie, just an hour or so." Doc packed up his things and stood. "Why don't you take a little nap and I'll be back with some medicine." He winked at both Ben and Laurie. "And maybe some ice cream."

Ben followed Doc back downstairs and into the kitchen. Louis was already chopping a whole chicken into pieces for soup and Callie was taking care of the vegetables for it. "I have no idea right now what's causin' the fever," he answered Ben's question that hadn't left his mouth yet. "I'll be back with some general antibiotics and I'm gonna start an IV. She's dehydrated."

"Shouldn't she be in the hospital for that?" Ben asked.

"Not yet. Tryin' to get her to the hospital right now would probably do her more harm. I'll give her a day or so; see if we can get her eatin' and drinkin' and maybe the fever'll break. Then, if

she's not doin' better, we'll have to take the bull by the horns."
Ben walked Doc through the café and to the front door.

"I'm surprised she allowed the window to be open," he said.

"Laurie needs baby steps which Jamie, who I love like my own daughter, sometimes doesn't do so well at. She would have just barreled on in there and thrown the drapes back and opened all the windows. Laurie, in turn, would have high tailed it into the darkest corner of the room. I suggested somethin' small and reassured her that if she wanted, she could shut the window after tryin' it for a while. It's nothin' different than tryin' to get a little tater tot to eat his broccoli. You don't give him the whole stinkin' head of broccoli; you give just a couple little pieces and ask that he just try it." Doc shook Ben's hand. The strength in the elder doctor's grip belied his looks.

Chapter Nineteen

Dinner and a Worry

After dinner, Louis and Callie offered to take care of cleaning the kitchen up so Ben could take Laurie's dinner to her. The chicken soup was steaming and Callie made a batch of Laurie's favorite cherry Jell-O while Ben added some hot tea. Doc came by a couple hours earlier to start the IV and give her the first dose of antibiotics, then gave Ben directions on when to give her the medicine. He also gave Ben a quick lesson on changing out the IV bag. Ben wasn't so sure about this task but since it didn't involve actually sticking Laurie, Doc told him he had faith that he could do the plugging in of the tubing. Doc also brought several flavors of ice cream. He reported to Ben that she was working on a small dish of chocolate when he left.

"Soup's here," Ben said when he entered the apartment. Surprisingly, he found Laurie sitting in one of the straight back kitchen chairs a few feet away from the open window. The IV stand that Doc paid one of the local kids to carry for him was standing next to her. He smiled at the fact that Laurie appeared to be enjoying the fresh air. *Baby steps*, he heard Doc's voice in his mind. He set the tray down on the counter of the kitchenette and then got an idea. "Would you like me to move the table to the window?"

"No," Laurie said after thinking it over.

"Do you want me to shut the window?"

"No," she replied, this time without hesitation. She stood and moved herself and the IV pole to the table where Ben placed the bowl of soup and hot tea. He then took the bottle of antibiotics from his pocket and doled out two, making sure to return the bottle to his back pocket so he wouldn't forget and leave them behind. Ben didn't need an explanation of why Doc emphasized not to leave them in the apartment. He kept his distance as Laurie settled in at the table.

"Is there anything else I can get you?" he asked and took a few steps towards the door.

"No," she said after sipping a little broth. He took another step but Laurie stopped him.

"You could stay, if you want, unless there's a lot to clean up downstairs," Laurie said. Ben felt this was an indicator of progress.

"No, I can stay," he replied, hoping not to sound too overeager. Ben sat down opposite Laurie.

"Any news from Marcus or Jamie?"

"He called about an hour ago. She's only dilated to three centimeters and Doc Jr. said it's going to be a very long delivery."

"I hope everything goes smoothly," she said. Laurie continued to eat her dinner and they chitchatted a little but not much. Her voice seemed worse than normal after raising it earlier in the day and he tried to keep the chitchat to simple answers for her. When she was done, he took the tray back to the kitchen.

Ben was unable to sleep that night. The fact that he was now responsible for Laurie wore on him heavily and he plopped himself down at the worktable in the kitchen to watch the monitor in the cabinet. Part of him felt guilty, almost creepy, for doing so but he didn't want anything to happen to Laurie on his watch. He brought the small notebook with him to try and finish what he needed to cover for the talk he wanted to have with Laurie when, and if, she said it was time.

It was a three-fold approach. First, the overall goal. That was easy; the goal was to let Laurie know how wrong he was to leave her five years earlier and also for not coming back when she needed him. He needed to try and explain his thinking behind those two very poor decisions and also apologize. Then, he wanted to tell her the reason he's doing this; that he thinks, and hopes, it will help in his goal for life-long sobriety. It was part of the program, after all, but even if it wasn't, forgiveness was something he needed to ask for. Ben was going to ask for Laurie's forgiveness for leaving her. He truly felt that that forgiveness would help him; that it might help the urge to drink to go away. And the third part, the part he hadn't figured out yet, was what role he wanted to play in Laurie's life. He had a list – nothing, acquaintance, friend, caretaker, significant other. *Significant other.* Yes, significant other. There's no doubt in Ben's mind that he made the worst decision in his life leaving Laurie and he still loved her.

He had always loved her; first as friends until they hit high school and then the hormones started. He made his decision that Laurie was the one in tenth grade. Everyone could see it and supported it, except for Mei obviously, so when he moved into the studio upstairs that was Laurie's the day after their high school graduation, no one gave it a second thought. The Old Man had become Laurie's foster father after her own family issues and Ben was a little worried about what his reaction would be but it was The Old Man's suggestion that he move in. *There's never been a more perfect match. You may be young but you have old souls. No one else can understand what you two have been through. You belong together.* Ben was pretty sure if The Old Man was still alive today, he would have kicked Ben's ass from Memphis to kingdom come for what he did.

Ten years they lived together and it took one very bad decision for Ben to destroy it all. If the only thing they needed to overcome was the fight from that night, he could see their hearts coming back together. But the fight wasn't the only barrier. In fact, it was just a very tiny one. The big barrier was what happened after the fight and how it damaged Laurie physically and mentally. That barrier was immense, to say the least.

Ben made it through the night after several cups of coffee and began breakfast preparations before Louis and Callie arrived. Without Marcus in the café, they opted again for a more simplified menu. No one complained; all the customers were regulars and knew the birth was imminent. They had everything covered so Ben could slip upstairs to check on Laurie. He noticed on the monitor that she woke early although it appeared all she did was move from the bed to the couch and lay back down. Her temperature needed checking, the IV bag switched out, and pills along with her breakfast. Callie dished up a hot bowl of brown sugar oatmeal and raisins and again, Ben made tea.

Laurie was still asleep when Ben quietly approached. He did what he could without waking her but that was basically hanging a new IV bag. She slept through his clumsiness as he followed the directions he wrote in his notebook. Ben then sat on the edge of the coffee table and looked down at Laurie. Again, he felt a little creepy but he couldn't help himself. She was trembling slightly as she slept and the slight blush in her pale cheeks indicated she was still running a fever. The old fashioned quilt that she lay beneath was the same one they laid beneath together for ten years. Ben recognized the blue plaid of the flannel pajamas she wore and had the random thought that she had not added to her wardrobe in five years.

She moved in her sleep and her left arm slipped from underneath the quilt and Ben saw the scar that mimicked the one from the day before. He held his emotions in check for about five seconds before they became too much for him. The scars on her face and neck he could handle. The scars from her own father were nothing compared with his own but the ones she inflicted on herself, those were a different story. He went out onto the patio through Laurie's door and walked around in circles as the tears fell.

When he had himself under control, he went back into the apartment. Laurie was just stirring and he quickly shut the door before she noticed it was open. He put on his happy, non-threatening face and brought a plastic cup of water for her pills. "Good morning," he said as Laurie awkwardly sat up. She looked worse than the day before and when he took her temperature, he muttered a not so nice four letter word.

"104°," he announced after apologizing for the f-bomb. She accepted the antibiotics and two Tylenol but wanted nothing to do with her breakfast. His first instinct was to try and push at least the warm cereal on her but he caught himself in time. "Text me if you change your mind," Ben said and made sure she had her cell phone. Marcus and Jamie provided one for her to communicate with them easier. He knew she wouldn't text if she needed anything. Laurie was unable to ask for anything. It was just another one of her issues that caused him to walk five years earlier.

The morning was steady with no lull at all. Ben covered the front while Louis took care of the kitchen with Callie floating between the two. Marcus's mother got behind the counter to refill coffee mugs despite Ben saying everything was under control. He didn't really feel like he had anything under control but he hoped it was at least coming across that way. The lunch rush came earlier than normal and stayed late and Ben felt awful for not getting anything up to Laurie until after two. This time she topped out at 104.6° and when he asked if her fever had broken at all, she said no. Her lunch was left untouched and when he had a chance, he called Doc to give him an update. Doc wasn't too concerned yet so Ben went back to the café for the dinner rush. They were on their toes a good half hour after the café officially closed and Ben rushed up the stairs with Laurie's dinner. She was asleep and barely opened her eyes when he woke her long enough to give her medicine. Back down the stairs he rushed to the kitchen to help with cleanup and again spent another sleepless night watching Laurie on the monitor. Her sleep was restless and several times she woke up almost as if she was having a nightmare.

The next day was just as busy as the previous day and it didn't help that Laurie's temperature was flirting with 105° and on top of that, Mei was holding court in the café. Ben took Louis up on his offer to serve her table which eased Ben's tension slightly. The only thing Laurie would touch on her breakfast tray was the tea Ben brewed for her. Doc visited her in the morning and officially declared himself worried. After Ben refilled several waiting coffee cups, Doc followed him into the kitchen.

"If her fever hasn't wavered by dinner, we're gonna need to get her to the hospital," he said but they never made it that long. When Ben checked on Laurie on the monitor just past noon, he saw that she was crumpled on the floor by the couch. He took the stairs two at a time and then realized he forgot to grab the keys to the door.

"The keys!" he yelled at Louis and Callie who were several steps behind him. Louis ran back to the kitchen and tossed the keys up the stairs to Ben. He fumbled with the locks and damned them silently in his mind. "Laurie!" he called to the prone figure as he finally came through the door and rushed to her side. Not only did she rip the IV out of her hand when she fell, she must have hit her forehead on the coffee table. Ben pulled off his apron and applied pressure to the deep laceration.

"I called 911," Callie said, holding out her cell phone. "I called Doc also."

"Thank you," Ben replied. "Can you and Louis handle the café by yourselves with your mom helping? I can't let Laurie go to the hospital by herself."

"We'll be fine, Ben. Don't worry about it."

Ben's heart was beating out of his chest; he could feel the heat she gave off from the fever. Ben knew that she'd been sick longer than the last few days and he worried about what was causing it.

The paramedics arrived and quickly put a temporary dressing on her forehead, then started a new IV as Ben gave them the rundown of what was going on. They bundled her up and carefully maneuvered her down the steps and into the waiting ambulance in the alley. Ben climbed in the back for the short drive to the hospital.

DANA MANSFIELD

Chapter Twenty

Absolution

Jamie looked down at the small little human that slept peacefully in her arms. David Benjamin Bailey was 97 minutes old. He had a shock of dark brown hair and Jamie joked the first time she saw him that he was already due for a haircut. The delivery was long and hard and she declared herself a one-child mother early on in the process but for the little guy they named after Marcus's father and Ben, it was so worth it. Baby Davy made a few adorable baby noises, gave a little wave of his fist, and went back to sleep. Jamie was enveloped in complete happiness and she leaned back against the pillows, smiling.

At some point, she fell asleep and when she woke she panicked because Davy wasn't in her arms. Marcus, though, stood near the window and was smiling down on their son. "Hey," she said, surprised at how tired her voice sounded.

"Hey," Marcus said back to her and delicately lay Davy down in the bassinette. When he turned to face Jamie, she could tell something was wrong and she sat up a little bit too fast for her very sore body. "Take it easy," Marcus said and sat on the edge of the bed.

"What's wrong?" she asked after the pain subsided a bit. "I can tell in your face that something's wrong."

"It's Laurie."

Jamie's breath caught in her lungs. The only thing she heard for several ticks of the clock on the wall was her heartbeat as it steadily increased. And then the image that often haunted her nightmares appeared before her of Laurie leaning against the pale blue metal cabinets in the apartment, her arms hanging limp in her lap. A pool of blood quickly spreading around her and Laurie's face a deathly white. She was mumbling unintelligibly; her chef's knife lay on the floor in front of her. There were bloody paw prints surrounding the scene as a stressed Clementine skittered about her owner.

"No," Jamie breathed out as she came back to the day of her son's birth. "She didn't kill…"

"No, god, no," Marcus said quickly and Jamie slumped backwards. "She's pretty sick with a high fever and they're bringing her in an ambulance. Ben's with her."

Twenty minutes later, Marcus wheeled Jamie towards the ER. He tried to talk her out of going downstairs but she insisted. Laurie was her best friend and also her charge. If any medical decision needed to be made, as power of attorney, Jamie would need to make it. They arrived in the ER and spotted Ben pacing outside one of the rooms. He looked like shit with dark shadows beneath his brown eyes. His worry creases between his brows were deeply etched. "Ben," she called.

"Jamie," he replied and bent down to give her a peck on the cheek. "Congratulations, Mama" he added with a forced smile.

"What's going on? What happened?"

"She's running a high fever but they don't know from what. They're working on getting her stabilized to move her up to the ICU." Ben's voice was strained. "Doc's in there, telling everyone what to do. The fever is over 105°." The intonation in his voice was a cross between disbelief and fear and Jamie could tell he was pretty close to losing it. She grabbed his hand and gave it a squeeze. Ben needed to talk so she sent Marcus back up to the maternity ward and ordered Ben to wheel her into one of the small family waiting rooms. He kept looking back into the hall but Jamie needed him focused.

"Sit," she said and pointed to the chair across from her. "Doc will come get us when we can see her." Ben nodded and sat down with a frustrated yet tired sigh.

"What's going on?"

"What's going on?" he repeated with confusion in his voice. "Laurie's sick…"

"No, not the obvious. With you. You look like shit."

"I'm just worried about Laurie."

"Have you slept at all lately?"

"No," he said after a moment of hesitation. "I was afraid to sleep in case Laurie…"

"In case Laurie tried to kill herself again," Jamie finished Ben's sentence.

"Exactly."

"I used to be like that. Marcus finally threatened to remove the cameras if I didn't stop watching the monitors like it was one of my granny's favorite soaps from back in the day. I realized that even with the cameras, it just wasn't feasible to watch her all the time and I had to have some faith that she wasn't in that bad place. She said she wouldn't try to kill herself again even though the cameras were her idea."

Ben sat looking at his hands for several minutes. Jamie noticed the tears but said nothing. There were no words she could form; it was the first time she ever saw Ben cry.

"I saw the scars…" he said after a while and pointed to his own forearms. "The other scars are just scars but those… those got me here." Ben placed a hand over his heart but didn't look up. He'd always been that way; whenever he was having a heavy discussion, he could never look anyone in the eyes. It was a leftover reaction from having to deal with his father. "Marcus tried to tell me not to blame myself for the suicide attempt but how can I not?"

"Because what did Jamie do every night after closing down the kitchen?"

"Go for a run," he said after a pause.

"Right. And what did she do even though you just left her?"

"She went for a run."

"Exactly. Regardless of what happened leading up to that run, the kidnapping was probably going to happen. Her rapist did not know that she had just been dumped. It wasn't your fault. The only person I blame is her rapist." Jamie slumped in the wheelchair. This conversation had a ton more mileage to go but she didn't have the strength for it right now. She didn't think her words really sunk in but Ben made a half-hearted attempt to nod in understanding.

"There's the new mama," Doc bellowed from the doorway. "You should be up with your tater tot. Benji and I are lookin' out for Laurie."

"How is she, Doc?"

"She'd be a lot better if we could get that darn fever down. They're settlin' her up in ICU right now and we're gonna hold off on antibiotics until some of the blood tests come back tomorrow so we're not just tryin' to shoot blindly. We really don't know what we're lookin' at right now but we're all pretty darn worried."

"Oh, god," Jamie said.

"Let's not be talkin' to Him just yet, Jamie," Doc said. "She's also dehydrated and that's messin' her up pretty good also. Like I said, we'll know more tomorrow. Now, let's get you upstairs and back to your baby. Show him off for Benji and by that time they'll have Laurie all settled in the ICU and Ben can go sit with her."

Ben was stunned to learn Marcus and Jamie gave the baby Ben's name and more stunned when they asked him to be the godfather. He said yes and then held his godchild. Tears came to Jamie's eyes but she quickly shooed them away.

"He's perfect," Ben whispered as he handed Davy back to Jamie.

"I kind of think so," she said and looked up at Ben. There was still so much pain in his face and she made a note that as soon as she was back home and had a chance, they would sit down to have their own talk. Perhaps their talk would help him with the talk he wanted to have with Laurie.

DANA MANSFIELD

Chapter Twenty-One

Beginnings

Ben hesitated to enter the glass ICU room where Laurie lay. She appeared so fragile and vulnerable and he was afraid that his presence would do harm.

"You can come in," the ICU nurse pleasantly said as she came up beside him. "I just need to hang some more fluids."

He used the nurse's presence almost as an emotional shield and he felt rotten with himself. With a deep breath, he entered the antiseptic smelling room.

"Here," the nurse said and placed a stool next to the bed.

He sat and looked down at Laurie. There was a snowy white bandage over the cut on her forehead and Doc said it took twelve stitches to close. It would be another scar.

She was pale and the hospital lighting really showed the contrast between her pale skin and the scars. The room was chilly and Ben wondered aloud if Laurie should have a blanket but the nurse said no as they wanted to try and keep her as cool as possible. She checked the new IV in her hand and the bandage over the old IV site, then returned quickly with a plastic pitcher of water and matching cup. "Encourage her to drink," the nurse said with a smile and then left the room.

Ben looked back down at Laurie; she appeared to be sleeping. Gently, he picked up her hand that held the IV. It was the first time he touched her in five years. Even over the last two days there was no need for physical contact and the feel of her hand warmed up a long buried feeling within him. It felt so comfortable, so normal, but also so frightening.

Laurie stirred and he worried about how she would react to finding herself in the hospital. That's why he couldn't leave her side; he didn't want her to be alarmed by the new surroundings. She needed a friendly face, or at least a face she knew. His role had yet to be defined.

"Laurie?" he called gently. Ben's hand automatically went to touch her face but he caught himself just in time. "Laurie? It's Ben." Her eyes fluttered several times until they finally opened up about half way. She spent the better part of a minute just looking at the muted ceiling. Ben took a quick look at where the nurse call button was just in case she panicked. "You're in the hospital," he told her, hoping that might help. Her blue eyes began to dart around the room and the monitor beeping the staccato of her heart increased unevenly. "It's okay, Laurie," he tried to calm her but her heart continued its climb. The nurse came rushing in.

"Doc warned us this might happen," she said and injected something into Laurie's IV.

"What is that?" Ben asked.

"A very mild sedative. It'll just take the edge off. Doc doesn't want her to be completely out unless she's asleep." The nurse gave Laurie's shoulder a slight squeeze and despite her friendly manner, Laurie clumsily moved away from the nurse. "My name is Lurinda," she said. "And I'll be your nurse until tonight. I'll be back in a little bit to check on you."

Laurie was fighting the sedative and that didn't seem to be helping the situation. Ben wished he could do better for her but all he could think of to do was try and calm her through his voice. Back in the day, when she would seek solace from her father and sneak into his room at Jamie's house, he would talk quietly about their future to ease her troubles. The run-ins with her father would leave her terribly upset and anxious. Once he fixed up any injuries she had, they would sit on the roof outside his bedroom window and talk under the shelter of a huge weeping willow tree. "You're safe here, Laurie," he started, just as he started back in the day. "You've got your own room and Doc's looking out for you. So am I," he added and gave her hand a squeeze. She pulled it away and Ben's heart sank a little. "Do you want me to leave?" Laurie seemed to give his question a great deal of thought and he realized he was once again holding his breath waiting for an answer from her. Eventually, she gave it by a shake of her head – *no*. "I'll stay with you, until you want me to leave. I'll make sure you're safe; I'll protect you, okay?"

"Okay," Laurie said very slurry and let her eyes fall closed. For the remainder of the day she dozed on and off while the chills ebbed and flowed. Ben stayed by her side, only leaving when Marcus swung by for a few minutes to give Ben a chance to hit the restroom and grab some bad coffee from the vending machine. Teddy came by in the evening and they both watched over her silently.

Laurie's fever raged on and when she would wake up she didn't seem to be cognizant of what was around her. Just past ten that night, Laurie grabbed at Ben's hand. "You came," she whispered with unfocused eyes. "I kept asking Jamie to call you. I knew you'd come." Laurie's words were like a dozen ice picks directly into his heart. She was confused, thinking that it was the week after the attack and he had fulfilled her request to return to Memphis. He remembered that time vividly and still had the last message Jamie left him saved in his voice mailbox. *Damn it, Ben. Please, I'm begging you. Come back to Memphis...* It was just after listening to that message that Ben had taken his first drink and it was that drink that sealed his silence.

Her delirium continued through the night but she didn't return to that time in her incoherent ramblings and eventually, her damaged voice wore out. Exhaustion weighed heavily on Ben and by dawn he found himself having a hard time staying awake. It was his third night in a row without sleep. He needed to close his eyes for just a few minutes and sat down in the easy chair that was in the corner of the room. The next time he opened his eyes, Jamie hovered over him with a blanket.

"I'm sorry I woke you," she said quietly. "I thought you'd like a blanket because the room is so cold."

"No, no," he said and rubbed his face. "I'm fine." He stood up quickly and the room began a slight twirl. Little sleep and only coffee for sustenance for three days was catching up to him.

"Whoa there, buddy," Jamie said and pushed him back down into the chair. "I think you need to go back to sleep."

"I just wanted to rest my eyes a few minutes," he said and checked the clock on the wall. Was the clock right? Was it really nearly noon?

"You need food, too," she noted. Slower than last time, Ben stood and walked over to Laurie. She was sleeping. "The fever's a little less, 104.6°, but it hasn't broken," Jamie explained. "So far, the blood tests have all been inconclusive and they want to start a series of tests to begin ruling stuff out. MRI, CT and PET scans, the whole ball of wax." She leaned forward and dabbed a wet washcloth on Laurie's face. "I've got her covered for right now, Ben. Why don't you go grab Marcus out in the waiting room and head down to the cafeteria?" He hesitated but Jamie wouldn't have it. "You're not going to do her any good if you're the next one to collapse and smack your head. I'm not asking you to eat a seven course meal. Grab a sandwich, maybe a soda. That's all I'm asking."

"Okay," he replied reluctantly. "I'll be back in fifteen but text me if something happens."

"Thirty and make sure to chew your food before swallowing."

Thirty minutes turned into nearly sixty as the hospital's cafeteria was a busy place for Sunday's noon meal. Marcus chatted about how many of the customers weren't even visiting anyone in the place and were only there because the cafeteria happened to be the only food place open in the neighborhood on Sundays. He and Jamie were talking about opening the café on Sundays for either a midmorning brunch or mid-afternoon Sunday supper. Ben gave proper responses in support of the idea but his thoughts were more on Laurie than on the café. They finished their cheeseburgers and fries and Ben went back to ICU while Marcus headed for the nursery. Ben relieved Jamie and he took up his spot on the stool.

Chapter Twenty-Two

Ice

For three days they put Laurie through test after test and Ben was there by her side for each and every one of them. He ran back to his apartment for only as long as it took for him to grab a quick shower and change into a pair of clean jeans and t-shirt but only if Teddy, Marcus or Jamie sat with Laurie. He napped only when he absolutely had to and only if Laurie was asleep. He would set the alarm on his cell phone for an hour and settle into the easy chair. Her fever never abated and the delirium came and went. Sometimes she was aware of her surroundings while other times she bounced around her history. Nothing the doctors prescribed broke the fever or even lowered it and after three days, they were no closer to figuring out what was wrong.

"She's sleeping right now, CJ," Ben told Jamie on his cell phone on that fourth day. She and Marcus brought Davy home two days earlier and were ecstatic that he was the perfect baby so far. Ben took that to mean he was allowing his parents to sleep through the night already.

"Is she getting better about leaving her room?"

"Not really and they often have to give her a mild sedative as long as it doesn't interfere with the test. Other times she's just so out of it she doesn't realize she's leaving the room. Doc suggested going old school today with an ice bath; just trying to get the fever down a little. They're setting it up now. I'm not sure how Laurie's going to like that." Ben looked through the glass wall into Laurie's room. The curtain was pulled so he couldn't see what was going on but he thought being submerged in a portable tub of ice and cold water had to be an awful experience. He was waiting for Lurinda to call him in as Doc insisted he be there. It happened slowly over the last three days but they arrived at the point where Ben could calm Laurie down with words when she panicked. *She'll probably be a might touchy about the ice bath,* Doc had said when he told Ben about the procedure. *Keep her calm, Benji. If that's somethin' we need to resort to a few times a day until we figure this out, we need to make sure she's as comfortable as possible with it.* There was a lot of clatter over the cell phone all of a sudden and it sounded like Jamie was calling from the café itself. Despite everything going on, Marcus decided to try the Sunday morning brunch idea. "Are you sure you don't need me to come back and help, CJ?"

"No, we've got everything covered, Ben. I want you to stay there with Laurie," Jamie said.

"I know, but I'm supposed to be there helping because of Davy."

"Ben, stop. You are right where I want you to be. End of discussion." Jamie was very insistent and he gave her an exasperated *fine.* "I'll be by this afternoon."

"See you then," he replied and ended the call.

He turned his attention to Laurie's room. Some excitement broke out and all of sudden he saw a small wave of water and a few crescent-shaped ice cubes hit the floor. Lurinda stuck her head around the curtain and waved Ben in with a look of exasperation. He was careful not to slip on the water or ice cubes as he found his stool next to the portable tub. Laurie was putting up a subdued fight, causing water and ice cubes to splash about.

"Try and get her to calm down," Lurinda said although she didn't need to as Ben knew what he should do. He gently pried Laurie's good hand from the side of the tub she was trying to weakly remove herself from and held it between his two.

"Laurie," he called and she looked at him with such pained eyes.

"Get me out of this," she pleaded in a very strained voice.

"I can't do that, Laurie. I know it's uncomfortable but it's hopefully going to bring your fever down a little." Laurie had no fight left in her and she slumped backwards, a pathetic half-sob escaping her lips. Lurinda added two more bags of ice and after a few more minutes began to check Laurie's temperature. It was a slow process but eventually the fever came down to the target of 102°. Ben left the room while Lurinda and another nurse got Laurie cleaned up and into a dry hospital gown. He went into the small kitchenette and grabbed some cherry Jell-O.

Ben waited until Lurinda said it was okay to enter. Laurie was back in her bed with her IV reattached. She was lying on her left side, her back to the door, and she had the thin sheet she was finally allowed to have pulled up tightly around her. The sheet gave her psyche the protection she was craving being outside of her comfort zone of the apartment. She curled up tighter when Ben sat on his stool and she avoided looking at him. He tried not to let this bother him. Although he was her constant companion while in the hospital, the history was still there.

"I brought you some Jell-O," he said in a slightly forced light voice. "Since you didn't eat the broth at breakfast I thought you might want something." She looked at the fancy plastic bowl and then nodded but when he held it out to her, she shied away. Ben picked the spoon up himself, captured a wiggly red square, and held it to her mouth. She took the bite and he continued to feed her in silence.

It was a scene so reminiscent of sixteen years earlier except that Laurie wasn't fearful of Ben then. It was her father she was scared of and with good reason. Three days earlier, on Christmas, he had locked Laurie in the attic of their house and then set it on fire. The police were after him and despite having a guard outside her hospital room door twenty-four seven, she was scared that her father would come after her while she recovered from smoke inhalation and burns to her legs. Ben had spent as much time as he could with Laurie in the hospital; she had truly felt safe when he was there.

He decided to take a risk and brought up that time with Laurie. "Do you remember when I would feed you all the cherry Jell-O you could eat during that Christmas break from school?" She nodded a *yes* after another jiggly piece and pulled the sheet tighter around her.

"You kept me safe," she whispered.

"And I'll keep you safe until you tell me to go," he replied. Laurie slyly looked up at Ben and he gave her a smile. It seemed to almost make her more uncomfortable and she dropped her gaze.

When she finished with the Jell-O, she sipped a little tea and then nodded off. By the time Jamie dropped by around three, Laurie's fever was back over 105°.

Chapter Twenty-Three

Broken

The ICU was quiet at midnight. Teddy left a few minutes before and Ben texted an update to Jamie – *L asleep, fever back up. More ice baths and tests tomorrow*. Lurinda, working a double shift, came in and silently switched out the empty bag of fluids for a full one and then left. He took a deep breath as he stood and stretched, then went to look out at the semi-darkened neighborhood. From the window he could see the top of the café's building four blocks over and beyond that the twinkling Memphis downtown. His family's history in Memphis went back to the Civil War where his long gone male relations upset plenty by wearing the Union uniform and those that died at Andersonville had been mocked by the neighbors after the War. How Ben's father could be cut from the same cloth as those who fought for what was right was unknown to Ben. The man was an evil and abusive drunk and there had been days where Ben wondered how he managed to survive Lemuel Polniacek.

Laurie had barely survived her own evil father and one of the worst days of Ben's life was the Christmas Day of their junior year of high school where John Grumman had set the shabby house on fire. By that time, his wife and Laurie's siblings were gone but Laurie, feeling obligated despite the abuse, stayed. It had taken the burns to her legs to finally get her out of that house. Ben could see the empty lot two blocks over where the house used to sit; the gaping basement long ago having been filled in. The lot was set to become a tiny park as the neighborhood was slowly being reborn and Ben liked this idea. That house was nothing but horrors for Laurie and where it stood would soon be a place of beauty. He wanted to tell her about it but was afraid it might also bring back so many bad memories.

Another worst day was the day he had seen his father bludgeon his mother to death when he was fourteen. Beaten himself, he was unable to gather enough strength that sultry summer day to stop his father as he repeatedly struck his mom about the head with his fists. The last hit, from an empty whiskey bottle, knocked her out and his father left with a new bottle of Jack Daniels. Ben crawled to his mother's side and was holding her hand as she took her last breaths.

But nothing compared to the span of time starting with the day he left Laurie and continuing through his entire stay in Panama City. Would another bad day be the day that Laurie decides on what role he would be allowed to play in her life? Or would it be something much worse related to the fever? For the first time since the night he walked out on Laurie, he pulled out his mother's rosary and prayed.

Another three days with more inconclusive tests and ice baths. Laurie hated them but Ben could calm her down enough for the staff to do their job. After the bath, her temp fell for a couple hours but eventually, back up it would go. When her temperature came down, her delirium seemed to wane temporarily, and Laurie rested. When she did, Ben would rest also in the easy chair. He shared pictures of Davy that Jamie sent him on his cell phone and when Jamie was there, Davy was all Laurie could talk about.

Ben hung out in the hall when the two women were visiting and he observed Laurie. She smiled, albeit weakly, with Jamie and occasionally he heard her light laugh. Smiles and laughter were something that was absent when he was with her even though he tried to lighten her spirits. Her somber mood around him he understood considering their history but it confused him also. If being there with her at the hospital brought her mood down, why tolerate his presence? Each day he asked her if she wanted him to go back to the café and send Jamie and each day she said no. He craved to ask her why she wanted him there but could never muster the courage to do so.

The next day things worsened with Laurie and whatever condition ailed her. It was a slow buildup in the delirium and by mid-afternoon Laurie was in the throes of what Ben could only describe as a waking nightmare. She thrashed about, muttered unintelligently until her voice disappeared, struck out at unseen evils. The mild sedatives weren't working and the doctors didn't want to give her anything heavier and by six in the evening, they put her wrists in restraints to keep her from pulling out her IV, something she did twice already. As the evening and overnight continued and the nightmare increased, it became apparent that the nightmare she was reliving was the abduction and rape. Her barely there cries of *no, no, no, please don't hurt me, please let me go* shook Ben to his core. He caught himself inching toward the door and was terribly ashamed with himself.

"Man up," he muttered under his breath and forced himself back to the stool. "Laurie, it's okay. You're safe now," he said close to her ear and took her bound hand in his. Ben gently squeezed it and continued to talk to her. "It's just a nightmare. That was a long time ago; it's over. You're safe now." Physically she was safe but he knew mentally she wasn't but it wasn't the time to try and differentiate that with her.

The chills running through her body became almost violent, another reason they chose to restrain her. The next day and night slowly wore on with Laurie crying and begging with the unseen. She held onto Ben's hand as if for dear life. Occasionally she would focus on him, beg him to help her but all he could do was talk to her in a calming voice or wipe her face with a cold washcloth. The severity of whatever she was going through was beginning to rattle even the doctors and a terrible feeling began to gnaw in Ben's gut. What if this was it? What if she was travelling towards death and fighting the journey? Ben delicately wiped the stray hairs that escaped her single braid away from her sleeping face and bent over. He gently kissed her on the forehead, then the tip of her nose, and then her lips, just as he did during those good years. Tears began to fall and he put his cheek next to hers. "Please don't die, Laurie. I'm so sorry for what I did, for leaving and then not coming back when you begged me to come back. Please fight, Laurie. Please fight as hard as you can. I love you so much, Laurie." He broke down harder than he ever had, falling to his knees and weeping into the mattress, all the while still holding onto her hand.

As dawn broke that morning, so did Laurie's fever. Ben was emotionally and physically drained but he still kept vigil. By nightfall, she was a cool 98.6°.

*

"And they have no idea what caused it?" Jamie asked in the cafeteria the next morning.

"No," Ben said and rubbed his forehead. "They say it happens and there are times when they have no idea what the cause is or if it'll happen again."

"When are they going to release her?"

"She's pretty exhausted and washed out and they want to make sure the fever doesn't come back. Doc is hoping by Wednesday." They sat in silence for several moments. Jamie looked at Ben as he rubbed his forehead again. He needed a few days of recuperation also but she silently told herself that he didn't deserve those days. The small and ugly part of Jamie was coming through; the same part that wanted to ask him about the dirty details of Panama City the night Ben came back to Memphis. If sitting by Laurie's side day in and day out, much as she had done after the attack and stroke, left him exhausted and weak, then so be it.

"Jesus," she said aloud, ashamed with herself.

"Jesus?" Ben repeated.

"Never mind," she replied and drained the rest of her coffee cup. The hospital coffee was disgusting after so many years of The Old Man's recipe. "Why don't you run back home and shower and change? I'll sit with Laurie until you get back." Ben took her up on the offer and she watched him exit the cafeteria, his gait slow and shoulders slumped. He was a broken man.

She returned to Laurie's room and sat on the stool while Laurie slept. It was so different than those days after Laurie was found bleeding in the alley. The rape left Laurie so fearful that she refused to rest even when she desperately needed it from the surgeries to fix the damage done by the knife wounds. Laurie would stay awake until exhaustion finally won over but what sleep came was not refreshing and Jamie always had to calm her down when she woke up screaming. Then came the stroke and it was nothing but a month of silence as Laurie lay in a coma. Those were the darkest days.

Laurie stirred and Jamie smiled down at her. Her best friend made a scan of the room.

"Where's Ben?" she asked in a whisper.

"He's grabbing a shower. He'll be back."

"He was here every day," she said and pulled her sheet up tight around herself. Jamie waited for Laurie to say something more but she stayed silent. Jamie wasn't sure what to make of that and let it slide.

DANA MANSFIELD

Chapter Twenty-Four

Journey

A few days later Jamie was back in Laurie's room helping her to get ready to go home. Doc discharged her with strict orders for Marcus and Jamie to plump her up. The amount of weight she lost over the last few weeks made Jamie nearly sick. Describing Laurie as skin and bones would be describing her as fat. The first thing she was going to do when they got back to the café was to make Laurie a big chocolate malt, one of her favorites.

Laurie sat on the edge of the bed. She wore the Sunset Park Café sweatshirt and jeans Jamie brought for her to wear home. On her feet were her usual running shoes. She used to go through a few pairs a year but her current pair was now well over a year old.

Jamie sat next to Laurie on the bed and pulled a brush through Laurie's thick hair. "Your ends need trimming," Jamie said. "I'll have Callie take care of that when you're feeling up to it."

"If she has the time," Laurie said quietly. This new quietness Jamie saw in Laurie the last few days bothered her. Yes, Laurie was always quiet but this was a different quiet and Jamie was afraid to ask her about it.

"She always has the time for you. We all do," Jamie added, a bit out of irritation. She was getting tired of this behavior from Laurie. It hit her right afterwards that Ben allowed this behavior to drive him away from Laurie five years earlier. "I'm sorry," she apologized.

"For what?" Laurie asked innocently.

"Never mind," Jamie said and finished braiding Laurie's hair. She noticed that Laurie kept throwing worried glances to the door of her room and she wondered if they were going to have a problem getting her out of the hospital and back to the café. Doc left orders with the nurse to use a mild sedative if needed. Jamie was hoping they wouldn't need that. Getting Laurie home would be difficult at best, she feared, and having Laurie be a little loopy wouldn't help. This could potentially be the longest four block drive ever.

*

Ben knocked on the door to Laurie's room. He fetched Jamie's Jeep from the parking lot and brought it around to the front of the hospital. Jamie opened the door and Ben entered with a wheelchair. Laurie was dressed but not looking all that confident. Her weak arm was wrapped around her front and her left hand fiddled with the end of her braid – classic nervous Laurie posturing. Ben tried to give her a reassuring smile but she refused to look at him. She was extremely cold to him since the fever broke and he had no idea why. Although they didn't make any headway in their relationship during the two weeks in the hospital, Ben didn't think he did anything to deserve an even colder reception from her.

"Okay, let's get going!" Jamie said in a voice that was overly cheery and Ben noticed Laurie inching away from them towards the window. He really wanted to tell Jamie to bring it down a notch or two but he didn't want to add more stress to the tense situation. As soon as Doc said Laurie could go home earlier that day, he began worrying about actually getting her home. There were four floors and a big lobby to get through and although they waited until after visiting hours to start the task, Ben doubted they would encounter a completely empty hospital. "This is going to be easy-peasy, Laurie. Just hop on into that wheelchair and we'll soon get you downstairs and back home. Let's go!" This time, Jamie clapped her hands and Ben knew right away that the situation just got ten times harder.

Laurie's legs buckled and she sat hard on the easy chair. "Fuck," Jamie said, her voice dripping with frustration.

"I'm... sorry..." Laurie stammered and dropped her gaze to the tiled floor.

"No, I'm the one that should be sorry," Jamie apologized. Ben pulled her keys from his pocket and jingled them at her. "I'd better go wait in the car." He gave her a not so nice look as she passed him and she mouthed an *I'm sorry* to him. As soon as Jamie was gone, he slowly approached Laurie.

"She's just a little wound up. You know how she gets sometimes," he explained and hoped Laurie bought it. "She's eager to get you out of the hospital and back up to the apartment. Seeing you in here hasn't been easy."

"You don't need to make excuses for her," Laurie said quietly. "I've put you all out at a very bad time."

"Don't be silly. Despite everything," and that everything meant the whole thirty-three years of their existence, "we're all family; none of us have been put out." Ben felt the familiar irritation rise a bit in him from Laurie's low self-esteem but he quickly squashed it. He was now next to her and he crouched down so he could get on her level although she still refused to look at him. "I've got the wheelchair all ready. The hospital's pretty quiet. It's after visiting hours so we should just run into a few nurses. It'll be a lot less people than when we went for all those tests. We'll go when you're ready, okay?"

At the fifteen minute mark, Jamie sent her first text. After the tenth text, Ben shut his cell phone off. He glanced out the window as the evening grew darker. Was she waiting to go home under the cover of night? Sunset Park was like a small town and no doubt there might be some folks not minding their own business and waiting for a peek at Laurie. That kind of behavior always irked Ben. Busybodies plagued him and Laurie during their tumultuous childhoods and they didn't subside when they moved into their adult lives.

Finally, after an hour of waiting, Laurie said it was time. He tried to guide her to the wheelchair by the elbow but she shied away from him. Keeping his confusion to himself, he slowly wheeled her from the room. They encountered a handful of individuals and each time Ben gently gave a supportive squeeze to Laurie's shoulder. This action was not rebuked by her.

When they wheeled through the front door, Ben saw that Laurie was shaking and he quickly got her to Jamie's vehicle. "How are you doing so far?" he asked as he slipped into the back seat next to her.

"I just want to go home," Laurie replied in a trembling voice. She leaned forward and shielded her eyes with shaky hands. He didn't care about taking things slow at that moment; he just knew that she needed comforting so he scooted closer to her and pulled her against his chest. She hid her face against his t-shirt.

"We'll be home soon," he said and slowly began rubbing her back. Jamie returned from returning the wheelchair, started the car, and pulled away from the curb. Ben paid more attention to Laurie than exactly where Jamie was maneuvering the vehicle. If he had noticed that she was heading to the alley behind the café, he would have told her that that was a very bad idea considering Laurie's experience with the alley. But he didn't notice and Jamie had the car parked and turned off by the time he did.

"Jamie…" Ben started but she held up a hand.

"I know where you're going with this, Ben. They've got the street in front blocked off and set up for the start of Sunset Park Days. This is the only choice," she explained a touch forcefully.

He released his anger at the situation in a long exhale of breath. Ben let go of Laurie and talked to her calmly.

"Laurie, we have no choice but to go into the café through the alley." As soon as he said that, her head snapped up with an utterly frightened look on her face. She fiercely shook her head.

"I can't," she stammered.

"It's just about fifteen feet to the back door of the café; then you'll be home. You can do this, Laurie, I know you can." She scooted farther into the Jeep.

"Should I get Marcus so he can give her a sedative?" Jamie offered, a bit frantically.

"We can't go and drug her every time to make it easier on us," he replied a bit testily.

"Calm the fuck down, Ben," she said through clenched teeth. Ben's patience with his cousin was wearing very, very thin and he turned his attention back to Laurie. This bickering wasn't helping her at all.

"Would you allow me to carry you inside? That way, you can close your eyes and you don't have to look." Laurie's frightened eyes bounced around as she contemplated the option. Finally, she nodded a slow okay.

Very carefully, Ben picked her up and she buried her head in his neck. He heard her crying as he quickly moved her away from where her endless nightmare started.

DANA MANSFIELD

Chapter Twenty-Five

Sunday Supper

Ben felt immense relief that Laurie was well and back home yet he edged out of Laurie's apartment unnoticed as Marcus, Jamie, Callie and Louis celebrated her return with chocolate malts. Ben wanted to be alone and needed fresh air so he headed for his usual chair in the farthest corner of the patio from Laurie's apartment. His mind needed clearing so he could wonder about what tomorrow would bring. Laurie's increased coldness threw a wrench in the situation and he wondered if he lost any chance at making amends. This thought brought Ben down quite a bit.

Sunset Park Days brought in many new customers to the café starting the next day. Ben and the others were busy from the time the café opened at six until it closed at its usual eight-ish. The steady business lasted all the way through Sunday's brunch and supper. Despite the morning's thunderstorms, the day was a success. Marcus and Jamie originally decided to alternate the two Sunday meals but for the busy weekend they went with both. When Ben finally pulled off his boots early Sunday evening, he was exhausted. He wasn't afraid of working hard and the busyness of the four day celebration kept his mind off Laurie. He did not see her once during those days but Jamie let him know she was resting comfortably in the apartment.

His cell phone chirped at him. *Leftovers – 20 minutes.* Although his body said no to anymore movement, his stomach said a definite yes. He hopped in and out of the shower, pulled on a pair of raggedy shorts, t-shirt, and lazy flip-flops and went next door. When Ben ate supper with Marcus and Jamie, they did it family style around their antique dining table. He enjoyed it. Traditional family dinners had not been something found in his house while growing up thanks to his father and it wasn't until he moved in with Jamie and his aunt and uncle that he really experience a leisurely 'What did you do in school?' type dinner.

"There's an extra set of hands," Marcus said to Davy who was camped out in his infant seat. Marcus held out a bottle to Ben, which stopped him in his tracks.

"Seriously?" Of course Ben had held his godson/cousin already but feeding? That seemed more complicated.

"Don't worry. He's not going to bite; he doesn't have any teeth yet."

"Well," Ben said with a touch of nervousness. "Why the hell not?" He sat down on the couch, accepted the burp rag over his shoulder, the little bottle of formula, and finally, Davy. "Hello, there, Little Man," he said quietly. Marcus stayed just long enough to see that Ben wasn't screwing the task up, then headed downstairs for what Ben assumed were the leftovers.

It was peaceful feeding Davy who alternated between sipping at his formula and gobbling it down. Halfway through he stopped for a huge yawn and for a few moments, Ben thought he was done but when he went to put him back in his infant seat, Davy woke up from his power nap and went for more grub. Even with the task at hand, Ben's thoughts circled back to Laurie. In their long relationship there were a couple pregnancy scares where they both tried to put on excited faces while waiting for the test results yet as soon as the test read negative, they would both breathe sighs of relief and vow to be more careful next time. Neither of them were sure about having children; spending a lifetime together yes, children not so much.

But the lifetime part didn't work out and Ben realized he was frowning down at Davy who was looking up at him with the most perplexed look, probably because Ben let the bottle drift from Davy's mouth to his right cheek as he reminisced. "It's empty anyway," he said to the baby and then laid him on his shoulder for the burping part. It was very successful and Ben slipped him back in his infant seat, then gently bounced it until Davy was sound asleep.

Marcus arrived with the first load of food and Teddy.

"You look beat," Teddy said as he helped Ben set the table with a hodgepodge of retro and antique plates and silverware.

"Busy day," Ben replied.

"I think there's more to that." Ben shrugged at the suggestion by his best friend. "Do you need to get something off your chest?"

"No," he said and looked around the apartment. "Where's Jamie?" he asked.

"She's bringing the rest of the food," Marcus answered and took the sleeping Davy to his room.

Jamie came in the door a few moments later and following her was Laurie. It was the first time Ben saw her in four days but what surprised him the most was the fact that she actually left her apartment.

"Laurie asked if she could join us for dinner," Jamie explained.

"Wonderful!" Teddy bellowed in a very Doc-like manner. "The more the merrier!" Ben fetched a fifth plate. Marcus and Jamie took their usual spots opposite each other which left Ben to take the spot across from Laurie, who still had not even acknowledged that Ben was in the same room. She looked better than a few days ago; color having returned to her cheeks and he noticed she gained a little weight. Teddy squeezed in next to Ben.

"Progress," Teddy whispered to Ben.

"I agree," he replied but he wasn't exactly confident about it.

Marcus and Jamie outdid themselves with the Sunday supper theme they served from two to four that afternoon with ham, mashed potatoes and gravy, greens, and biscuits. Discussion at the table was over continuing the Sunday experiment.

"Sunday's our only day off," Jamie said. "And now with Davy, it would be nice to do stuff with him. The zoo, a drive out to the country, family shit like that."

"I know but the Sunday opening has definitely been a success. Not to get all money-grubbing but the books don't lie," countered Marcus. Ben chewed the problem over in his own mind while sneaking glances at Laurie. She was eating but quiet; her typical self. Ben wanted to see his cousin be a success but he also didn't want them to overwork themselves, especially now with Davy.

"Why don't you compromise?" he suggested and lay down his fork and knife.

"How so?" Marcus asked. Ben took a drink of iced tea and wiped his mouth.

"There's typically four Sundays in a month. Open the café for only two of them. Offer brunch one Sunday and supper the other Sunday. A little supply and demand works too; people really enjoyed themselves today and if this is something that's only going to happen a couple times a month, you can bet business will be great. Then you have the other two Sundays to yourselves."

"I like," Marcus drawled out slowly.

"So do I," Jamie added. The rest of the dinner went enjoyably slow as they talked about the Sunday plans. Laurie stayed quiet but Ben didn't think she seemed overly nervous. He noticed her actually looking up at the others several times and on occasion, a smile crossed her face when something amusing was said. They all pitched in to clean up after dinner and retired to the patio for dessert, including Laurie. She took the chair closest to the door. There was definitely something going on with her, and Ben wondered what that something was.

Dessert was Laurie's pound cake and Jamie's pecan pie; both recipes that the ladies added to The Old Man's menu while he was still in charge of the place and if memory served Ben right, it had been their first two additions and created while they were still learning their trade. Ben had no willpower and ate a piece of both and was miserable. It was a good miserable; the type of misery that only good food, and good company, can make. The sun began to set and Ben's eyes were droopy. It was a good day; one of only a few since returning to Memphis.

"Well," Jamie said with a sigh. "'Tomorrow is another day.'"

"She's quoting Scarlett O'Hara," Marcus noted. "Definitely time to get her to bed." There was light laughter and Ben thought the idea of bed sounded very good. He stood with Marcus, Jamie and Teddy and took a step towards the door.

And then Laurie spoke up.

"Ben," she said. "Could you stay out here? I'd like to talk, please." You could have heard a pin drop three blocks away.

"Of course," Ben said. Jamie was the one that hesitated, though.

"Do you want me to stay, Laurie?" she asked.

"No," Laurie replied. "The talk, it needs to be just between me and Ben." *The talk!* Ben's full stomach lurched. Laurie was allowing the talk!

"Are you sure?" Jamie asked slowly. "What about Teddy? Maybe he should stay."

"No," Laurie said with a touch of annoyance in her voice. "Just Ben and me."

"Come on, sweetie," Marcus said and started to guide Jamie towards the door. "Let's give them privacy." Jamie seemed to want to object but Marcus wouldn't let her, although the look on his face wasn't one of support either. Ben never talked to Marcus about his plan but it was too late now. Teddy stayed a bit longer and gave them both advice.

"Be honest and make it count."

Chapter Twenty-Six

Hope

"May I sit?" Ben asked and motioned to the chair next to hers. He didn't want to make her uncomfortable but he also didn't want her to raise her voice either.

"Yes," she said quietly in a nervous voice as her left hand fiddled with the end of her braid. Ben sat, then realized that his notebook with his 'script' was back in his apartment.

"I need to go grab something..." Ben stood back up and took a step towards the door but Laurie stopped him.

"I know Marcus had you write a bunch of stuff down but could you please talk to me from here," Laurie patted her heart, "instead of just reading off of a piece of paper?" She made this request with definite eye contact and he slowly sat back down.

"Of course, Laurie," he replied. The night was muggy but not uncomfortably warm and through a few breaks in the clouds, Ben saw the twinkling stars.

"First, I want to thank you for staying by my side at the hospital," Laurie said, which brought Ben into focus.

"I had to be there, Laurie. There was no way I could leave you alone." He looked at her; her face tensed and she clenched her jaw.

Ben knew the look; Laurie was pissed. This was something new for him. Although he saw her angry about things or food in the café before the fight, this was the first time he felt her anger directed at him.

"But you did before," she said with more force than she should have used and her hand went to her throat. So this was how the talk was going to begin, about his distance when she needed him. He dreaded this topic but knew it was going to happen sometime. "Why didn't you come back, Ben? I begged and begged for you but you never came." Laurie's voice was so raw and emotional and the reverberations jack-hammered into his soul. He felt sweat trickle down his back. "I needed you so much and you weren't there." She was already crying and he wasn't too far behind her.

"I don't think there's anything easy I can say, Laurie," his voice dangerously low with emotion. "My actions after you were attacked are inexcusable. Saying 'I'm sorry' doesn't even come close to apologizing for not being there for you." She stood and he was afraid that she was going to retreat into her apartment but instead she began a slow pace in front of him. The patio was lit sporadically with electric luminaries but there was enough amber illumination for Ben to see Laurie in the soft light. It created such a perfect yet somber atmosphere for the talk.

Laurie continued her slow pace so he continued talking, from the beginning. "Those last two years before I took off were... were..."

"Awful?" she offered.

"Yes, awful. With Uncle Jack's death and you losing The Old Man and your own old man being released on compassion... All those things were just grinding on us and when you started to close yourself off..."

"You did that too, Ben; I wasn't the only one."

"I admit that I internalized so much and wouldn't talk to you, Laurie, like I used to and then your other issues started to intensify, I just... I..." He stammered to a stop. "I thought that was it and I made the worst decision of my life, our life. I couldn't handle it anymore and I felt I had to walk away."

Laurie stopped pacing and began to cry harder. Ben took a huge leap of faith by walking over to her and wrapping his arms around her. She didn't fight the embrace and she spent a good five minutes crying into his chest. He let his own tears slide and when she seemed to be calming down, he led her back over to the chairs.

"I know we were both at fault but that night, when you started talking and then began to yell, I just couldn't process what you were saying. I was hearing it but it wasn't sinking in," she explained through a few more tears and a voice he wondered would last the task. "I wanted another chance; to show you that I could be better. I thought I could but then I realized that that's who I was at the moment and you didn't want me…"

"It wasn't like that, Laurie," he interrupted but then realized she was partially right. "No, it was a little bit like that. I didn't want the Laurie that was so hurt by what you'd struggled with during those two years because after everything we both went through in our whole lives, I just didn't know how much more you could take." He stopped himself and shook his head. "That doesn't even make sense." He rubbed his forehead and tried to remember what he wrote down. That was of no help as none of what was in that damn notebook came from his heart. "No, it does make some sense. I didn't know how much more you could take and the way your problems were overcoming you was scary for me to see. It was so hard to see the woman I loved, who I still love, and who used to be strong, slowly shrink inward." He paused to collect himself. "I could see how you were withdrawing from life. You spent all your time in the kitchen or the apartment and when you did go out it was only to run and even then you stuck to the shadowy alleyways so no one would see you. I felt like I was losing you and that just tore me up inside. I didn't know how to help you, how to make you feel better." He paused again; it was becoming harder and harder for him to vocalize what he needed to say. "I threw you away so I didn't have to see you, afraid of what you were becoming, when I should have been afraid of what I was becoming. I was doing the exact same thing but in my own way." Ben stopped and took a deep breath. "I know leaving you must have hurt so bad…"

"Don't you dare try to think you know how I felt, Ben," Laurie said, the force returning to her voice but this time, although there was the pain on her face, her hand didn't flutter to her throat and she didn't back down the energy behind her voice.

"I lost some of my memories from the stroke but I didn't lose a single memory of us. I remember clearly the pain I felt when I was running that night, when I finally realized what you did. I remember the tears on my face and how my lungs felt like they were going to explode because I kept running and running, harder and harder, trying to run away from those words. I loved you so much, Ben, and you left. I couldn't believe you actually left! And you're right, you did throw me away. I felt like a piece of worthless garbage. I still feel that way."

Laurie paused for a few moments to catch her breath. Her words were so painful for him to hear but her words were so correct. "You didn't know how to help me? All you had to do was show me some of the caring that was inside you. You always made me feel so safe when we were together and your words left me feeling so afraid that night, so frightened, so absolutely worthless. The only other person who left me feeling that way was my father. Every time he hit me or made me do those awful things, I was left so scared, but in those days I had you as a friend and then eventually as a lover, and you knew how to comfort me. I let you into my heart; you're the only person I allowed to get that close to me and in a span of an hour you ripped my security away from me.

"And then, when I was in that hospital bed after being raped, I was so frightened all I wanted was you to be there with me so that I could feel safe again. I thought that even though you left me, what I went through was enough to at least bring you back as a friend. And you never came."

Laurie broke down again and he held his head in his hands. Ben knew that when they got around to it, addressing those issues from five years ago was going to be beyond hard but what he felt at that moment was raw pain. His head pounded and his chest hurt. He was shaking and if he didn't know better, he would have thought it was a heart attack. Instead, his body was just dealing with the consequences of that one night and that one decision.

"I made such a colossal mistake, Laurie, and the only thing I can do right now is ask for your forgiveness," he said through his own tears. "My love for you has never waned and I needed to tell you that. I told you that night I wasn't even sure if I could love you and those words were so... so... so wrong. I said them but I didn't mean them. It just sounded like the right thing to say for what I was doing." It was his turn to pause and take a few breaths. "I never should have said those awful things and I should have come back when Jamie told me about the kidnapping. I should have come back when you asked for me but I was so ashamed of myself that I couldn't even under those horrific circumstances and then I took my first drink and then another and the shame grew. When I hit rock bottom a year ago, I knew there was no way I could ever be completely sober again if I didn't have your forgiveness for both that night and then not coming back. And then when Mei told me that you tried to kill yourself, I was shocked and again, ashamed that my actions caused you to be in so much pain that you tried to commit suicide." Ben stopped talking to breathe. The urge to drink and shoot up at that moment was unbelievable. He rubbed the crook of his arm and yearned for the sharp prick of the needle and then the feeling of... nothing. No shame, no pain.

"I didn't try to kill myself because of you," Laurie said in a small voice. "I don't blame you and you shouldn't blame yourself."

"That's what Jamie said, too."

141

"She's right, Ben. To be honest I don't know why I cut myself. I don't really understand what happened that night; it's something that has bugged me since it happened. I don't have clear memories of me making that decision. That's why I asked Marcus for the cameras." Silence crept onto the patio and the crickets provided an uneven soundtrack of the somber moment. "I didn't know you started drinking until I overheard you and Mei in the alley a few weeks back. I'm so sorry, Ben. You told me so many times that you would never drink because of your dad." She paused a moment. "I feel responsible for that." Ben couldn't help but laugh sadly.

"I was the one that walked into that bar and took a drink. You shouldn't be sorry, Laurie."

"And you shouldn't blame yourself for my suicide attempt. Can we agree on those two things?"

"Yes," Ben replied with a deep sigh. He was exhausted and leaned back in the wooden Adirondack chair and Laurie did the same in hers.

"I love you, Laurie, whether you grant me your forgiveness or not. If you want me to leave the apartment, Memphis, even Tennessee, I will abide by your wishes." The silent minutes that followed were nerve-wracking and he led himself to believe that the long passage of time was Laurie's silent answer telling him to leave. But then she spoke, her voice quiet but sure.

"If I tell you to leave, you'll die, won't you?"

Even the crickets seem to stop their song to hear his answer. He didn't want to answer, didn't want the obvious answer to jade Laurie's feelings. It would be a silent way of forcing her to do something she may not want to do. And so he remained silent.

"I don't want you to leave." She paused and Ben felt her hand on his forearm. "I care about you too much and I know that if I were to turn you away, it would be your turn to try and commit suicide by drinking yourself to death. I know you too well, Ben."

"If you tell me to stay, I feel like I'm forcing you to tell me that because I'm so weak." It was so hard to get those words out. "I don't want to force you to do anything."

"You're not forcing me. I know exactly what I'm doing. I admit I have days where my brain just doesn't seem to work right, I have the stroke to thank for that, but when it comes to you, I know I'm thinking clearly. When I say I don't want you to leave, there are two reasons. The first is that I don't want you to end your days at the bottom of a bottle. I admit it; I am afraid of what will happen but..."

Another pause but this one felt different. Very different. He looked over at her and expected her to drop her gaze like she had done so often before. This time, however, she looked at him squarely. "Ben, the other reason is that I still love you and I can't ignore what I feel in my heart. If you leave Sunset Park again, it won't be because I told you to."

"Then where does that leave us? What's next? What role do you see me playing in your life then?"

"I don't see you 'playing' a role, Ben." She stopped and took a deep breath. "Call me crazy, and I know Jamie does sometimes, but providing I can trust you again, I see you... us... sharing a life again." There was a brief moment where he thought he had heard her wrong but after a moment's thought, he realized he heard each word perfectly. Ben's heart both glowed yet trembled in worry. It was his hope for another chance but he also knew that they both had a lot of work to do to get to that point.

"Are you sure, Laurie? To be honest, this is what I hoped for."

"Even after everything, I want this. When Jamie said you were coming back to walk her down the aisle, I really didn't react because I thought you'd be here and then gone again."

"But then I didn't go."

"No, you didn't. I missed what we had so much, even some of the bad stuff, but I didn't know what you wanted. Then I got sick and you were at my side the whole time. I saw that you still cared.

At first I tried to ignore it, ignore you, but I couldn't. Since I was released from the hospital, I've done nothing but think about us. I couldn't ignore what was in here." Laurie put her hand to her heart again. "I make no promises, Ben. I was raped. I may not be able to move past it and you may not be able to love me in the same way because of how it left me." Those words were heartbreaking to Ben. He wasn't naïve; he already prepared himself for something like that. After all, he wrote down *nothing* as a possible role he could take.

"I understand," he replied.

"I don't know what details you know about what happened," she said in a shaky voice. "But for us to try and come back together, I feel like I need to tell you about those days... when he kept me in that place and what he did. I need you to know so you really understand me."

"Of course, Laurie, but only when you feel the time is right and you're comfortable."

"Thank you. I will need time. I have good days and bad and I hope you understand that there may be some days I just want to stay in the apartment with the curtains closed. Jamie stresses me enough when she tries to force me to change; I don't need that from you also."

"Forcing you to do anything if I was given this chance was one of those things I promised myself I wouldn't do when I came back. I was prepared to even accept you refusing to talk to me and leave it at that."

"But then you would have started drinking again."

Ben felt his cheeks glow in embarrassment. Now was not the time to hide anything from Laurie.

"More than likely, yes," he admitted. "If you would have said no or asked me to leave, I honestly think it would just be a matter of days before I succumbed to my temptations and let them kill me."

144

"You asked for my forgiveness, Ben, and I give it to you without any strings."

Ben's emotions peaked with Laurie's absolution and he didn't trust himself to voice his gratitude. He fought a valiant war but lost as he broke down. Laurie kneeled in front of him and just as he had done for her, she brought him in for a comforting embrace and he cried a cleansing cry of hope and possibility.

DANA MANSFIELD

Chapter Twenty-Seven

Acceptance

Ben stood at the bottom of the kitchen steps and craned his ear up. For a good half an hour, thankfully during the morning lull, Jamie and Laurie fought. Actually, it was more like Jamie doing a lot of yelling and Ben guessed that Laurie was doing a lot of listening, or maybe ignoring. He had no idea what was going on between the two best friends and even Marcus didn't know. He went upstairs just as the yelling started but Jamie ordered him back downstairs. The only words Ben could make out were the words that a Southern Belle usually didn't use but then Jamie wasn't your typical Southern Belle.

"I hope they finish soon," Marcus said and looked at the old school clock that stood above the door to the walk-in fridge and freezer. It was a little after ten and their early bird lunch regulars would be arriving within a half an hour. Ben knew from growing up, especially the early teen years, that Jamie and Laurie could go round and round for hours at a time. But they were women now; he didn't know if that made things better or worse.

The back door of the kitchen opened and Mrs. Bailey entered with Davy in his car seat. It was an inopportune moment as

Jamie's voice rushed down the stairs in a tumble of what was a colorful combination of four letter words. "Sweet Jesus!" Mrs. Bailey exclaimed and put Davy on the metal worktable. "I haven't heard that in years! Marcus Arthur, what is up with your wife?"

There was a slam of a door and then Jamie's clogged feet stomped down the stairs and when she appeared, everyone took several steps back. Her cheeks were flushed and she was breathing heavily. Ben had seen this anger in her before and knew the best thing to do was to remain quiet.

Jamie glared at everyone but her mother-in-law; even Jamie knew better than that.

"You're a might upset," Mrs. Bailey said. "Perhaps you need a few minutes to cool off?" Ben knew that truly wasn't a suggestion from the tall and stocky matron of the Bailey family.

"Thank you, Bea," Jamie said in a very controlled voice. "But for right now, I would love it if you could settle Davy upstairs for his nap so I can speak with Ben." Ben's eyes grew wide and he quickly looked over at Marcus who was shooting him a very sympathetic look.

They went into the rough basement where no voices would carry at all. He followed Jamie into the darkest of the storage rooms. Ben was more worried about smacking his head on one of the low hanging ceiling lights and wasn't expecting what came next. Jamie whirled around and hit him so hard in the chest with her open palms that he stumbled backwards and hit his head on the last light. When he touched the back of his head, he felt stickiness and his fingers came back bloody.

"What the hell, CJ?"

"What the hell?! What the hell?!" Jamie screamed at him and he took another step back.

"Are you angry that Laurie and I talked last night?" he deduced in question. That's the only thing he could figure out.

"I. Am. Very. Angry," she said and punctuated each word. He noticed her clenching her fists; Ben wasn't sure if he ever witnessed her so irate before. "I have been angry for five years and I can't take it anymore."

"And this anger is at me."

"Damn right, you fucker," she spat out and began pacing. Ben gave her a wide berth. "That night you left Laurie I just couldn't believe what you were doing; I couldn't believe that you were leaving her because you just 'couldn't deal,' if I may quote you. You were in the most important, most stable, relationship of your life and you were refusing to realize that it was a two-way street. You were only thinking of yourself. I didn't even recognize you that night, Ben; you rarely put yourself ahead of anyone and the fact that the first time you did that was with Laurie, I... I..." she faltered as her pacing grew more intense. "You left and Laurie was still not back from her run. It wasn't until midnight when Marcus and I started to worry. Unofficially, we knew we had to wait for forty-eight hours before calling the police but we had Marcus's dad on our side. He asked the night patrols to keep an eye out for her. I was so afraid because instead of talking with me about what happened, Laurie took off.

"The next morning David came by with Detective Nolan. They used to walk the neighborhood together and David asked if he could help. He called in a favor and they started unofficially looking at all the security cameras in the area and that's when they saw Laurie being grabbed and forced into the trunk of a car." Jamie stopped and covered her eyes with her hands. "Ben, I saw the fucking tape. He just grabbed her," she said incredulously. Ben knew only the basics of what happened in those days from a series of increasingly irritated voice mails and texts from Jamie. "They started an investigation right away but the trail was weak. Her abductor kept his face away from the camera and there was no license plate on the car.

"I kept the café going so I had something to distract me from my worry. I really don't need to remind you that Laurie's like my sister and I was so afraid of what was going to happen, what might be happening to her. Marcus cancelled all his appointments to help out but what I really needed was my best friend, you. Ben, the woman you loved had been kidnapped and you fucking refused to come back! I couldn't believe it and what was worse, you wouldn't even pick up the phone for me, you son of a bitch! I don't want you to tell me why because nothing you could say short of you being abducted by fucking aliens could change how I feel about your sorry ass right now."

Ben didn't need the adjective; he did completely feel like an ass. It was a familiar feeling, five years old.

"Four days later, she was dumped in the alley. The image of Marcus's father with his fingers trying to stop the bleeding is so vivid," she explained with her eyes closed. "I never told you this, Ben, but in the ER her heart stopped; Laurie was fucking dead."

Ben felt as if his own heart beat its last beat. He thought he understood how close he came to losing Laurie but in reality, he had no idea.

"She lost so much blood but I begged them not to stop trying to save her; begged Doc to go into that ER room and talk some sense into those that wanted to stop. It worked and they did everything they could and she came back." Jamie was crying now and under a different set of circumstances Ben would have consoled her. Now, all he wanted to do was escape the basement. The problem was Jamie was between him and the stairs. Running, that's what he still wanted to do instead of face what he did.

"She came back and they rushed her into surgery for the knife wounds. The ER doctor was the one that told me she'd been raped. If Marcus wasn't standing right next to me, I probably would have fainted. I knew that with her history with her father, the rape was going to cause more damage than all the stabbings and the blood loss. That's why she wanted you there, Ben. She needed to feel safe and you were the only one who could provide that for her. She fucking needed you, Ben, she wanted nothing to do with me," Jamie screamed. "And you didn't come!

"A week later she suffered the stroke and was lying in a coma for a month. You needed to be there but you weren't. I sat by her every day, hoping the café could survive without me, and then when she woke up, she was so helpless. I took care of Laurie, bathed her, fed her, dried her tears when she faltered with relearning to walk and talk. Even before she voiced anything she was scribbling your name on a little whiteboard. You should have been there at her side; she wanted you and not me. I kept calling and texting you and you ignored me. She needed you; I needed you, Ben, but I got over it because we go back too far but Laurie... well, I thought Laurie was never going to get over what you did and that made me feel better. I felt like I had won whatever game you were playing. I knew that I wouldn't have to worry about picking her up again; I just needed to maintain her with Marcus and Teddy's help. But then you moved back and then you wanted to talk to Laurie and you got the fucking nerve to ask Laurie for forgiveness. How dare you!? Are you going to leave her again? Are you going to throw her away? Do you know how fucking exhausting it is to try and keep Laurie from falling so far she wants to kill herself? I do, Ben, because I was by her side the whole time despite the fact that she wanted you and only you."

Ben, in a stupor, didn't realize what happened until it was too late. Jamie reared back and delivered a hard right hook to his left eye and just like that, Ben was standing in front of his father. He dropped his gaze to his feet and waited for the next blow. He was shaking and his stomach quivered in fear. His father screamed at him, calling him worthless and a screw up because he had trouble in school. But then he came rushing back to present day and it was his cousin in front of him and not his father. His stomach reacted like it did twenty years ago and he stumbled to the corner and vomited into a garbage can. Ben's heart began to race and a cold sweat broke out. The bricked room began to sway before him and he sat down hard on his ass. He could hear Jamie calling to him but she sounded like a million miles away. Darkness that resembled his father crept in on him and he was too weak to fight against it.

*

Jamie's anger disappeared as she watched Ben react to her stupidity. She saw this before, just once, when Ben hid her in his closet out of fear. Her uncle, Ben's father, was raging for some reason she didn't understand and through a small crack in the louvered door, she watched as Ben was slapped and backhanded several times before being ordered to strip so Uncle Lem could use his belt on Ben. Jamie watched in horror as his backside was turned into a sickening roadmap of cuts, bruises, and welts from the heavy leather belt. When Uncle Lem was finished, Ben puked on the floor of his room and nearly passed out. They were fourteen, just days past their shared birthday, and that night Jamie told her own father what she witnessed. Two days later, Uncle Lem bludgeoned Ben's mother in front of him after being confronted about the abuse.

"Ben!" she finally shouted out of fear and not anger as he collapsed on the floor. His eyes rolled into the back of his head and she ran to the stairs to get Marcus.

"What the hell happened?" Marcus said as he came upon Jamie kneeling next to a very unconscious Ben.

"I got carried away," she cried. She was losing it. "It just happened."

"Jamie, he's bleeding. What did you do?"

"I didn't do that," she said but then corrected herself. "I didn't physically do that. He hit his head on the light." She kept Ben's secret, how he reacts to physical abuse, just as she promised to do so many years ago.

"Go get the First Aid kit," Marcus ordered and she collected the red bag from the kitchen. Luckily, Bea was in the apartment and only Louis was in the kitchen.

"What's going on?" he asked.

"Don't ask," replied Jamie. When she got back down to Ben, she was relieved to see he was sitting up. He looked pale and shaky; his left eye already starting to puff up. Marcus cleaned the two-inch cut on the back of Ben's head but didn't think it was deep enough for stitches. Finally, he broke two of the instant ice bags; one for the back of his head and the other for his eye.

"How are you doing, Ben?" Marcus asked and Ben looked at Jamie with a combination of confusion, fear, and anger.

"I'm confused," he said.

"You took a hit to your head..." Marcus tried to explain but Ben waved him off.

"No, not from that," he interrupted. "CJ, what the hell is going on?"

"It's a valid question, Jamie," added Marcus. Two of the most important men in her life were waiting for her answer.

"I'll talk to you later, Marcus. I promise," she added, knowing he would want to object not knowing right then and there. "I just really need to talk to Ben right now, just him and me."

"Should I leave this down here?" Marcus asked, holding up the First Aid kit.

"No," she replied shortly.

"You're a beautiful woman, sweetie," Marcus said and gave her a kiss. "I worry when you get like this. And you bet we'll talk later." Jamie waited until Marcus was gone.

"I'm so sorry, Ben," she apologized and didn't hold back the rare tears. "I let my emotions completely control me and I can't believe I hit you. I saw what that bastard of a father did to you but I still hit you." She looked at Ben but he wasn't looking back. His gaze was once again on the dusty concrete floor as he held the ice bags to his injuries. "I hit you."

"You don't need to tell me that," he said, "I felt it." They sat in silence until he spoke again, "If you were so angry with me, why didn't you say something during the last five years?"

"Ben, I couldn't even get you to call me back when Laurie was kidnapped and then when we finally did speak, I was just so afraid to bring anything up out of fear."

"Fear of what?"

Jamie found herself speechless. How could she put into words that fear? She had to try; that fear was so close now and she needed to keep it at bay.

"This whole nightmare has us all messed up. Well, except for Marcus and Teddy. Thank god they've got even keels on them." She moved closer to Ben. "Do you remember back in seventh grade and Laurie's mom left her dad?"

"Of course, CJ."

"Laurie refused to go with her mom and siblings because even though her dad was a son of bitch who abused them all and... and... did those things to Laurie, she didn't want the family to be broken up."

"And she stayed because she was afraid that son of a bitch would be sad that his wife left with four of his five kids."

"Did she tell you what her mom did before she took off?" Jamie caught herself; of course Laurie would have told Ben. "I witnessed that; Laurie's mom just screaming at her. Her dad wasn't the only one that was messed up. Her mom told her that she was stupid for staying and deserved what he did to her and whatever he would do to her after she left."

"And then she hit Laurie."

"I watched Laurie's family disintegrate in front of my eyes and in the aftermath of your fight and the rape, I felt like my family was disintegrating. I wanted to hold on to what little was left and I was afraid that if I expressed how angry I was at you, I'd lose not only Laurie, but you, too. We all have too much history together."

Muffled footsteps from the kitchen above provided a comforting barrier to the silence. Ben reached over and put his arm around Jamie's shoulders.

"I'm sorry. I know that seems too simple for all the pain I caused but I don't know what else to say."

"I know Laurie forgave you, Ben, but it's going to take a little longer for me. But let me tell you this. I've aged over the last five years and I have Marcus's family and Teddy and now Davy. And Laurie. If you hurt her trying to appease your demons, I'll have no problem banishing you from my life. You have one shot in my eyes and if that shot fails, that's it." She looked over at Ben who was finally able to make eye contact. "I'm serious."

"Noticed," he said and pointed to his soon-to-be black eye. "Trust me, Jamie," he said, using her real name. "I understand that not only do I have just one shot in your eyes, I only have one shot in Laurie's. The last five years have been hell but I've also realized that I belong here with Laurie and you, of course. I would like to believe I won't screw things up. If I do, that would be the end of me also."

"I need to apologize to you, though, Ben."

"What for? I'm the one that's pretty much screwed everything up."

"Well, not completely but you're actions didn't help." She took a deep breath and let it out as a sigh. "I just assumed that you were moving on and away from Laurie down in Panama City. I thought the drinking was just a slight blip, nothing more than a year but when Marcus told me that you struggled with it much longer than what you let on with me and then also the heroin abuse, I realized that you were in pain also. I'm not excusing your actions but I never once really thought how everything was affecting you." It was her turn to provide a reassuring arm around the shoulders. "When I hit you, I recognized your reaction. You seemed to go back in time," Jamie noted slowly.

"It was like I was standing in front of him again," Ben said quietly and leaned back against the brick wall. He pulled his knees up and rested his forearms on them. Jamie hadn't seen her cousin looking so vulnerable in a very long time. In fact, the last time she did was right after the beating she witnessed. "I'm thirty-three years old and I feel like that stupid fourteen year-old again."

"You are not stupid now and you were not stupid then."

"Even at fourteen, I couldn't stop him from hitting me. I just took it. I knew it was wrong but I didn't know what I could do."

Jamie's heart ached for Ben. He was still in so much pain from his childhood, just like Laurie. And just like that, she understood why he asked for Laurie's forgiveness and she gave it.

"I sometimes wonder if you hadn't told your dad about that night if my dad would have eventually killed me." Jamie wanted to say *of course not* but the beating she witnessed was still fresh in her memory even after twenty years. The chances were good that if she hadn't told her dad, Ben wouldn't be sitting next to her.

"Let's just be glad it didn't come to that," she said. They sat in silence for quite a while until Jamie asked a question that she wanted to ask since he came back. "I know you go to AA and NA meetings for help with your drinking and the heroin but have you ever talked to anyone about what happened back then?"

"No," Ben replied. "I'd rather just forget about it."

"Understood but look at what just happened." From the look on his face, Jamie knew he realized that talking to someone was a good idea. "Even if it's unofficial..."

"You mean Marcus?"

"Yes, Marcus, maybe even Teddy. I just think that it would be a good idea, especially since you and Laurie are going to try to work through things. It may help with that."

⚜

Both Marcus and Jamie insisted on giving Ben the rest of the day off. It was Monday, their slowest day, and it had been quite the emotional morning for him. Ben insisted he was fine but eventually, he grew tired of the harping and headed upstairs with a bottle of Advil and a bag of frozen corn for his eye which was almost swollen shut. His head was pounding but he wasn't sure if it was from hitting his head, the right hook, the pounding to his chest, or the overall stress of the morning. His steps were slow and plodding and when he got to the top of the stairs, Laurie stood with her door ajar a few inches. Just the site of her, even what little he could see through the opening, melted a little of the tension away.

"Hi, Laurie," he said and did a miserable job of hiding the stress in his voice. Her gaze went from his eye to the bag of corn in his hand.

"You don't fight," she noted, her voice still rough from the previous night. "What happened?" she asked with concern. He wasn't sure how to answer the question. Truthfully? Gloss it over? Lie? Then the childhood shame rushed back into his psyche and he couldn't look at Laurie. He was a mess. The cold sweat broke out again and he felt shaky, just like he felt in the basement. The last thing he wanted to do was pass out in front of Laurie. "You don't look so good," she said. The door shut and then reopened after she undid the chain. "Why don't you come in?"

Ben accepted the invitation and for a moment he thought the last five years hadn't happened. All the curtains were open and the room once again glowed. But then the memory of the morning came back along with the shame. His stomach was queasy and he really just wanted to go to his own apartment and hide out. But that would be running away and it was that action that caused so much pain for everyone.

"And what happened to your head?" Laurie inquired as he sat on the couch.

"I hit it on one of those lights in the basement."

"What were you doing down there?"

"Getting yelled at by Jamie." Laurie brought Ben a cup of water and he downed four Advil. He rubbed his forehead and wished for the pain medication to bring instant relief.

"Dare I ask what happened down there?" Again, Ben debated how to answer her and in light of their conversation from the previous evening, he realized that the truth was necessary. By the time he was done, Laurie was a bundle of different emotions.

Angry with Jamie for hitting him, concerned about Ben's reaction, and sad that he was still dealing with their childhood.

"Thank you for being honest with me," Laurie said and took his hand in her good one. She moved closer to him as the emotional retelling got the best of him. The Advil finally took hold and talking about what happened made him feel a little better.

"I didn't think glossing over what happened would be a good move," he admitted. "There used to be a time when we told each other everything."

"That was my fault; I started that," Laurie said quietly and Ben wasn't going to argue with her. She kept the news from him that her father had won release from prison out of compassion. Dying of cancer, he was allowed to live out his final months as a free man despite nearly killing his daughter. It had been Laurie's own estranged mother and siblings who were behind the request for release. Her mom then contacted Laurie and said she wasn't welcomed to come by and see her father or even go to the funeral when he finally died. Laurie kept all this away from Ben and inside and things started to become so different. When he found out, from Mei of all people, he confronted Laurie and that was the basis of their first fight of that difficult two year period.

"But we're trying to move on," he noted with a smile that was meant to be comforting and his heart warmed when she returned one. A knock on the door caused Laurie to jump and look panicked. She had taken a few baby steps that day but Ben could see how easy it might be for her to regress. "I'll get it," he said and went to unlock the one deadbolt Laurie threw when he entered the apartment. It was Jamie and she was holding Davy.

"I went to your apartment to check on you but tried here when I found your place empty," she explained nervously. "Am I interrupting anything?"

"We're just talking." Jamie seemed torn about something and to be honest, Ben hoped it was about her actions that morning. He was still quite rattled by the level of her anger and her actions.

"Can I come in and talk to you both?" Ben looked back at Laurie who nodded her permission. When they settled in the living area, Ben and Laurie on the couch and Jamie in the antique rocking chair that once belonged to Ben's grandma, Jamie apologized.

"I'm sorry about this morning," she began, a little weepy. Davy cooed and she smiled down at him. Ben wondered if she brought the baby to ground her after a wild morning. "It's just that I care so much about you both and the last five years have been hell and I just want to make sure you're doing what's right for both of you."

"I believe we are, Jamie," Laurie said. "As I told you this morning, Ben and I had a good talk last night and we want to see if we can resolve the last five years."

"And we are going into this knowing there's a chance it won't work but we have to try," Ben added. "We understand that Laurie and I affect you and Marcus and now the next generation. Hopefully, by dealing with what we have to deal with, that'll ease the tension on you guys. We appreciate all that you've done for us and hope that you'll give us the time and space we need." Ben did a lot of we talking and he hoped Laurie didn't mind.

Jamie choked on either a sob or a laugh but in the end, she smiled through her tears.

Chapter Twenty-Eight

Baby Steps

The early summer days passed and waned and Ben took over the Laurie jobs that the others were used to holding. It was a smooth adjustment and having Ben bring her meals helped ease Laurie into what they needed to do. Neither expected her issues to resolve overnight and Ben was willing to work with them; something he failed to do leading up to his walking out on her. He began to rise earlier in the morning and hit the gym across the street to help combat some of the softness that was setting in from a combination of good food and not working construction anymore. Running around the café helped some but he also needed an alternative outlet for working off any frustration. He learned early on in the process that he could not talk clearly while frustrated and that just created more issues than they needed.

The cafe took the next few hours of his day with the breakfast rush and then as soon as the lull came, he would take his breakfast and Laurie's breakfast up to her place. On the good days she felt comfortable enough to leave her door unlocked (Ben always knocked first) but there a few bad days where all five deadbolts were engaged along with the chain. He would need to wait until she opened the door and yes, there were a handful of days where Laurie wouldn't even unchain the door for him.

Later they would eat lunch together and while Ben helped prep for dinner, Marcus would have a session with Laurie. Sporadically throughout the day, Laurie would text Ben for a pot of tea or a snack and he complied. Sometimes she would just text a simple *hi* and those moments made him smile. Dinner would again keep everyone busy and when everything was cleared and cleaned and put away, up the stairs Ben would go again to have dinner with Laurie. She usually asked about the day in the café and Ben was happy to tell her; he was pleased that she was showing an interest in the place she loved so much before everything went to hell. After dinner they would talk either in the apartment or out on her side of the patio. Sometimes they even just sat and watched TV. Teddy continued to stop by and on Sundays, all five of them would eat a family style meal in Jamie's apartment.

Even the quiet times were considered progress. When they talked it might just be chitchat but they did spend a lot of time on the issues they needed to work through. They started with the easy things but as the days added up they moved towards the more difficult topics.

Those talks would leave them exhausted, both emotionally and physically. Or, in Laurie's case, silent for a few days as she used up her voice. They both agreed to continue talking until they were finished with a topic and sometimes that didn't happen until the sun was coming up and it was time for Ben to scoot down to the café. By the time the end of June rolled around, they hit on many things but still needed to cover Ben's drinking in Panama City Beach (and Mei), Laurie's suicide attempt and the attack itself.

But then, on an appropriately stormy, late June day, the fight happened.

Chapter Twenty-Nine

Words to Ruination

Three days of blistering heat irritated those in Sunset Park. Instead of bringing a few degrees of relief, each night brought escalating storms. That first night, a Saturday, the rain was so heavy for such an extended period of time that Ben, Marcus and Jamie stood at the front window of the café and watched, inch by inch, as the rainwater came close to invading the café through the front door. They were lucky for the most part; there was just enough of an incline going into the café that the water ended up rushing away. However, the next day, an off Sunday, the men spent a grueling eighteen hours emptying the stone basement of six inches of water and cleaning the gunk left behind in hopes of heading off any mold issues. It had been The Old Man who insisted on keeping very few items on the floor of the basement, apparently for good reason, so most everything was safe and dry on metal shelves. There were just a few old fruit and vegetable boxes to be tossed.

Ben was in desperate need of sleep after that grueling task but just past midnight the next storm came through. Not a gully washer, thank goodness; this storm though was heavy on hail which shredded the patio greenhouse and took out one of Ben's windows and two of Laurie's. They opened the café the next day but kept the menu to quick sandwiches and plenty of iced tea as people cleaned up the mess in the neighborhood in temperatures that soared into the triple digits.

Jamie's language as she cleaned up her beloved greenhouse made anyone within earshot blush. Ben helped Laurie take care of the broken glass from her apartment floor and after boarding up all three windows, he ran over to St. Anthony's to help there. Luckily, or divinely, none of the beautiful stained glass windows of the church were even chipped. When Ben walked back to the café with sweat pouring off of him, he marveled at how much damage the hail storm had done. He couldn't remember the last time his home neighborhood had been so physically damaged. The park was the saddest part as nearly every large tree had been shredded by the hail and the green grass was littered with leaf bits. They lay about almost like a green snowstorm had moved through the area.

When he returned home, he found Marcus slamming around the kitchen, a rarity. "She is so impossible sometimes!" he announced to Ben as he came in the service door.

"What's wrong? Is it Laurie?" Ben quickly asked, anxiety exploding within him.

"No, your cousin," replied Marcus testily.

"You mean your wife," Ben corrected with a little confusion.

"No, right now she's your cousin. You go talk to her!" Marcus retreated into the walk-in refrigerator. Ben looked at Louis and Callie who were standing by the work table looking very awkward.

"What's going on?" he asked them but all the two did was point upstairs. At that moment, Ben heard the sound of hammering alternating with Jamie's foul language. Ben found her in Laurie's apartment. "What the hell are you doing?" Jamie was at one of the broken windows that he had boarded up a couple hours earlier. She had pulled the plywood off the window and proceeded to use the hammer to knock the remaining pieces of glass through the bars and onto the patio.

"How could you fucking do this?" she yelled and continued to smash the glass. "I can't believe how fucking stupid you can be." Angry, Ben grabbed Jamie's arm before she could attack another jagged piece.

"Stop!" he ordered but when Jamie was angry, she had quite the force within her as Ben knew very well. She shoved his arm away and for a very split second, he thought the hammer she held might become a weapon. "Hadn't you even noticed that Laurie only has plastic cups in the apartment? Really, leaving a bunch of jagged glass in the window frame?" Jamie rolled her eyes at him; he wasn't getting it. She bent down and picked up a large piece of glass and held it up in front of him. "Fucker," she growled and his eyes focused on the blood that covered one of the edges. His stomach fell and a sharp coldness zoomed around his body.

"Where's Laurie, CJ?" he asked and quickly looked around the room. She was nowhere to be seen and the curtains to the sleeping nook were open. Ben's heart began racing and a new type of sweat broke out on his brow. "Jamie, what happened?"

"It's your turn to deal with this shit," she replied and shoved the First Aid kit into his chest. "I locked her in the bathroom." Ben ran to the shut bathroom door. The door had been constructed wrong decades ago when the building was built and instead of opening into the bathroom, the door opened outwards. Jamie had taken one of the kitchen chairs and jammed it under the handle of the door.

"You are fucking crazy!" Ben yelled over at Jamie. He rarely used the f-bomb but he thought the current situation would benefit from it. Jamie imploded at that moment and with considerable force, chucked the hammer at Ben's head. Luckily, he was able to react quickly but the poor TV had no chance. The heat and terrible storms were taking their toll on everyone in the building. "You need to get out of here, Jamie." She advanced quickly on him and with a flashback to their confrontation in the basement, he backed up several steps.

"Don't tell me what to do," she warned with a jab of her finger. Turning on her heel, she left. For several moments, Ben stood stock still in shock. His world that was just beginning to make sense again was once again a clusterfuck.

Then, a tiny voice broke through his shock. "Ben?" Laurie's voice quickly shook him from his reverie. He pulled the chair away from the door and opened it. Laurie stood a few feet from the door. A bloody towel was wrapped around her left hand and wrist. Her t-shirt was also covered with blood and so were her scrawny and scarred legs. For the second time in less than two minutes, he was paralyzed with shock.

"I w...wasn't trying to hurt m...myself," Laurie hiccupped. She was crying. "Please believe me, Ben. Honestly, I wasn't trying to cut myself. Believe me, please," she begged. "Believe me." Her crying intensified and Ben quickly jumped into action.

"I believe you, Laurie," he said honestly and led her out of the sweltering bathroom. The apartment was now cooled nicely by the window unit but with the door closed, the bathroom became an oven. Laurie was drenched in sweat and Ben ran a washcloth under cold water and wiped her face. She cried the whole time and this clawed at his heart.

He was still only certain about part of what transpired in the apartment. Ben understood why Jamie was upset with him; with Laurie's past it hadn't been wise for him to leave all the easily accessible broken glass where she could get to it. He hadn't been thinking but Jamie's reaction was just so overboard, especially if Laurie wasn't trying to harm herself. She was calming down and he wanted to ask her what happened but first, she needed attending to. Carefully, he removed the bloody towel. The cut going across her palm was deep.

"I think you need stitches," he said and Laurie immediately reacted in a panic. Ben kicked himself mentally for not phrasing it a different way about what needed to be done. "No, no, calm down, Laurie," he said quickly. "You don't need to go to the hospital. I'm positive Doc can take care of this here. I'll give him a call, okay?" A visibly shaken Laurie nodded and Ben made the call. Doc said he'd be over in about a half an hour and after Ben gently wrapped her hand up in gauze to curtail the bleeding, he brought a pitcher of iced tea up from the kitchen.

Doc stitched the hand easily but didn't ask for details. He didn't seem concerned and bid adieu to them both with a damnation of the heat. "It's makin' the whole neighborhood the devil's playground," he practically shouted this proclamation on his way out the door. This made Ben smile but when he turned to see Laurie's reaction, she was very morose. Again, his heart hurt to see her this way. They had made progress over the last month but Laurie appeared to be very... different.

"What happened this afternoon?" he asked and sat next to her on the couch.

"I wasn't going to hurt myself," she insisted once again without raising her gaze from the floor.

"And I believe you, Laurie," he said.

"And I don't blame you for what happened," she added but this just confused him more. "That was nice of you to help me clean up the glass. After you left, well, you know how curious Clementine can get. She jumped up into the window and I was afraid she might cut herself so I thought I should remove the broken pieces that were still attached to the frame so she wouldn't hurt herself." Laurie paused her rushed explanation and she started crying again. "I don't have any tools so I was trying to use my nail file to slip under the glass and break it from the frame. I'm not having a good day; I'm so uncoordinated and I can't think clearly. It's such a bad day. I admit it was stupid to do what I was doing but I was so afraid Clemie was going to cut herself. I was so clumsy and the nail file slipped and I cut myself. Jamie came in right after that and saw the blood and assumed I was trying to kill myself again. She locked me into the bathroom and then went..."

"Berserk?" Ben offered and Laurie agreed.

"I make so much trouble for her," Laurie said and her crying worsened for several moments. Ben frowned and a familiar irritation began to rise inside of him.

"You're no trouble," he told her but she wouldn't accept his words.

"I am and I've probably made you feel bad because you left those broken pieces in the window and..."

"I don't feel bad," he said, cutting her off and understanding why she said she didn't blame him. "Please don't think that, okay?" All Laurie did was sniffle. She wasn't having anything to do with what he was saying.

"I'm just a bother to everyone," she said. "I'm such a screw up." The irritation rose a little more and he thought it best he busied himself and finished the job that Jamie started. He kept thinking about what Laurie said and he was getting angrier and angrier. By the time he finished, Laurie disappeared into the sleeping nook.

It stormed all night. Not bad enough to do any severe damage but bad enough to crawl under everyone's skin and tense them up something awful. Ben couldn't sleep and he joined Marcus down in the dining room to watch the storm. The lightning was nearly constant and the rain came down in sheets in ebbs and flows. It wasn't as bad as two nights earlier although they both took turns checking the basement.

The café was dull in the morning; everyone was tired and on edge and by nine the first tornado watch was issued for Memphis. The air felt like something awful was going to happen and the café was empty when the sirens pierced the air just before eleven. Marcus ran to grab Jamie and Davy from their apartment and Ben went to Laurie's as Callie and Louis ran to lock the doors to the café and head for safety. Ben went into the apartment without announcing himself and found the main room empty along with the sleeping nook. Laurie was huddled in the bathtub with Clementine in her carrier. Laurie looked scared to death.

"We need to get to the basement," Ben said and went to help her out of the tub. She slapped his hands away.

"I'm not leaving the apartment," she said, her voice shaking with fear and pain to make herself heard over the sirens. "You go and be safe with the others." She awkwardly picked up the carrier, her bandaged hand making it difficult. "Take Clemie with you. Keep her safe."

"I will keep her safe and you," he said tersely and looked out the window. It was as dark as night and Ben would be lying if he said he wasn't scared. "You are going to the basement. No arguments."

"No!" she screamed at him, her voice cracking, but he ignored her and easily picked her up and put her over his shoulder. He grabbed the cat carrier and despite Laurie trying to pull herself out of his grasp, he managed to get all three of them safely down to the basement. Marcus, Jamie, and a whimpering Davy were already down there along with Louis and Callie. Ben set Laurie down; she limped over to the corner and buried her face in her hands, her back to them all. Suddenly, an awful feeling came over him and he took a step towards Laurie. He was stopped by a hand on his arm.

"Give her space," Marcus said. Ben didn't want to; he wanted to tell her that he did what he did to make sure she was safe.

"Please let me talk to her," he almost begged his friend but Marcus shook his head. This angered Ben and he pulled his arm out of Marcus's reach. He was tired of always being careful about talking to Laurie. They had been talking for over a month and he saw no reason not to talk to her now.

"Laurie," he said quietly as the warning sirens still wailed outside. Ben lightly touched her elbow and she scooted away from him. He followed. "I'm not sorry for bringing you down here."

"Leave me alone," she said in a rough voice and started to inch towards the stairs.

"Where are you going?" he asked.

"I'm going back upstairs," she replied and put her foot on the first stair.

"No, you're not," Ben insisted and she struggled up two more stairs. "I'll just haul you back down here." She wasn't listening to him and he grabbed her around the waist.

"Let me go," she demanded and managed to get a good kick to his knee.

"Damn it, Laurie," he said through clenched teeth as the irritation that had been rising in him exploded. "Will you stop being stupid?! I'm just trying to save you from a damn tornado."

"I'm not worth saving," she countered and with those words, Ben let his anger get the best of him.

"Will you just stop with that damn talk!?" He grabbed her by the upper arms and gave her a small shake. He was on a roll; the frustration of her low self-worth was going to come out and he couldn't stop it. "I'm so sick and tired of you putting yourself down like this. You make me so angry when you do this."

"Ben!" The angry voice that cut through the difficult moment was one not heard often. It was Marcus but Ben ignored him and stupidly continued.

"How do you think I feel, Laurie, when you say stuff like you don't matter or you're not worth saving? I think the world of you; I always have. You're worth everything to me and I hate that you can't recognize the fact that you mean something to all of us. God, I'm so sick of this." And then came the nail. "I'm so sick of you."

It was like the air was sucked right out of the basement; even baby Davy stopped whimpering. Ben was breathing heavy and it took him a few moments to realize what just came out of his mouth. And when he did, he knew it was all over. As the sirens outside moaned to a stop, the feeling to run was too strong to ignore and Ben took the stairs two at a time. He didn't know what to do and ran out into the alley. The skies had lightened up but there was still the low rumble of thunder in the distance. The storm, wherever it had hit, did nothing to ease the heat and heavy humidity.

Ben wildly looked around and took off running down the alley. Around the corner he went and to the south. Sweat soaked his t-shirt and the few people that came outside to look at the clouds gave him an odd look. When he stopped running, he looked at the building in front of him and he knew it was fate. Before he could back out, he pulled open the door and in a voice he barely recognized, he addressed the man inside.

"Jack Daniels."

Chapter Thirty

Change of Heart

Marcus watched in shock as Ben ran from the basement. An uneasy silence filtered down the stairs and Marcus looked at Jamie. Her face was blotchy with anger and he noticed her fists were clenched. He'd never seen her look so angry, even when Ben refused to come back to Memphis in those dark days.

"I'll go put Davy down for a nap," Callie said, her voice shaky and when Marcus looked at his little sister, he saw her face was tearstained. Even Louis was shaken as he announced that he would unlock the café doors and get ready for lunch. With the elimination of those three, it was just Marcus, Laurie and Jamie left in the basement. *Laurie…*

She was shaking where she stood and her face was easy to read – shock. Their gazes met but she quickly looked away and took an uncertain step backwards. Her good hand reached out for the wall as if to steady herself. Laurie didn't look too well. Marcus approached her and she shrank away from him. "Can I help you back upstairs?" he asked in a very non-threatening manner.

"No," she replied in nothing more than a whisper. "I've put out too many." It was painful to watch her ascend the steps and then it was just Marcus and Jamie. He put a hand on her back; he could feel her tension through her Sunset Park Café t-shirt.

"It's over," she said with finality and went over to the large safe that was pushing half a century old. After opening it, she pulled out the only bottle of alcohol in the building. It had been a congratulatory gift from one of their wedding guests who didn't know how dangerous it was to have the liquid in the building. Instead of just tossing it like he should have, Marcus locked it up instead. Jamie opened the bottle of vodka and took a long drink. She coughed as it must have burned going down and after a second long drink, she held the bottle out to Marcus.

"No, I don't want any," he said.

"I'm not offering," she shot back at him. "Just get rid of it." He took the bottle from her and dumped the rest of the vodka down the utility sink in the corner. Marcus kept an eye on her; he was worried about her reaction to what Ben had just done. He was afraid that her volatile anger, which already caused problems the day before, would consume her and she might hurt herself. And if Ben was anywhere around, Marcus was concerned she'd do something very stupid.

"Do you need a moment to yourself?" he asked and got the answer he wanted.

"Yes."

Marcus exited the basement and made a quick search of the building. Ben was nowhere to be found and although he hadn't searched Laurie's apartment, he was sure Ben wasn't in there. He debated at least checking on her but when he unlocked her door, the chain was pulled. Checking the monitor in the kitchen, Marcus saw her sitting on the edge of the couch. Her body language read very sad.

Jamie appeared with Clementine's carrier. The cat was crying mournfully which was very fitting to what transpired over the last twenty minutes.

"I'm going to slip Clemie into Laurie's apartment," she said quietly and without asking if it was possible to get into her best friend's apartment. Jamie went upstairs and Marcus stood at the bottom of the stairs as his wife tenderly slipped the cat through the small opening allowed by the chain. She then stood, locked the door back up (all five locks), and tossed the key ring down to him. Marcus listened as Jamie walked out of his sight and instead of entering their apartment, he heard her walk towards Ben's. Was she trying to find him? Marcus was glad that Ben had left the premises.

Callie entered the kitchen with two lunch orders and Marcus pulled his mind from what was happening upstairs. Fifteen minutes later Jamie came downstairs, put on her apron, and went into the dining room. The lunch rush was on and it thankfully took Marcus's mind off of the basement. Jamie's mind was definitely still on what happened as she checked the monitor every time she brought an order from the dining room. With each viewing, she grew more and more distressed and finally Marcus pulled her into the alley to talk. Or at least try to ease her. He wasn't sure he could actually voice anything in regards to what happened.

"Lunch was busier than I expected considering the weather excitement," he said and gently massaged Jamie's shoulders. The knots he felt were not a surprise.

"There was a funnel cloud across the river but it never touched down," she explained. "More bad weather tonight." Marcus turned Jamie around and looked into her dark brown eyes that were twins to Ben's. He was surprised to see sadness in them.

"I knew he would fuck it up," she admitted without an ounce of rage in her voice. Marcus wondered where her fury went. He knew that she gave Ben only one chance at fixing things with Laurie and he assumed that when she had said *it's over* in the basement that she meant the attempt at reconciliation.

"I hate to say this but I'm not surprised either." It actually pained Marcus to say that but it was true. The task was rather monumental considering everything they both needed to overcome. "I still hoped it would work out. I could see a great improvement in Laurie these last few weeks."

"I had hope also," she said and sat on the hood of Ben's rusty truck. Marcus joined her and they sat in silence for a few minutes. The change in demeanor still bothered him.

"You were very angry with him after he took off but now you seem... calm?"

"I was angry, very angry."

"And now you're not."

"I'm not sure what I am." She let out a big sigh and he put his arm around her shoulders. "After letting Clemie into Laurie's apartment I went to Ben's. I was going to pack up all his shit and throw his sorry ass out. I wasn't going to allow him to ever see Laurie again, especially after the way he grabbed her. He had one chance and I thought he destroyed his chance today."

"But what happened?" After a moment of hesitation, Jamie pulled something from the back pocket of her jeans. It was a creased photo of Ben and Laurie when they were perhaps nine or ten years old. They stood side-by-side with their arms around each other's waists and were smiling from ear to ear despite the fact that they both sported ugly black eyes. "I've never seen this picture before," he said.

"Neither have I." Jamie turned the photo over and there was writing on the back. The same sentences were written twice; once in the flowery script of a girl (complete with i's dotted with hearts) and the second time in the impatient script of a boy. *Friends forever – nothing will keep us apart. You for me, me for you.* It was touching to read. "Ben left his wallet behind and it was inside. I think he's carried it forever."

"You went through his wallet?"

"Water under the bridge," she quickly said. "When I saw that photo... I don't know. I guess I saw the black eyes and their goofy grins and... I just don't know, Marcus, but all that anger I had towards Ben just rushed out of me. I know I gave him one shot at making things right with Laurie but something about this picture made me realize that ultimately, it's not up to me. I don't even think I had the right to say he had just the one chance."

"You were just protecting Laurie," Marcus ventured. "When it comes down to it, that's what we all want to do when it comes to her. She's been hurt by both her family and strangers." He debated whether to say the words that were on his tongue. They sounded odd when he said them in his mind. "I think that's even what was driving Ben this morning when he lost it. He was trying to protect her from the constant demeaning thoughts she has about herself. The weather has us on edge and it was just a bad, bad moment."

"But what he said to her, Marcus. He told her that he was sick of her."

"I'm not making excuses for him but in a way he was right. He's sick of her putting herself down and speaking so poorly of herself. It just didn't come across very good. It just wasn't the right situation to address it."

"She was so hurt by those words," Jamie said and dropped her head into her hands. "The look on her face was awful."

"I know," he concurred.

"I know I have to go talk to her but I don't know what to say," she confessed.

"Knowing Laurie, she's probably not up to talking. Just go sit with her." Marcus's cell phone chirped at him and he pulled it from his pocket.

"Who is it?"

"Teddy," he replied and hopped down off of the truck. "You take care of Laurie, Teddy and I will take care of Ben."

"Why? And how does Teddy know what happened?"

"Not sure but I better get going." Marcus gave Jamie a kiss and a reassuring hug.

Chapter Thirty-One

Hopeless

Teddy sat next to Ben. When they arrived at Feeney's Pub a few minutes earlier, Jimmy the bartender pointed to the darkest corner of the establishment. There, Ben sat in a corner booth. It was a sad sight and one that Teddy wasn't surprised to see. When Jimmy called him and said he thought something was wrong with Ben, Teddy had a suspicion that something had gone wrong between Ben and Laurie and Marcus confirmed his thought on the walk over to Feeney's. Regrettable words were voiced and now Ben was in a bar.

His hand was around a full highball glass.

He had yet to make eye contact with him and again, Teddy was not surprised. He was sure falling off the wagon was not an admirable action and if Teddy could pop open Ben's head he was certain he could see his friend self-punishing himself with self-directed regrettable words. Ben and Laurie were a lot alike in that way. When Marcus explained to Teddy what Ben said to Laurie, he found it so ironic as Ben often said the same things about himself when talking with Teddy. Neither of them had very much self-worth. Teddy could relate to what Ben said and did that morning; he himself had wanted to shake Ben around a bit on numerous occasions and tell him that he wasn't a loser or a mistake; that there were people who cared about him and thought the world of him. He tried the same thing with Laurie but both she and Ben were unable to accept the words he wanted them both to believe so much.

"How many drinks have you downed, Ben?" Teddy asked in a voice that ended up being stern.

"None," replied Ben.

"I don't believe you." Ben's shoulders slumped as Marcus slid into the both across from Teddy.

"What was his tab?" Teddy inquired. Marcus explained when they arrived that Ben's wallet was still in his apartment and figured he'd spent the last few hours running up a tab. Marcus offered to pay it so they could get Ben out of the bar.

"He was paid in full," Marcus replied. "Jimmy said he had enough cash in his pocket to buy one drink." He pointed to the one that Ben was holding. "That one right there. Jimmy says he hasn't had a sip of it the entire time." Teddy felt awful; Ben had told him the truth.

"I'm sorry, Ben," he apologized but was met with half a shoulder shrug.

"Doesn't matter," Ben said with his gaze still on the table. Teddy frowned. Ben was in a bad place.

"Do you want us to call your sponsor?" Marcus asked.

"No," Ben replied quickly. Teddy didn't like his best friend's answer. His sobriety was hanging by a thread and Teddy felt that this was exactly the right moment for someone in recovery to contact his sponsor. He ignored Ben's answer and picked up his cell phone that was lying on the table. Scrolling through what few contacts Ben had in his phone, he easily found the name of the sponsor and was just about to call him when Marcus grabbed the phone.

"Ben said no," he said calmly, then pointed to Teddy's own phone. He checked it and saw a text from Marcus. *Let's just see where this goes.* Teddy cocked a doubtful eyebrow at Marcus but eventually nodded his approval. Ben took his phone from Marcus and laid it back down on the table. Using a shaky finger, he brought up a picture of Laurie. Teddy was surprised as it was a recent photo. He was amazed that she had allowed Ben to take it.

"I ruined my chance," he said and Teddy noticed that Ben pulled the whiskey an inch or so closer to him. "I knew I was going to screw up." He hid the picture and the caustic drink moved a little closer. He closed his eyes and rubbed his forehead with his free hand. It was an action that Teddy saw Ben do often in his life. He knew his pained friend was aching inside. Several quiet minutes passed by. A text lit up Teddy's cell phone. It was from Jamie. *What's going on? Where are you guys?*

Feeney's, Teddy sent.

Fuck was Jamie's appropriate response.

First an hour crept by, then two. Ben never let go of the drink and he said nothing more. For the first time in a very long time, Teddy didn't know what to say and Marcus stayed quiet also. As dinnertime approached, Ben spent more and more time rubbing his forehead. Finally, he let go of the glass of whiskey and dropped his head into both hands. His shoulders were shaking and Teddy reached out to put a reassuring hand on his arm. None of his theological studies or training prepared him for a moment like this. He could deal with the sick and dying, he could counsel rocky marriages, but to sit by without knowing what to say as a man won the battle but lost the war against his demons caused Teddy to question his abilities.

"Please," Ben said in a strained voice. "Get me out of here." Teddy felt relieved with this request and he and Marcus eagerly removed themselves from the booth and led Ben from the drinking spot.

"Where do you want to go?" Marcus asked as Ben looked around with confusion on his face.

"I can't go back to the café," he said with a touch of fear to his voice. "I don't want to do that to Laurie."

"Then you'll come back to the rectory," Teddy offered. "My couch is lumpy but maybe you'll find a little peace under St. Anthony's roof."

"Peace is not something I deserve, Teddy." Ben turned in the direction of St. Anthony's and began a slow, defeated walk. Teddy could see the heaviness in the situation weighing Ben down and he let out a big sigh. For the first time since Ben returned to Sunset Park, Teddy's hope wavered.

Chapter Thirty-Two

Helpless

Jamie knocked softly on Laurie's door. It was her third attempt that afternoon at speaking with Laurie and she hoped the cliché held true. Although she could see on the monitor in the kitchen that Laurie hadn't physically harmed herself, Jamie wanted to talk to her to see how she was doing mentally. It was almost as if five years ago was happening all over again and Jamie was so afraid of what it would do to her best friend. How far was Laurie going to retreat? This scared Jamie a lot.

Her cell phone beeped at her and she quickly read the text from Marcus. *B settled in @ St. A's.*

How is he?

We'll go over our limits if I try and honestly answer that in text. Let's just call it sad for simplicity. Jamie sighed. Although she was hugely relieved that Ben hadn't given in to his desire for a drink, she worried that it would only be a matter of time considering. Another beep announced a new text. This one was from Teddy.

Talked to M and he said you weren't angry w/B. Any chance you could come talk to B and let him know? It might help.

Yes, when M comes home. Trying to talk to L now.

Good luck.

I need it.

She knocked again. "Laurie? I just want to come in for a little while. I want to make sure you're..." Jamie stopped herself from saying *okay*. She knew Laurie wasn't but she needed to be with her best friend for her own nerves. "Can I just sit with you for a while? You're probably not in the mood to talk." Jamie held her breath. Again, her cell phone interrupted her.

Door's open.

It was from Laurie. Even though Laurie was expecting her, Jamie was slow in her actions just to be on the safe side. After closing the door behind her, she automatically locked all five deadbolts and then spent a few moments letting her eyes adjust to the dark of the apartment. The drapes were pulled shut and the air in the apartment hot as the air conditioner wasn't on. Actually, hot didn't adequately describe the extreme heat in the place. It wasn't good for Laurie and Jamie turned the small window unit on without asking. Because she had to pull back one set of drapes to run the unit, the apartment lit up a little bit and Jamie saw Laurie lying on the couch. Her friend was drenched in sweat and she brought a glass of ice water over for Laurie. She accepted the glass and after a few moments, took several sips from it after sitting up. Jamie sat next to her.

"You're upset," Jamie said. Laurie looked at her with sad eyes. *Sad.* Yes, it was the simplest word to describe everything at that moment. Then, Laurie surprised her by talking.

"Where's Ben?"

"He's going to stay at Teddy's for a few days." Actually, Jamie had no idea how long Ben was staying there but thought it best to say that for Laurie. In reality, she had no idea about anything, really. She always thought that if Ben screwed up, he'd be gone. Case closed. But that's not what happened and Jamie hated being in this atmosphere of not knowing.

"So he didn't leave Memphis today," Laurie said and frowned. Jamie had to venture on this topic.

"Do you want Ben to leave?" For several minutes, Laurie appeared to be contemplating the question.

"I know you told him he only had one chance," she said, "Ben told me about the conversation you two had after you hit him but Ben can't leave. I know you want nothing to do with him but he can't leave, Jamie, he can't." There was a touch of panic in Laurie's voice and Jamie didn't want her to get more upset than she already was.

"I've changed my mind, Laurie," she said calmly. "You know how I can get sometimes, all bark and no bite."

"No, that's not you. You bite all the time." Laurie was clearly getting agitated and Jamie recognized the beginning of a panic attic. "You told him that if he screwed up he was gone but he can't go, Jamie, he needs to stay. Please trust me when I say that he cannot leave us."

"You're right; I still have my bite but in this case, I really have changed my mind. I had no right to get angry when he asked for your forgiveness and I had no right to set that ultimatum. I am not going to force Ben to go."

"Then why isn't he back here?" Laurie was crying.

"I don't know, Laurie," she replied honestly. "All Marcus said was that he was going to stay with Teddy." Laurie sank back into the couch and covered her eyes with her one good hand. Jamie contemplated her reaction. Ben had said some awful things to Laurie but she didn't seem to be upset about that but was upset about whether or not Ben had left. Did that mean she wasn't angry with him for what he did?

"Do you want Ben to leave?" It was the second time she asked that question.

"He can't leave. He needs to stay here with us." Laurie was answering the question but also not answering the question. She was answering the question for Ben and not herself.

"Laurie, I'm asking you a yes or no question. Do you want Ben to leave? I want you to answer how you feel, not if there's some other reason why you think he should or shouldn't go. Please, Laurie, answer the question from your heart. Do you yourself want Ben to go?" There was no hesitation from Laurie.

"No," she said and broke down into a heavy crying fit. Jamie pulled her into a hug and held her. It was a big cry and Jamie felt it was a long time coming. Even after she stopped crying, Jamie held on to her. Marcus was so right, all any of them wanted to do was protect the two people who needed protection from themselves.

Eventually, Laurie pulled herself out of Jamie's embrace and excused herself to the bathroom. When she came back out, she looked even sadder, something Jamie didn't think was possible. She sat back down on the couch and Jamie pulled out the photo that she found in Ben's wallet earlier that day. She debated showing it to Laurie but decided that it was important that she knew he had kept the photo with him all these years. She seemed surprised to see it and looked at their images closely before turning the photo over and reading what was written on the back silently to herself. For a moment, her sadness seemed to lift but it quickly returned.

"My copy was destroyed in the fire," she explained. "Where did you find this one?"

"In Ben's wal... apartment."

"He kept it all these years, even after I told him I didn't have mine anymore." Laurie seemed a little surprised at this. She continued to look at the picture as she curled up on her end of the couch. Within a few minutes, she appeared to be asleep and Jamie quietly crept out of the apartment.

An hour later she wimped out and drove over to St. Anthony's instead of walking in the awful heat. Storm clouds were already brewing on the horizon and she worried about how bad the weather was going to get. Flooding, hail, endless lightning and thunder, funnel clouds. It was beginning to be too much and Jamie actually blamed the weather for partly causing the personal storm in the basement that morning.

"It was probably just a matter of time before it happened," Marcus explained as they were in Ben's apartment packing a few items for his stay at Teddy's. "The weather was the instigator today but it could have been something else on a different day." Jamie couldn't disagree with her husband's logic.

"Hey, Jamie," Teddy said as he let her into his living space. He gave her a much needed friendly hug.

"Where's Ben?" she asked and looked around the sparse space.

"Bathroom," answered Teddy and took the small bag she brought with Ben's things from her. "I think he's afraid that you're here."

Guilt rose within Jamie. The conversation they had in the basement the day she clocked him was still fresh in her memory.

"I didn't say anything to him about you not being mad because I'm sure he wouldn't believe me. He needs to hear it from you."

Jamie understood this and was going to need to take the same tact with Ben. She knew Laurie didn't want him to leave but that was something Ben would need to hear directly from Laurie for him to believe it.

Teddy slipped the white notch into his black collar. The craziness of the day had backed up his schedule and he was overdue for his daily visit to the hospital. "Don't push him, okay?"

"I won't," she replied honestly and watched as Teddy left the apartment. She was suddenly very nervous but she knew the longer she waited, the worse she would feel and the harder it would be to talk to Ben. Again that day, she faced a door and quietly knocked on it. "Ben?" Silence. "Ben, I know it's been a bad day but I want to talk to you." She paused for a moment to think about what she wanted to say next; she didn't want to screw this up. Enough screwing up had been done that day. "I'm not mad at you; I know you think I am, especially what I said after I hit you in the basement a while back. But you need to believe me, Ben, I'm not mad. I really, really want to talk to you but only if you want to. I won't force you." She checked her watch. "I'll stay for an hour or so and if you don't want to talk now, then maybe tomorrow. Okay?"

She didn't want to pressure him so she made herself comfortable on the couch and checked in with Marcus. Dinner was slow in the café and he believed it was because people were wary about being too far from home with storms due to hit the area within a couple hours. Memphis was under another tornado watch and Jamie said a short prayer that they would be spared any more damage.

How's L? Jamie asked in text.

Took her a sandwich. Don't know if she ate it yet. How 'bout B?

Better ask me later.

A few minutes later the door to the bathroom opened and Ben stood in the doorway looking a little unsure. Jamie felt a sense of déjà vu come over her; she had seen this same scene so many times before but it was with Laurie and not Ben.

"Hi, Ben," she said in a calm voice.

"Hi," he replied back. "I just need a couple days here and then I'll pack my stuff up and leave Memphis. Unless you want me to leave sooner; I'll do whatever you want." He approached cautiously and pulled out an envelope from his back pocket. "Could you make sure Laurie gets this? I apologized for what I said and I didn't want to leave without doing that." He put the envelope on the coffee table.

"I don't want you to leave," she told him. This was clearly not what Ben was expecting from the look of shock and confusion on his face. "I don't want to spend a lot of time explaining myself because I'm tired of hearing myself talk but please just know that giving you that ultimatum was wrong. It was wrong of me to get mad at you for asking Laurie for her forgiveness and then getting made at Laurie for giving you that forgiveness and it was wrong of me to think that this process you're going through with Laurie would be smooth sailing. What happened this morning was bad, I admit it, but I'm not going to throw you out because of it. To be honest, that would be giving up on you and I don't want to do that." Emotion welled up in Jamie and she took a couple deep breaths to keep those emotions from consuming her.

Ben sat down in a chair opposite Jamie. *Sad.*

"I have to go," he said quietly. "I said awful things to Laurie. I hurt her again."

"Do you think Laurie wants you to leave?"

"Isn't that a given?"

"No," Jamie answered and again, Ben showed shock on his face. He needed to know that Laurie didn't want him to go. Jamie pulled her phone out and sent a quick text. Where she was damning modern technology earlier, she now was thankful for it.

A few moments later, Ben's phone vibrated. He was slow to check it but when he did, he stared at it for several moments before slowly tapping a reply. After hitting send, he put the phone on top of the letter that sat on the table. Ben hid his face in both his hands and Jamie sat stone still.

It was only the second time ever that Ben cried in front of her and it bothered her. Despite knowing that he had a multitude of demons inside of him, she always thought of Ben as a rock but that was before he walked out on Laurie five years earlier. She knew about the alcohol, knew about the heroin, knew about the pain inside of him but Jamie just couldn't see, or wouldn't see, the true Ben and it was at that moment that she realized how truly fragile he was. Even the incident when she hit him didn't reveal this.

Jamie's phone lit up; the text was from Laurie. *He's staying.*

DANA MANSFIELD

Chapter Thirty-Three

Tables Turned

Business picked up once the heat wave and storms subsided over the next couple of days and a typical July commenced. Marcus and Jamie worked hard in the café, Teddy took care of the spiritual needs of the neighborhood, Laurie stayed safe in her apartment, and Ben stayed safe at St. Anthony's. The reconciliation between Ben and Laurie was on hold and not because of Laurie. Although she had been hurt by Ben's words, she wanted to continue talking with him.

"It's just different this time," she confessed one morning as Jamie braided her hair. "I must sound stupid."

"Hush up," Jamie said sharply, then softened her tone. "You're not stupid. You, and Ben, just really want this to work out."

"How is he doing? I'm worried about him. I text him a *good morning* every day and he replies but that's it." Laurie said quietly. Jamie sighed; Ben's situation was complicated. The words he spoke that day seemed to affect him more than Laurie. Teddy told Jamie and Marcus that he was torn up inside. He wanted to come back to the café, wanted to continue talking with Laurie, but he didn't trust himself. That's why he was basically hiding out at St.

Anthony's. Ben and Laurie had not spoken since exchanging texts the night of the fight other than their morning salutations.

"I think we're all worried about him," explained Jamie. "He just wants to make sure he doesn't make the same mistake again."

"He's afraid," Laurie deduced.

"Yes."

"I wish he would talk to me but I understand the time he needs." Where it was Laurie that needed time originally, it was now Ben's turn.

The gossip machine was working overtime with Ben's disappearance from the café. No one directly said anything to Jamie so she was unable to address the rumors. Some people had Ben leaving town (and Laurie) again while others said that he had taken a construction job elsewhere in the city. The only people that directly spoke to Jamie about Ben were the ladies in Mrs. Bailey's group. Jamie was pretty sure that they knew what happened between Ben and Laurie but the ladies were very respectful and asked that Jamie pass on supportive wishes to him.

And then there was Mei. Nearly every piece of gossip Jamie heard in the café was preceded by *According to Mei* or *Mei told me that*. The bitch had not shown up in the café since the fight and this irritated Jamie. She was too busy to go out into the neighborhood and find Mei herself so she really wanted Mei to make an appearance on her turf so she could give her a piece of her mind.

Jamie would visit Ben during the afternoon lull. She wanted to make sure he understood that she was definitely not angry with him. He spoke some over coffee and dessert she would bring from the café but he was eerily quiet most of the time. Ben did always ask how Laurie was and seemed relieved when Jamie would tell him that she was okay. When Jamie would ask Ben how he was, though, he was unable to answer for the first several days after the fight but eventually, he could reluctantly give her a simple answer. First, it was *I've been better*, then it improved to *okay*, and then one day about three and a half weeks after those regrettable words were said, he gave Jamie a good answer to the question she asked every day.

"I feel good," he said. "And I'm ready to go back to the café. I'm ready to talk to Laurie again."

Chapter Thirty-Four

Back to Business

Laurie's heart pounded in her chest as she made her way over to Ben's apartment. Busy noises from the kitchen floated up from the steps and that actually helped Laurie's nerves a bit. She knew that Jamie and the others were busy taking care of the lunch rush and wouldn't be up to the second floor anytime soon. Going over to Ben's was a big deal and she didn't want anyone to know.

With a shaking hand, she knocked on his door. She had heard him come up a little earlier and she was desperate to exchange even just a word or two with him. Footsteps approached the door and Laurie took a small step backwards.

"Laurie," Ben said in surprise after opening the door. Despite looking a bit off with dark circles beneath his brown eyes and needing a shave, Laurie was relieved to see him.

"Hi, Ben," she said quietly, then gave him a small smile. He looked scared to death. "Can I come in?"

"Of course," he replied and stepped aside to let her in. It was the first time she had stepped foot into the apartment since The Old Man passed away in it so many years ago. Laurie wished she had thought about that before deciding to visit Ben but shoved that sadness away and looked around. Ben had done a nice job of fixing the place up since moving in back in April. He motioned her to the couch and she sat on one end while he took the other.

After a few uncomfortable moments of silence, Laurie pulled two things out of the back pocket of her cut offs. She placed them on the cushion that separated her and Ben.

"How did you get this?" he asked and picked up the photo that Jamie found in Ben's apartment the day of the fight.

"Jamie. She found it in here."

"Yes, in here would be technically correct but it was in my wallet," he explained with a shake of his head. Laurie couldn't help but chuckle and even Ben joined her.

"Jamie will always be Jamie," she said. Ben's sad smile faded as his gaze fell on the envelope. Laurie picked it up and held it out to him. "Thank you for the letter," she said. "I accept your apology."

"I'm so sorry for…"

"No, Ben," she said sharply and was met with a sharp pain in her throat. She waited until it died down before continuing in a softer tone. "You've apologized to me and I've accepted it. Let's move on."

"But I said such awful things," he continued. "What if I do it again?" His hand went to his forehead. Laurie recognized that he was stressed and worried. She scooted closer to him and pulled his hand down so she could see his face.

"If it happens again, please, Ben, just don't run away. Let's just try and work through it. Promise me, Ben; promise me that you won't run away again." Laurie knew she was asking for a big promise so she added an incentive, one that had taken the last three and a half weeks for her to accept. "I finally understand how much I mean to you. You care about me. I really have known that for a long time but it's so hard to actually believe it."

"That I understand also," he replied. "Like I said that afternoon, you mean the world to me."

"And you mean the world to me," she insisted. "Let's start there. Okay? We both do the same thing and it's because of what we went through as kids. After never hearing that we meant anything to our families, it's hard to believe it when other people tell us that. We're in our thirties and still can't accept that. I'm surprised you didn't yell at me sooner than you did five years ago."

"You've had a breakthrough," Ben noted sadly. "Marcus would be so proud that he finally broke through to you."

"It wasn't Marcus, Ben," she said and turned his face so she could look into his eyes. "It was you. You were willing to put this monumental task we have to complete on the line to try and get me to believe what you were saying that morning."

"That so wasn't my plan. Don't give me any credit for that."

"Whatever, Ben, but although it was hard to hear it again from you, it finally sunk in. I get it now and I want you to get it also. We still have a long ways to go and do I think it will be all hunky dory? No, I would be stupid to think that but we can just try and hope for the best. If you get angry with me, we have to talk about it. Running is not the answer. It never was."

Ben looked at Laurie for a long time but finally promised not to run again.

"Thank you," she replied and smiled at him. "We both need to take baby steps; it's not just for me anymore."

They ate a nice, quiet dinner that night. Laurie asked if he would grill steaks for them on the rooftop grill and he complied. Jamie provided sliced baked potatoes from the café and a simple salad. Desert was sliced peaches and strawberries. Afterwards, they sat and began talking where they left off a month earlier.

*

The next day, Ben returned to work in the café. He felt sick to his stomach as his first few patrons asked where he had been. He didn't know what to say so he fibbed. "I was sick and needed a couple weeks to recuperate." Everyone bought the excuse and by the end of the lunch rush, the tension in Ben's stomach disappeared. Then, Mei showed up.

"Well, well, well," she said and slid onto a stool at the counter. "Back again, I see." Ben took a deep breath and moved to the other end of the counter but Mei followed. The café was empty at that moment so he went into the kitchen. He didn't like the fact that it was empty also. He knew Mei and it was no surprise to see her follow him into the out of bounds area for the usual clientele. Mei, however was not usual.

"You need to get out of here," he warned and put the work table in between them.

"I have a little birdy working in Feeney's Pub," she said in a low voice. "You nearly ruined your sobriety. What happened, Ben? Did your Loony Laurie get the best of you? I'm sure she's a handful with all her little... issues."

"Shut up," he warned with anger beginning to flow through is veins.

"Or did you try and have a romantic moment with her and..."

"Get out!" It was Jamie and she was angry. Ben was glad his cousin showed up at that moment. "Get the fuck out of my restaurant!" She advanced on Mei quickly but Mei didn't back up. Ben did, however. "I have put up with your shit my entire life but no more. I never want to see you again. You're nothing but fucking trouble, bitch." Mei was quick and had slapped Jamie across the face before either Jamie or Ben realized what happened. Once the realization came to Jamie, she raised her own hand for retribution but Ben knew this didn't dare go any farther and stepped between the two. Ben was glad that Marcus came through the service entrance at that time.

"What's going on? Mei, why are you back here?"

"Mei's leaving," Ben said. "And she's never going to show her face around here again. Right, Mei?" Mei gave him a dangerous look through half closed eyes. She was definitely angry with what

Ben said but it was something that needed to be said for everyone's safety and sanity.

"You can all go to fucking hell," she said and stomped out of the kitchen. Ben turned around and Jamie was rubbing her red cheek.

"Are you okay?" he asked.

"I'll be fine, especially if that bitch follows orders and stays away." It was a hope that Ben shared also.

Chapter Thirty-Five

Scrambled Eggs and Stories

The Bailey family was having a huge family reunion Labor Day weekend in Monteagle so Marcus and Jamie decided to close the café on the Saturday before Labor Day. Ben and Laurie would have the building all to themselves. He was looking forward to this, actually. Not for any nefarious reasons, that thought had not come up at all over the weeks of talking nor did he expect it to, but just for the peace and quiet. It would just be him and Laurie and they planned to paint her apartment. Several times leading up to the holiday weekend he ran to the hardware store around the corner and brought back paint samples for Laurie to consider. Finally, she chose a very pale yellow to replace the light olive green they picked out together over ten years earlier.

That Saturday started out cloudy but Ben was in a good mood, something that had been slow to return since that ugly fight in June. He was trying to keep himself in check though. Only two weeks earlier, Laurie had a very bad stretch of days. There was no obvious cause, no bad words between them, but she had warned him early on that she might have days like that. He did his best to help Laurie when she allowed and they were able to get through another bump in the road. However, with three days together coming up, he wanted to make sure his expectations weren't set too high in case Laurie needed some quiet time. And if she needed quiet time, he would be there for her, if she wanted.

"Laurie?" Ben called just past seven and lightly knocked on her door. Just as he was about to open it, he heard the sound of metal hitting the tile floor in the kitchen below. He frowned; Ben and Laurie were the only two that were supposed to be in the place. He crept down the stairs expecting to find a burglar but instead he found Laurie. She struggled to pick up several stainless steel mixing bowls that had fallen to the floor. Marcus warned him about over helping Laurie but she was clearly flustered.

"I just wanted to take a look around without anyone here," she explained her voice cracking already. Her slur was worse and he noticed that her right side seemed weaker than usual.

"Are you okay?" he asked and knelt down next to her.

"Just clumsy today," she replied and managed to get the bowls nestled together but with just one good hand, she couldn't pick them up.

"Let me," he said and placed them back on the counter and then helped Laurie to her feet and over to one of the stools at the worktable.

"Thank you," she said without looking at him. She was clearly both frustrated and embarrassed. Ben took a chance and tipped her head up; he could see exhaustion in her face.

"You didn't sleep last night," he deduced. It was something he noticed early on in their talks along with the time in the hospital; the more tired she was, the worse her slur became and her weak right side caused her problems. Laurie didn't respond right away but eventually nodded in the affirmative. "Do you want to talk about it?"

"Not yet." It took a lot of effort for her to get those two words out. Whatever kept her awake was weighing on her. Ben decided to set the situation aside for the moment.

"How 'bout breakfast then? What would you like?"

"Make whatever you like; you know I'm not picky." Familiar frustration rose in Ben. Laurie rarely ever offered up what she wanted when it came to anything and it used to make him so mad, especially when he wanted an answer from her like what she wanted for her birthday. The frustration he felt was an indicator that it was time to address this with her.

"I know you're the type to eat anything," he tried to keep his voice light as he continued. "But honestly, what would taste really good to you this morning? We've got the run of the kitchen." He chewed on his lip as he watched Laurie. Her gaze was on her hands in her lap. For any ordinary person, answering the question was a pretty simple request but for Laurie, it wasn't. She'd never been given a chance to offer her opinion while growing up and even when she did escape that rule, it was so deeply engrained in her that she rarely could answer such a simple question.

Ben kept his cool. In those last two years before he walked, he often would say *Come on, Laurie, make up your mind* or *What's taking so long? I'm not asking for the meaning of life.* He never thought to offer suggestions to get her thinking or even to give her the time she might need to make the choice. But he was trying now. He had to. "How 'bout some orange juice first?" he suggested and put two juice glasses on the table and grabbed a carton of fresh squeezed from the walk-in cooler. Since it was just a suggestion and she didn't accept it right away, Ben poured himself a glass and left the carton on the worktable. He busied himself slicing a loaf of homemade bread for either regular toast or French toast. He didn't know yet.

Out of the corner of his eye he watched as Laurie slowly reached out for the carton of OJ. He should have left the cap off but he wasn't thinking; he was still getting used to Laurie and her limitations. She braced the carton against her upper body with her weak hand and opened it with her good one. Not a natural left hander, she spilled a little pouring it into the glass. She frowned at this at first but then Ben noticed a flash of anger in her face.

"Scrambled eggs," Laurie said.

"Scrambled eggs it is," Ben replied and took a step towards the walk-in but Laurie stopped him.

"No," she said. "I want to make them." As far as Ben knew, Laurie had not fixed any food since the day he walked; Marcus and Jamie always brought her food from the café or Teddy brought a pizza for their Monday movie nights. Of course his first thought was if this was a good idea, letting Laurie make her own breakfast. It was a recipe for frustration and one thing that Ben wanted to keep low was her frustration level.

"Okay," Ben said slowly. "I'll get the…"

"No, I want to do it all." She slipped off the stool and made her way to the walk-in. Ben had a bad feeling about this and he wondered if what kept her up that night had something to do with her limitations.

The door to the walk-in was heavy but that didn't bother her and she disappeared inside. His heart was racing and he itched to just rush in there, grab the eggs, and start cooking but Laurie seemed to be on a determined mission and he was willing to let it play out for a while. He waited and waited and waited. Five minutes passed and that was too long for Laurie to be in the cooler. Looking through the window, he saw she was sitting on a low shelf and at her feet was a pile of broken eggs, at least a dozen and a half. Laurie was crying.

Quickly, he entered the cooler and cleaned the mess up. Laurie sat shivering but he didn't want to send her into the kitchen while he was cleaning; he felt he needed to keep an eye on her. He worked quickly and efficiently and had the mess cleaned up in no time. As he worked he thought frantically how to turn this situation into something helpful. His first inclination was to pull Laurie into a hug, tell her everything was going to be okay, and make her breakfast but Ben knew that this was how Jamie typically dealt with things. If she wasn't being bossy to Laurie, she enabled Laurie's issues.

Ben ran into the kitchen and grabbed one of the smaller mixing bowls and ran back to Laurie. She was still crying and shivering and just an overall mess. He crouched down and held the bowl out to her. "For the eggs," he said. "It'll make it easier for you to carry them." Ben stood back up and held out his hand and with her own shaky hand, Laurie took his and pulled herself up. She took the bowl from him and filled it with six eggs. Tucking it against her body, she slowly walked out of the cooler using the shelving as a light support. It took a very long hour but she eventually made them a simple bacon and egg breakfast. Ben was in charge of the toast.

They ate at the worktable and cleaned up together. It was the first time Ben felt that familiar closeness they shared before their worlds started spinning out of control. Even Laurie appeared more relaxed but still tired so he suggested they wait a day to start painting. She was not against this.

Back in her apartment, Ben made himself comfortable on the couch with the *Commercial Appeal*. He had his Uncle Jack to thank for his newspaper reading. Uncle Jack was the principal of their old elementary school and a former teacher. Knowing that Ben struggled with reading (because he often missed a lot of school during those early years, no thanks to his father), he told Ben one of the best things he could do to help his reading was to practice. If he didn't want to be seen with a book, pick up the paper. And so Ben did and his reading improved along with his performance in school. Even after graduation he continued to read because he liked to be up to date on what was happening around the city and world, something his father never wanted to be. Many Sunday mornings would find Ben, having returned from early Mass, and Laurie curled up on the couch with their preferred reading material – Ben with the newspaper (and later a novel) and Laurie with a cookbook.

Back in the day, Sunday was the quietest day for Ben and Laurie. The café was closed and neither of them had work obligations. They would enjoy a leisurely breakfast and then some time reading. They would go for walks down by the Mississippi, see the ducks at the Peabody (one of Laurie's favorite things to do), or see a movie. If it was cold out, they would snuggle on the couch for a nap. For dinner they would go to a nice restaurant. Nothing too fancy but a place where they could enjoy the food and each other's company. He enjoyed how Laurie tried to figure out how something was made and she often would jot notes down in a little notebook for when she tried the recipe back in the cafe. Sundays were their favorite day until one chilly Sunday in January when Uncle Jack dropped dead of a heart attack.

Ben shook himself out of that memory and focused on the paper in front of him. His concentration was broken again, this time by Laurie. Instead of sitting on the opposite end of the couch, as usual, she sat right next to him. In the weeks that passed as they were working on their relationship, they shared a handful of close moments, usually a hug or a hand hold, but that was it. Ben didn't make a big deal out of where she sat and instead, just went with it. Where it eventually ended up was with Laurie falling asleep with Clementine curled up in her lap. She was leaning dangerously forward and he didn't want her to tumble off the couch so he very carefully leaned her back against the cushions. Clementine gave him an evil eye.

"Get your mind out of the gutter," he whispered to the cat who flicked her tail at him. All he did was lean her backwards and then move on with his paper. It was Laurie, a few minutes later, who slumped against him. He gently put his arm around her shoulder and in her sleep she nuzzled against him. Ben finished the paper a few minutes later but didn't want to move for fear of waking Laurie. She obviously needed the sleep.

On the end table was one of Laurie's photo albums. Without disturbing her, he picked it up and began strolling down memory lane. It was from 2000, the year before Uncle Jack died and the last year that Ben and Laurie were really happy together. Once out of her father's house, Laurie became big about photos and her organizational issues dictated that each year required a separate album and the pictures placed in chronological order. This album commenced just as 2000 began with snapshots of Marcus and Jamie's annual New Year's Eve party. Once a year they threw a formal to-do in the café for their friends. Jamie went all out with fancy hors d'oeuvres and requiring black tie and Louis, usually very reserved, came out of his quietness and kept everyone in stitches as he alternated between stand-up comic and DJ. Good food, good friends, and of course the kiss at midnight and the hope for a good new year.

Ben smiled at the picture that Marcus took (he was the official photographer of the festivities every year) of him and Laurie. It reminded him of the homecoming or prom pictures from high school, which was cheesy Marcus's goal. Ben wore his rented tux and Laurie looked absolutely stunning in her quiet way. Her hair was done up in a fancy 'do and she wore a retro formal gown from the 1950's that she bought at the vintage clothing shop in the neighborhood. The dark blue velvet brought out the blue in her eyes and on her left hand was the small antique diamond ring Ben gave her for Christmas just a week earlier.

The ring itself caused confusion for both of them. They were out Christmas shopping together, on a Sunday, when she fell in love with it. He bought it for her but neither of them knew what kind of ring to call it or which hand for her to wear it on. They spent the entire night talking about it. At that time, they'd been living together for six years but were a couple for eight and friends their entire life. They never talked about marriage; each was happy with what they had without having to make it all official.

It's a ring from the man who loves me regardless of my problems, Laurie finally said and slipped it on her left ring finger. Of course, the rumors started about an engagement, Sunset Park was as bad as a small town, and Ben and Laurie just made the choice not to confirm or deny anything. They knew what the ring meant to each other and they didn't really care what anyone else thought.

"You looked so handsome," Laurie whispered and he looked down. She was awake now and he wondered how long she had been staring at the same picture.

"And you so beautiful," he said. She reached her thin finger out and ran it over the glint of the ring in the picture. They sat together and flipped through the entire album reminiscing about the memories. Every time the ring showed up, she would finger the picture. He wanted so much to ask her about it but opted to assume that after he left, she removed it and tucked it away some place dark so it wouldn't remind her of him. Ben was very, very wrong on that assumption.

"The man who... raped me took the ring," she said in a very quiet voice. It was the first time she came close to mentioning what happened when she'd been abducted. Laurie sat up and continued talking, her gaze at Clementine in her lap. "I don't remember everything about what happened but I do remember running for over two hours that night and was just about home when he grabbed me; I could see the service entrance door. I should have been more careful; you were always warning me about running through the alleys." Laurie stopped and took a couple deep breaths through pursed lips. Ben reached out and took her hand. "I was so focused that it wasn't until I was halfway into the trunk of his car that I realized what was happening." Her voice was becoming dangerously shaky and creaky but she continued. "I remember that he drove a long time but it was in circles, or at least it seemed that way because he made a lot of right-handed turns. Then we stopped. When he opened the trunk, I could smell the Mississippi." She clamped her eyes shut. Ben didn't want her to think so hard to remember such a bad thing but he knew with an aching heart that it needed to be said.

"He dragged me into this awful place. It was small and dark and smelled like rotting fish. I remember being surprised that it had a basement. It was so damp that I worried the river was about to break through the walls." Laurie began to tremble. Ben was finding it hard to keep his emotions in check. Hearing Laurie's side of the incident was going to be very hard and he pulled out one of his sobriety chips to feel for strength. "There was this old bed…" She hiccupped a sob and the tears began to flow.

"Laurie…"

"No, don't stop me. I have to do this now; if I wait I don't know if I'll ever be able to tell you."

"Okay," he said and began rubbing her back, something he often did when they were innocent teenagers and she was having problems telling him about her home life. She cried for several minutes, putting her good hand over her mouth and shaking her head.

*

Laurie concentrated on the comforting feel of Ben rubbing her back. She had to tell him what happened; otherwise they could never move past this wall. Reliving those days was not something she wanted to do but she had to. The memories of what happened were first very scattered after the stroke but unfortunately, most of them returned and haunted her often.

A light rain fell during her run and as she lay petrified in the trunk, she grew very cold and began shivering. She knew it was partly from fear but mostly from running two hours in the chilly, early April rain. The car moved calmly but made uneven right turns; if she had to guess, she would say she spent a good two hours in the trunk which did nothing for her nerves.

The car stopped and Laurie tried to move as far back into the trunk as possible hoping if he had to work at getting her out then a moment of escape may present itself. The trunk, however, had been so full of junk that it was next to impossible for Laurie to move very far. She did the best she could and waited. When the trunk opened there was no chance for her to do anything as a musty smelling blanket was thrown over her. The loss of vision increased her fear and she had been unable to do anything to try and save herself.

"Scream and I cut you," a rough voice said loudly. The man pulled her out of the trunk and she immediately could tell by the mixed smell of wet sand, soil, and rotting fish that she was near the Mississippi. "I'm taking the blanket off. Remember what I said; I'll be pretty pissed off if I don't get to have a little fun with you."

"Please don't hurt me," she had managed to stammer out when she saw the man who abducted her. He was a stranger; no one she recognized from Sunset Park and not a regular at the café. He was big, a touch overweight and very tall. His hair was black and his eyes so light blue that they were unsettling. The ruddy face was pockmarked and he dressed in jeans and a greasy denim jacket.

"Come on," he ordered and he grabbed her arm. His grip had been strong and coupled with her fear, there was no way she could get away. He led her to a small, run-down cabin in an isolated spot. Looking around, she couldn't see if they were still in Memphis or crossed over the river. The area was dark; only a bare bulb lit the front of the shack and inside Laurie couldn't see much at all. Down a flight of wooden steps he forced her into a very damp basement. The sand and dirt floor actually felt wet beneath her running shoes and when he flipped on the light, the stone walls were shiny.

The only furniture in the space had been a wooden bed with a stained mattress. The man shoved her towards it. "On the bed," he ordered with a sick grin, "after you strip." The words were like ice and she froze. This angered the man and she took a hard punch to her gut, knocking the wind out of her. He backhanded her so hard everything went black.

When she came to, she had been handcuffed to the bed and naked. It was a nightmare and she just wanted to close her eyes and rewind her life by twenty-four hours; a Sunday instead of that horrific Monday. Her breathing was erratic and she focused on the only thing she knew would help her calm down – the mental image of Ben. Although he had just walked out on her, it was the only thing she had. *Help me, Ben*, she said over and over in her mind. Above her she could hear the heavy footsteps of her abductor and his muffled voice. Was there more than one of them? This new thought sent her heart rate through the roof.

Eventually, Laurie figured out that there was only the single man and he was speaking on a cell phone; she doubted there was land line service in the shack. She lay on the bed for a long time, shivering in the dampness, waiting her fate. Her wrists were cuffed tightly and her hands tingled with numbness; she wished the same for entire body but knew that would never happen. Laurie was facing a woman's worst nightmare – rape. Sadly, it was not the first experience with that horror but at least this time she wasn't an innocent child.

Heavy footsteps coming down the stairs caused her fear to increase. He came into her field of vision and sneered down on her. "Got my okay," he said. She had no idea what that meant.

"Please, don't," she begged but it was of no use. As expected, it was soul killing and painful and when he finished, she wanted to die. It took nearly two years of Ben's reassurances and gentle actions for Laurie to forget what her father had done to her and allow herself to be intimate with Ben and in the span of ten excruciating minutes, all those awful memories were back. Her rapist ripped the tender moments from her and when he climbed off of her, she felt half dead. There were no tears for her to cry; all she did was do her best to curl up on her side as he laughed at her.

That started four days of hell. If he wasn't forcing himself on Laurie, he was beating her with his fists and when she was left alone, she fell into a fog of pain and fear. If she was lucky, he would allow her some water; her toilet was a bucket.

As the third day dawned, she began dry heaving and her vision was cloudy. He no longer cuffed her to the bed; she was too weak from lack of nutrition and the beatings to try an escape. When the fog lifted slightly she could hear him upstairs, talking. As the days wore on, he seemed more intense in the conversations and on the fourth day, as she lay on the damp mattress dreading another appearance by him, she clearly heard him shout *finally*. Was the hour of her death now upon her? If it was, Laurie would embrace it. She saw death as the only way out of the hell she was trapped in.

But instead of killing her, he dragged her naked up the stairs and back outside. The late day sun felt good on her chilled body but it lasted only a few moments until he dumped her back into the trunk. Again he drove without incident and this time with a series of left hand turns. The car stopped and a surge of adrenaline lifted her briefly from the fog. When he opened the trunk, the first thing she saw was the knife. Using a small burst of adrenaline, she curled into a ball as the first slash came and the knife sunk into her right shoulder. His strikes had been methodical and all she could do was count. After seventeen he stopped for a moment, then came the last two. Too weak to stop him, the knife burned across her face and with the final one she finally felt death coming for her as he dumped her naked on a pile of collapsed boxes.

As he sped off, Laurie realized he dumped her right behind the café. The vision of her home wavered and then disappeared as she saw the hulking figure of Officer Bailey. *Hang in there, baby...* His voice had seemed so far away and she followed it into a dark nothingness.

*

Laurie stopped crying and was somber. "That's that," she said in a whisper, her voice giving out. Ben was shaking from her words; to hear her tell the story was beyond awful for him but he knew now; he would be able to comfort those torturous memories.

"You've been through so much and to live through that... I'm sorry," he said quietly.

"Don't blame yourself."

"I don't, not anymore." Ben explained to her what Jamie had said about the attack probably happening anyway. She had not made eye contact with Ben during the whole telling of her ordeal. Ben tilted her head up so she was now eye to eye with him. "Thank you for telling me what happened. You've said these last few weeks that you don't feel very strong because of how the attack left you but you must believe me that what you just did took a lot of strength and courage."

"I still don't feel strong," she confessed. The apartment was silent as the words of the ordeal echoed in their hearts. "Will you hold me?" Laurie asked in a small voice. Ben didn't answer; he just pulled her into the gentlest hug. She began weeping into his chest.

They stayed as one on the couch for nearly an hour; both emotionally drained. It was the toughest day since he came back and he felt numb inside. He couldn't even imagine how Laurie felt.

He held her until she broke the embrace. Her eyes were droopy; she looked exhausted. "Do you want to rest?" he asked. She shook her head and then in a grating voice, asked if she could have some tea. "Of course," he answered with a smile and returned as quickly as he could with tea and leftover apple pie for both of them. As he set the tray down on the coffee table he noticed Laurie running her finger along the long scar on her forearm.

"That was over three years ago," he said and placed his hand over hers. "If you weren't strong do you think so much time would have passed?" Laurie appeared to really think the question over.

"No," she finally said.

"You've said you don't really remember that day. What do you remember?" Laurie looked a little uncomfortable and he wondered if talking about the rape and the suicide attempt was too much for one day. "You don't have to answer now. You've done a lot of talking today. You sound like you're in a lot of pain." He gently touched her throat but she shrugged.

213

"I'll be okay. I'd rather get it over with so we could move on to your drinking." Ben couldn't help but frown and Laurie noticed. "It's not easy but we have to, Ben."

"I know but like you said, it's hard." *Especially since I was a heroin addict also* he thought to himself.

"We've been doing good so far," she replied and it was her turn for giving reassuring hand squeezes. He smiled at her and she returned a genuine smile, one that he remembered from so long ago. "Let's get this over with and then we'll have pie." She said it as if it was a project to cross off a to-do list. Technically, it kind of was and Ben nodded his agreement. "It was April; such a bad month for me."

"Me, too," Ben said. They sipped at their tea quietly.

"I thought I was doing okay. I wasn't going outside but occasionally I would go down to the kitchen after the café closed and talk to Jamie as she prepped for the next day. Other days I would enjoy visiting with people up here. I didn't feel so scared."

"Who would come by?" Laurie listed several of their former friends and acquaintances, including Mei which set Ben on edge. Ben wouldn't classify her as a friend or acquaintance but he knew Laurie's relationship with Mei was odd. Mei was just one of those people who Laurie could not stand up against so if Mei managed to worm her way into the apartment, Laurie wouldn't have been able to ask her to leave. Laurie was always nice to her regardless of how mean Mei was to Laurie.

"Most of the time she wouldn't stay long; she was actually delivering that tea I like from her aunt and uncle's store. We'd talk a little while and then she'd leave but by the end of March I started to get more nervous and paranoid. It was like this fog would come over me and I just wanted to hide in the corner. I couldn't sleep or eat. I was miserable."

"And then what happened?"

Laurie closed her eyes and took a deep breath which she let out slowly.

"It was April then and I hadn't slept in several days and I was so, so tired but I was also so afraid to fall asleep. I've said this before but I felt like I was in this haze but then…" She stopped and looked embarrassed.

"It's okay," Ben said encouragingly and held her hand.

"I guess I was hallucinating from lack of sleep but I thought someone was in here with me. I tried to turn on the lights but they wouldn't work, or at least I thought they didn't work. I was so afraid so I went and got my chef's knife; that was before Marcus and Jamie took away any sharp objects from me. The hallucination was so real, Ben. I could have sworn someone was in here; I was certain I could smell him."

"What did he smell like?"

"Old Spice, just like my dad, but he was dead by that time so I knew it couldn't have been him." Laurie replied somberly. "The hallucination was following me around the apartment, goading me. I thought I was going crazy because the hallucination knew so many things about me, especially the bad stuff."

"How long did this last?"

"It seemed to go on for hours. I would have called for Marcus and Jamie but they were at Mrs. Bailey's house for Easter. I was so scared and I finally hunkered down by the sink." Laurie struggled to her feet and walked over to the kitchenette. Ben followed. "The hallucination stood right here and started saying awful things; things I already felt about myself like how I was worthless and had made you run away. I was so scared and I was crying and I tried to slash out at him with the knife. I thought I even nicked him because I could have sworn there was blood on the knife. The thought of hurting someone scared me and I clearly remember, or I think I remember, dropping the knife. It was so hard to tell between the hallucination and what was really going on. Then, just before Marcus and Jamie got home, he convinced me the only thing to do was to kill myself, that everything would be better for everyone else if I wasn't around. He said I could sleep and I would no longer feel the pain."

"And that's when you cut yourself?"

"I guess," she said.

"You guess?"

"Ben, I honestly don't remember cutting myself. I could have sworn it was the hallucination that did this." Laurie held out her forearms. "I don't remember the feel of the knife in my hand doing this, just the pain of the cuts. As I started bleeding the hallucination faded away and Jamie came in a few minutes later. I spent the next month in the psych ward at the hospital."

"Did you tell them what you just told me?"

"Yes, but everyone just assumed I was crazy. I thought I was doing so well but I guess I didn't realize how bad the rape affected me. That's when I asked Marcus for the cameras; I just didn't trust myself."

There was something unsettling about Laurie's account of her suicide attempt. He had no expertise when it came to mental illness or how the human brain reacts to a traumatic situation but after everything Laurie went through, he thought that her trying to kill herself still seemed like an extreme response. It was probably wishful thinking, wanting Laurie to not be so messed up mentally after the attack. But like he pointed out to her, that was three years earlier and she hadn't tried anything like that since.

The rest of that Saturday was restful. Laurie seemed in a lighter mood, albeit exhausted, after relieving herself of the final two topics under her name on their mental list of things to discuss. Ben spent the afternoon preparing the apartment for painting while talking with Laurie about innocuous subjects like the weather and what to have for dinner but in the back of Ben's mind, he replayed Laurie's suicide story over and over.

Chapter Thirty-Six

Ben's Turn

Ben stood back and looked at the paint job; the yellow brightened the room considerably. He moved all the furniture back and cleaned up the brushes and roller. Laurie was over in Ben's apartment. She tried to help but the fumes were getting to her. He took the extra paint and all the painting accessories down to the basement, grabbed the pitcher of iced tea he made earlier, and went to his apartment. Laurie sat on the couch, gazing outside and it was a few moments before she realized he was there.

"You're deep in thought," he said and handed a glass to her. "Tea?"

"Thanks. I was just thinking."

"Noticed that," he said and kicked off his paint splattered Chuck Taylors. He desperately needed a shower. Although overcast, the temperature was in the low 90's and he kept Laurie's windows opened while he painted. His apartment was nice and cool though, but he still stunk. "What are you thinking about?"

"Everything and nothing," she replied with a sigh. He grinned; it was a saying he heard come from her lips ever since they were little kids. Ben hopped in the shower and after pulling on fresh jeans and a t-shirt, picked up BBQ for their Sunday dinner per Laurie's request – barbecued ribs and chicken, broasted potatoes, coleslaw, and cornbread. For dessert they fixed ridiculously large hot fudge sundaes and sat on the patio to watch the gorgeous sunset. It was a good day. So far, two out of the three that holiday weekend.

Laurie woke Ben up just past three that morning. He had given her his bed while her apartment continued to air out and he chose to sleep on Marcus and Jamie's couch. "Ben," she said and poked at him with her good hand. "Someone's banging on the door downstairs," her voice was slightly panicked. He quickly sat up and listened; there was definitely the sound of a heavy fist on the front door of the café.

"Stay here," he said and pulled on his jeans so he wouldn't have to confront whoever it was in his boxers. Ben made sure he took his cell phone with him and followed the banging. The auxiliary lights were on but just to be safe, he hit the switch for the main lights also. He entered the code to disarm the alarm and disengaged the two deadbolts. When he opened the door just a few inches, he kept his foot in front of it in hopes of keeping whoever it was from barging in. The minute the middle aged man opened his mouth, Ben knew he was dealing with a drunk.

"Hotel," he breathed into Ben's face.

"Nope, try four blocks to the south," Ben directed. The man's choice of inebriate was beer and lucky for Ben, something he hated. There would be no desire to drink after breathing that stench in.

"Which way's south?" slurred the man.

"That a way," he pointed to the right.

"Thanks, man." Ben watched as the man stumbled away and nearly biff it off the curb. He must have been part of a group as several other gentlemen about the same age spilled out of DaVinci's Bar across the street and surround the man. They were all plenty happy but moved on down the street without incident.

Ben found Laurie sitting on the kitchen stairs after he locked back up.

"Who was it?" she asked.

"A very happy man," he replied and sat down next to her. "His buddies came to his rescue."

"Did you have drinking buddies in Panama City?"

"Nope," he replied. "I preferred just the quiet company of me and Jack Daniels." Apparently, it was time for his final topic.

"Just like your dad."

"Yup, just like good old dad." Ben felt a heaviness come over him. Now it was his turn to talk about something dark and he wasn't sure if he could. In one day Laurie was able to talk about both her rape and then her suicide attempt and now he was finding it hard to talk about being a drunk, certainly the least of the three evils. Laurie didn't think she was very strong but of the two of them, he believed she was definitely the strongest.

"You don't have to talk about it right now," Laurie said, mimicking a phrase he said many times over the last few weeks when she was struggling. They sat on the stairs, in the semi-darkness, for several minutes while he tried to gather the courage to speak. When he did, his voice was quiet and low.

"I took that first drink knowing that it wouldn't be the only one."

"When did you start?"

Ben swallowed loudly; he really didn't want to answer that question. He was so nervous all of a sudden. His meetings weren't like this. They were strangers; it was easier to talk to them. This was Laurie. He felt her take his hand. Tears were surfacing and he was having a hard time keeping his breathing even. Finally, he remembered that he had his cell phone with him. He put it on speakerphone, accessed his voicemail, and played the message he saved for five years.

"Damn it, Ben. Please, I'm begging you. Come back to Memphis." Jamie's stern voice cut through Ben. *"Laurie's asking*

for you. What do you want me to tell her? Should I tell her that you don't give a shit about her anymore? I know you left her, asshole, I was there at the fight but I also know you. I know you'll never not be in love with her. For a week she's been begging for you. Stop being a fucking chicken shit and come home now." He took several deep breaths; he was shaking.

"It was so easy to just drown the pain away in a bottle," he said sadly. "It numbed me, helped me forget what I had done, or so I thought. When I sobered up, the pain was back and worse. After a few months I knew that drinking wasn't the answer and I joined AA but that lasted for only a couple months."

"How long did you drink then?"

"Nearly three years but when Jamie asked me to be part of the wedding, I knew I needed to be clean for that and have been sober since April of last year." He pulled his latest AA sobriety chip from his pocket and handed it to her. She looked at it closely, ran her fingers over it, then gave it back.

"But you almost drank back in July."

"Yes," he said, frowning. Someone else must have told her about that as he had never brought it up out of extreme shame.

"But you didn't," she said. "That took something right there."

"If you say so."

"And you're still going to meetings."

"Yes, I have to," he said. "And before and after each meeting I listen to this message." Laurie asked him to replay the message and he complied. Halfway through it, Laurie deleted it. He felt like a piece of his heart was ripped out, leaving him speechless. That message had become so ingrained with him that he couldn't imagine not having it around to listen to in those weak moments.

"We're moving on, Ben, and that message doesn't help." It was still shocking that she did that but he knew she was right. "Now, tell me about Mei." Ben groaned. This was a different kind of difficult. This was just damn embarrassing.

"I can only say I'm sorry about that," he said, hoping to get off easy but Laurie was a woman after all.

"I don't fault you for sleeping with her when you were drunk," she said. "I know how Mei works but when I overheard you two talking in the alley she said that you weren't always drunk." Now Ben was just darn uncomfortable.

"It truly was only once," he admitted. "I was low, very low, and she came across like she always has."

"As loose as a greased up pig," Laurie noted. In a different situation he might have laughed but now was not the time.

"To put it colorfully," he said. "I'm not proud that I did it and yes, I could have stopped it. It was just a very poor decision on my part. I was so down and she was saying all the right things and it happened. I wasn't drunk and I tried to avoid her whenever she came around down in Panama City afterwards. She finally took the hint and I hadn't seen her for nearly five, maybe six months until that day I started in the café."

"Thank you for being honest about what went on with her," Laurie said. Silence fell over the stairway and Ben knew that it was time to introduce his other self. She knew of Ben the Drunk; now it was time for Ben the Addict.

"There's something else I need to tell you," he began. Nausea rolled his stomach and he wondered if he would make it through his heroin story without needing to vomit.

"What is it, Ben?" His heart raced and he forced himself to take several deep breaths. How was he going to tell her? This was worse than talking about the drinking. "Ben?" As he had done several times to her, she used her index finger to swivel his head so that they were making eye contact. Laurie's blue eyes were full of concern. He focused for several minutes on them and slowly felt a pool of confidence grow in his gut. It was small but enough to get him started.

Ben stretched out his left arm and ran his fingertips over the needle scars. Laurie reached out and ran her own fingers over them. "About halfway through my three year drinking stretch, I started shooting heroin," he said. His voice sounded tinny in his ears and his heart continued to race.

"Heroin?" Laurie repeated.

"Yes," he replied. The nausea continued to build and the small pool of confidence quickly disintegrated.

"I don't know what to say…" she began but to keep from puking on her and the stairs, he ran into the bathroom of Laurie's apartment and started vomiting. There was little in his stomach at that time but the bile needed to come out. His knees wobbled and he sunk to the tile floor. Sweat rolled off his face and it felt like his heart was on the verge of pounding out of his chest. Laurie's bare feet came into his view but he didn't dare look up at her.

"Ben," she said softly and he heard running water. It was a struggle for her to get down on his level. He kept his gaze away from her as she wiped his face with a cool washcloth.

"I'm a drunk and an addict, Laurie," he said, his voice weak with shame.

"And I have to have help to tie my own shoes," she countered. Ben didn't mean to but he laughed at what she said.

"God, I'm sorry," he quickly said and tried to stifle another laugh bubbling up. This time when it came out, Laurie laughed along with him.

"Don't you get it, Ben? We're just meant to be together." She reached out her hand and placed it on his check. "We both screwed up five years ago by not talking to each other and now that's all we've done. We even hit a little rough patch but…" Laurie looked a little hesitant. "I think it's worked," she said. Ben felt his shame melt away and relief quickly replace it.

Chapter Thirty-Seven

Leap of Faith

"So now what do we do?" he asked.

"I thought what we've been through the last five years changed us and I think it did but not as much as I thought after all the talking we've done the last few weeks. I realized we're pretty much the same. It's just that our troubles are heftier but I think we understand where we are each coming from. At least, that's the way I feel."

Ben thought about what she said and it made sense.

"You're right," he agreed. "But the question still remains. What now?"

"Move back in with me," Laurie said her answer so fast that he asked her to repeat it. "I know it sounds rash but it's like the next logical step, Ben. We've talked and talked and talked all summer long and we're nearly talked out. We've hit everything we needed to hit. You've said nothing to cause me not to trust you even with that fight in June. Even telling me you were addicted to heroin doesn't make me not trust you. I feel you've been nothing but truthful with me. Now I need to see your actions, to see how we cohabitate together. That's where I feel I've changed the most, because of the rape and stroke and how that left me physically. If we can't live together then I guess that makes the decision for us."

"We would just be friends if that's the decision?"

"Yes," Laurie said slowly. "But I love you too much. If we can't be together again, I don't think I could have you around. I hate that it's an all or nothing decision but that's what my heart is saying."

"All or nothing," he repeated. He closed his eyes and tried to envision them as just friends. He could do it but ultimately, it was Laurie that needed to have the comfort. "Okay," he said. "I agree."

Laurie asked him to move his stuff right then and there even though it was so early in the morning. She sounded nervous about the whole thing and frankly, he was so nervous he thought he might puke again. By the time the sun was coming up his clothes were put away in the same few drawers he used before, his toiletries sat on the glass shelves just as they did since the day he moved in at age eighteen, and the two footlockers that held his mementos were under the bed.

"Well, that's that," he said and sat on the bed. He was now officially exhausted. Laurie stood several feet away and looked very unsure of herself all of a sudden. "What's wrong?" he asked and went to her. She looked so scared in the t-shirt that he recognized was his. Had she been using it as a nightshirt the last five years?

"I don't know," she replied her voice a little emotional. "I'm a little scared all of a sudden." Tears began to roll down her cheeks. "I'm afraid this isn't going to work and now that you're back, I don't want you to go." She was voicing the concern he had. He wrapped his arms around her and held her as tight as he dared.

"You've come a long way this summer, Laurie. It's been a little scary all along but you've done fine so far; we both have. This is a big step and I would be concerned if you weren't a little scared. I'm scared too and for the exact same reason." He held her face in his hands. "We'll never know if we don't try but I promise, Laurie, to do my best to make this work. Understand?" She nodded. He continued to hold her face as he leaned in close. The kiss, the first one since the one he had given her in the hospital and she was unaware of, was nice and simple. There were no expectations in the kiss, no request for anything more. It was just a good first kiss. "Now, we've been up for a couple hours and I know I didn't get all the sleep I wanted. Why don't we try and get a little more and we'll see where Labor Day takes us. Okay?"

"Okay," she said quietly and he saw that she was blushing. Ben led her to the nook where the double-sized brass bed sat with its soft sheets and vintage summer comforter. He pulled off his jeans and they each slipped into bed on their usual sides. They lay facing each other. Ben was sleepy but he also wanted to look at her in the pale light of the single antique wall sconce that lit the intimate space. With the tip of his finger, he traced the scar that travelled across her face.

"It's ugly," she said.

"I don't see it like you do, Laurie. It doesn't bother me. I see you and not the scars. Besides, you never cared about my scars." She scooted closer and lay her head down on his chest. He breathed in the scent of her shampoo and he recognized the familiar scent of peaches; the same scent he breathed in for so long. He hadn't realized how much he missed it until that very peaceful moment.

"Do you remember the day The Old Man gave his permission for us to move in together?"

"Like it was yesterday."

"He was right, you know, we are perfect for each other. Our scars, they connect us." Laurie was quiet for a few minutes. "I don't want to grow old alone, Ben, and I don't think I could trust anyone else with my secrets."

"I know that feeling," he admitted. "We've known each other for so long, been connected for so long, I just don't think I could start over with anyone else."

"You said it perfectly." She laid her palm on his cheek and leaned over for a kiss. He returned it and there was just the slightest bit of something more in it but it was Ben that scooted a few inches away; he didn't want to make Laurie uncomfortable.

"I don't know how long it will be before we can..." Laurie's voice trailed off and she sheepishly looked up at Ben.

"Hasn't this all been about baby steps?" he asked quietly.

"Yes," she whispered back.

"And baby steps we'll continue. I don't want to mess anything up at this point. You've told me what happened when you were kidnapped and I'm sure that is something that is extraordinarily hard to overcome. I haven't pressured you about anything yet and I'm not about to start now. As I've said many a time, when you're ready."

"Thank you," she said and they snuggled back together. Ben reached up and pulled the chain on the sconce. Within a few minutes, they were both asleep.

*

They woke up at ten but spent another hour just lying in bed. Although asking Ben to move back in with her had been spur of the moment, the decision was not. That's what kept her up two nights earlier; she needed to know if she could physically trust him and the only way for that to happen was to have him move back in. If she didn't have him move in right then and there, she was afraid she'd talk herself out of it. It was a big step but so necessary. Laurie was nervous and she could tell that Ben was also but it needed to be done.

"What should we do today?" Ben asked as he tickled her nose with the end of one of her braids. She couldn't help but laugh.

"I would like to go back downstairs and try to cook something." She missed being in the kitchen. The kitchenette in the apartment was empty of any food and besides, she liked the feel of the café kitchen. Even though it took forever for her to make them breakfast earlier, it felt so good to cook again. It made her feel normal, something she hadn't felt in a very long time. "What would you like to do?"

"Figure out how we're going to tell Jamie that we're living together again."

"Cooking sounds like more fun," she replied.

"Agreed but aren't you a little concerned with how Jamie will react?"

"Are you?" Laurie looked at Ben but he couldn't make eye contact with her. He seemed uncomfortable and sat up on the edge of the bed, his back to her. She kicked herself for forgetting how Jamie went slightly off the deep end and hit Ben in the basement when she found out about Laurie forgiving him. He had his usual reaction to being hit and Laurie realized that he was anxious about telling Jamie out of fear of what she might do. It was so sad. But then he had fought with her and Jamie had managed to not be angry with Ben. Would this situation do the same?

Laurie sat up and clumsily moved over to Ben. There was no window in the nook and she didn't want to talk to Ben in the dark so she turned the sconce on. The soft light illuminated Ben's bare back and the site of it after five years took her breath away. His back, muscular from years of manual labor and construction, was crisscrossed with a variety of scars. Some were long from the belt while others circular from whatever Lem Polniacek was smoking. There were some scars that she didn't know what caused them and Ben wouldn't tell her. Those scars seemed to upset him the most. She reached out and placed a hand between his shoulder blades. Instinctively, he stiffened.

"Sorry," she said and meant it. "I forgot." Ben never liked to have his back touched. She scooted closer to him and instead of reassuringly touching his back, she squeezed his shoulder. "I don't think Jamie will be too mad, Ben. She's seen how we've worked over the summer; she knows we've both been talking to Marcus. Her anger went away after we fought in June. Will she be ecstatically happy for us? Maybe not, but I think she'll be smart enough not to overreact."

Ben rubbed the back of his neck but didn't say anything for several minutes.

"Let just not jump out at them when they get back and announce it," he suggested in a tense voice. "Let's just see if we can work it into the conversation naturally."

"Sounds fine by me, Ben, whatever you're more comfortable with." The moment the words were out of her mouth, she regretted them and explained herself so he wouldn't grow irritated with her. "I'm not trying to be how I usually am," she said quickly. "This isn't a case of me being unable to answer a simple question about what I want. In this case, because of how you reacted to Jamie when she hit you, we'll do this how you want to, so you feel safe and comfortable. You take the lead on this. Understand?" She gave his shoulder another squeeze and he finally turned around and looked at her. The tears rimming his eyes rattled her but she kept her calm; she needed to. Ben needed her to.

"Thank you," he said and put his hand on hers.

"You shower first," she said, wanting their day to get going. She wanted to move forward with Ben. "I take too long now. You can read the paper while I'm in the shower. All I ask is that you leave me a little hot water."

*

Ben was almost finished with the paper when Laurie exited the bathroom. The queen of the five minute shower was now barely able to make it out in twenty-five minutes and she still had wet hair and needed to get dressed. He watched inconspicuously over the top of the paper as she sat at the small vanity table and struggled to run the comb through her wet hair with her non-dominant hand. She then split the two sides of her hair and began braiding. Ben now realized why she wore two messy braids the last couple of days instead of the usual one; it was just easier for her as she struggled with raising her right arm. Apparently, Jamie was the one responsible for the single braid.

She finished with her hair, grabbed some clothes from the dresser and disappeared behind the curtains of the nook. After a few minutes she reappeared wearing a pair of worn jeans and a simple pink t-shirt, her favorite color. Around her neck was the locket he gave her; he since learned that their pictures were still inside of it. She carried her socks and a pair of running shoes and sat on one of the straight back chairs. Just the usual morning routine seemed to have exhausted her.

"Do you miss running?" he asked before he had time to think if that was a smart question to ask. She didn't seem to mind the question, though, as she worked her socks on.

"Yes," she replied simply but didn't elaborate. Laurie slipped on the running shoes which were already tied. He now knew from her admission in the bathroom that the shoes were not tied by her so it was one more thing that Jamie must do for her. He assumed that some of the physical aids Jamie provided would soon be his responsibilities. Although awkward at first, he would not shirk away from the added responsibilities. He was certain that they were what Laurie was testing him on. Many, many years ago they planned to grow old together and knew there would be a day where they might need to help each other through physical limitations; he doubted either of them thought that would happen before the age of 35.

Laurie hesitated at the locked door of the apartment. She'd been doing well all weekend but now her hand shook as she touched the top deadbolt. Ben noticed her face had grown pale and a slight sweat shone on her brow. She backed away and covered her mouth with her good hand.

"We can stay in the apartment," he offered. "It's okay." She shook her head in the negative.

"No, I have to do this," she said and she reached out again. Laurie insisted that all five deadbolts be locked that early morning after the incident with the drunk and Ben obliged. It now took her a full five minutes to gather the strength to undo each one.

"How are you doing?" he asked when she unlocked the last one.

"Nervous, but okay." She took a moment before opening the door. The journey to the kitchen was long; the usual minute on a slow day trip took them ten but Ben was there with her for every step, giving her reassurance and support. "Thank you," she said and sat wearily at the worktable. Laurie looked defeated and Ben didn't like that. He'd been back for four and a half months and the strides she made in that time were phenomenal.

"Laurie," he said and stood right in front of her and put his hands on her shoulders. "You did great. You probably don't think so, right?"

"Right."

"But you did. Can you do me a favor now?"

"Of course."

"Believe me, okay?" She looked so unsure of herself so he leaned over and gave her a kiss, a big one, and it did not go on one sided. He regretted breaking the kiss after several moments but he had a point to make. "You know I don't throw affection around lightly but would you have accepted that kiss a few weeks ago when you were still too afraid to come downstairs?"

"No, god, no," she said with a severe shake of her head.

"See how much you've progressed?" Laurie did seem to be thinking it over and after a moment or two, a smile appeared. He pecked her forehead with a quick kiss. "Now, I don't know about you but I'm hungry."

That night, Ben and Laurie sat on Marcus and Jamie's couch and listened to stories from the Bailey family weekend. Of course Davy was a hit but both Jamie and Marcus were glad to get back home; they looked tired.

"What happened around here this weekend?" Jamie asked after Marcus returned from taking the sleeping Davy to his room.

"I cooked," Laurie said and Ben smiled at the pride in her voice. "Just some scrambled eggs and later grilled cheese and…" She got to her feet and left the room.

"Cooked?" Jamie questioned.

"Yes," Ben answered. "Downstairs, in the café kitchen." Jamie's mouth hit the floor.

"Seriously?" both Marcus and Jamie asked in unison.

"It was a good weekend," he said simply.

"What is she doing now?" Jamie asked, leaning over to look out the door of the apartment. Of course Ben knew, Laurie wanted to make a little show of it, but he promised not to say a thing.

"Just wait," he said and did his part of the show by grabbing four plates and forks. Ben began to worry a little the longer they waited but soon he heard her slow footsteps on the stairs.

"I made my pound cake," she announced and set it down on the coffee table next to the plates. When the cake cooled that afternoon, Ben had wrapped it, still in the pan, in a large towel so she could carry it up the stairs easier. She looked so proud of herself and he gave her a big smile. She leaned over and gave him a kiss straight on the lips. The room grew awfully silent and Ben dared to look over at Jamie. Again, her mouth had hit the floor. Even Marcus seemed shocked. Ben felt a strong urge to vomit but he refrained. Instead, he manned up using Laurie as an inspiration. With a deep breath, he took Laurie's hand in his and began.

"Laurie asked me to move back in with her and I did," he said, hoping his voice sounded more confident than he felt. Marcus was the first to react.

"You've both done a lot of work this summer," he said. "As a friend, I'm happy for you both. Professionally, all I ask is that you keep talking to each other and to me. We'll keep Ben's old apartment open in case you two need a few days apart."

"Thank you, Marcus," Ben said. That was a good idea; one he hadn't thought of. He turned his attention to Jamie. She had a very blank expression on her face but it slowly faded into one of happiness. Ben felt so relieved.

"As long as you both know what you're doing, I support you," she said.

Chapter Thirty-Eight

Optimism

A new mood fell upon Sunset Park Café that autumn that even seemed to extend into the neighborhood. Baby Davy brought a much needed smile and hope of rejuvenation to the neighborhood but it was the renewal of Ben and Laurie's relationship that brought hope to a neighborhood that had seen its fair share of pain. Ben and Laurie were the epitome of that pain both as children and as adults. Hurt by those that should have cared and nearly killed by those unknown, it was a core group of individuals who worked together to drive out the unseemly and welcomed those with gentrification plans. There was a stipulation, though. Sunset Park still needed to be affordable for families. It was, after all, a family neighborhood. This wasn't going to be a neighborhood for uppity folks thinking they were "saving" the downtrodden.

And so the houses that saw better days were either torn down or fixed up and the empty lots either designated for green spaces, like the lot where Laurie's house used to sit, or for family friendly new housing. With the increase in construction, Ben was offered a job with the construction company the gentrification committee hired. He was torn, to be honest. Marcus and Jamie offered him a place to live when he needed a place and he did enjoy working in the café but he was also a man who liked to work with his hands. After discussing it with Laurie, he chose to move back into construction. Jamie and Marcus were completely fine with his decision. It was nice to have the extra set of hands for a while but they were used to running the place as a quartet.

Ben was engrossed into this new routine by the end of September and he felt happier than he had felt in a very long time. Since he was working in the neighborhood he would run back to the café for lunch with Laurie. She progressed to the point where she would help out in the kitchen during the small late breakfast rush and prep for lunch. Her actions were slow and methodical but her assistance acted as physical therapy and her movements became a little easier. Laurie could do this in a section of the kitchen that couldn't be seen from the main dining area. Mrs. Bailey's group knew that she was back there but no one else; that was a request from Laurie. By the time Ben arrived for lunch, she was starting to tire out and after eating at the small 'chef's table' Marcus set up in the kitchen, she would retire to the bedroom nook to nap while Ben went back to work.

They would eat a late dinner with Marcus, Jamie, and Davy and then spend the evenings talking on the patio if the weather was nice or in the apartment watching TV if not. Teddy would still come by on Mondays with a movie and a pizza. Bedtime came early where they would lie close together and whisper about more private thoughts. It was Laurie who would bring up their intimacy. She was worried that he expected more out of her in that department.

"Hush," he would say and put his fingertip over her lips. "You know where I stand on that and I wish you would stop worrying about it."

"But…"

"No buts," he insisted and pulled her into a reassuring hug.

Her bad days seemed to be a thing of the past. Now, that's not to say she didn't have frustrating days when her body was clumsier than normal or she seemed to plateau again in regards to her progress. By the end of September, she wanted to move beyond the doors, the actual doors of the café. Every Sunday they tried as she wanted to take a look at the neighborhood she grew up in. Ben would tell her of the changes and she showed a lot of excitement but when it came to taking a step outside, she couldn't. Ben began to dread Sundays because it was hard for him to see how frustrated and upset Laurie became. Five years earlier this caused him to run but he was done running and although it was tough, he stayed by her side.

He took those Sunday challenges and did his best. As soon as he was back from the first Mass of the day, she made the attempt and broke down in his arms and he held her, comforted her, told her that she was still a strong woman and reminded her how far she had come. "There will always be another Sunday to try," he would tell her and wipe her tears.

"You're getting mushy on me." She would then laugh. Laurie didn't give up and on November 1st, the dull day after All Hallows' Eve, Laurie stood outside in front of the café. It was early on a beautifully clear day. The air was crisp but Ben knew that the chill in the air wasn't the reason why she was shaking.

"I am so proud of you," he said with misty eyes and gave her a kiss. The passion returned in it from Laurie surprised him and from the look on her face afterwards, she surprised herself also.

"I have you to thank," she said later that afternoon on the patio. "If you hadn't come back, I would still be locked in the apartment."

"But if I hadn't gone in the first place…"

"Ben, no." She looked at him with knowing eyes and dropped his argument. Despite having received her forgiveness, the guilt he felt would sometimes still surge strongly within him.

On Thanksgiving, Laurie sat down at the large table in the café for the traditional dinner. In addition to Ben, Teddy, Marcus, Jamie, and Baby Davy, there was Louis and his new girlfriend; Cassie (who finally cleaned her act up and completed rehab), Callie and her fiancé, and finally Mrs. Bailey and her beau, who owned the hardware store. Laurie was nervous and stayed quiet but she never panicked or ran upstairs. And afterwards, instead of standing in front of the café, she and Ben took their first walk together in the neighborhood in well over five years.

Christmas came and New Year's Eve fast approached. Despite the successful Thanksgiving dinner, Jamie did not anticipate that Laurie would be ready for the annual to-do and neither did Ben. She was still in baby step mode and the difference between a few close friends and many was just too much for her.

"I just want to spend the evening with you," Laurie said a few days before when he broached the subject with her. "Plus," and she said this sheepishly, "I'm afraid something will happen and I'll panic and be back at square one."

"Then we won't push it," he said.

When the ball dropped in Times Square, Ben and Laurie shared a very passionate kiss and sipped sparkling cider. They kissed again, just as passionate as before, and Laurie did something that surprised him. In his ear she nervously whispered her request, then took his hand and led him towards the bed. He stopped just before they got there.

"Are you sure?" he asked her, his stomach fluttering from nerves and the upcoming possibility. She nodded her head in the affirmative. 2009 began with gentle love and Ben hoped that was a good sign.

Chapter Thirty-Nine

Downward

January continued optimistically but then February came and something began to happen. They no longer took walks on Sundays and by the end of the month, she stopped coming down to the kitchen. When he came for lunch, he would take a tray up just like he did in those early days. When she began locking the deadbolts, all five during the day, that was when Ben decided to return to work at the café so he could be more available to Laurie.

"Maybe we took those baby steps a little too fast," he said one chilly March evening as he held her on the couch. She was still dressed in the same flannel pajamas as two days earlier and her hair was not even close to being contained in the braid he fixed for her on the same day. Laurie didn't say anything in reply and the more he thought about it, the more he realized that she hadn't said much all day. She was grouchy and cross looking. The new TV was on but the volume muted and all of a sudden she threw the remote across the room. It clattered against the door to the patio and fell to the wooden floor.

"Laurie, what's going on?" he asked gently but all she did was bury her face in her good hand, her right one lay limply in her lap.

Something was definitely up. "Laurie?" Ben reached out and carefully moved her hand and tipped her head up "What's wrong?"

"I don't know, Ben," she sobbed, "and it scares me."

The next day Laurie continued to be in that bad place and Ben went and talked to Marcus. He was concerned and so was Jamie.

"Has she been this bad before?" he asked them during the morning lull. Ben kept staring at the open cabinet and the monitors. Laurie was still in bed; he'd been unable to talk her out of it that morning

"Once," Jamie said somberly.

"Just once?" Ben asked.

"April, four years ago. Right before she tried to kill herself."

*

Ben's nerves were at their limit as he thought about what Jamie said. The last time they saw her this bad was just before the suicide attempt. His was so engrossed in his thoughts that even the whistle of the teakettle didn't shake him and it wasn't until Jamie snapped her fingers in front of him that mentally he came back to the kitchen. He moved the kettle from the fire and went in search of the teabags. With the weather colder, Laurie was back to drinking hot tea throughout the day. Usually Jamie took care of this so she could visit with Laurie but Ben decided to do it that day. He needed to be with her more; he needed to make sure she was okay or, at least, not harming herself.

"Not that tea," Louis said as Ben pulled out the box of orange pekoe that he always used for her tea before. "Here," he said and handed Ben a small paper bag. He recognized the label on it as it coming from the tea and spice shop owned by Mei's aunt and uncle. "And you'll need this." Louis handed him a tea ball.

"Fancy," Ben murmured and proceeded to go through the motions. He wound the small chain around his finger and lazily bobbed the ball up and down in the hot water. Ben was tired; Laurie kept him up all night. It was the second night in a row. The pattern was eerily similar to the last suicide attempt. As the tea steeped, he ran the story she told him over and over in his mind. *Most of the time she wouldn't stay long; she was actually delivering that tea I like from her aunt and uncle's store. We'd talk a little while and then she'd leave but by the end of March I started to get more nervous and paranoid. It was like this fog would come over me and I just wanted to hide in the sleeping nook. I couldn't sleep or eat. I was miserable.*

Then it hit Ben and he let the chain unwind and splash into the pot. "Louis, when did you guys start using this blend for Laurie's tea?"

"Middle of February." Ben frantically thought back to when Laurie seemed to get worse. "Mrs. Zheng brought it over."

"It can't be," he said aloud.

"Can't be what?" Louis asked but Ben was already charging his way upstairs with the bag of tea. Marcus was just closing the door to Davy's room. He put his index finger to his lips and then pointed out towards the patio. It was cold but Ben's anger provided plenty of warmth.

"What's up? You look like you're out for blood."

"I may be," he said, his anger bubbling up quickly. "I know this is going to sound paranoid but I'm serious when I say this." He held the brown paper bag up to his good friend. "Is this the same kind of tea that Mei would bring to Laurie in those weeks leading up to the suicide attempt?" Marcus took the bag from Ben and read the label.

"Yes, I believe so. Mei brought it from her aunt and uncle's shop. Why?"

"She just started to drink this again a few weeks ago."

"I'm not following."

"It's the tea, Marcus. Something is in this tea and I think it's affecting Laurie's mind. She keeps telling me she doesn't understand what's going on and it's scaring her because she doesn't feel like she's thinking right. I think that whatever is in this tea might be causing Laurie to lose her mind." Marcus sat down on one of the Adirondack chairs. He seemed to be angry and Marcus was not one to become angry easily.

"Dad has a few buddies in the police department who still owe him favors. Even though he's dead, they said if I ever needed anything, just to give them a call."

"Do you think one of them can get this tea analyzed? If they find something, then we know for sure it's not Laurie."

"It could just be something odd they put in the tea that she's reacting with," Marcus followed through with Ben's thought. "Or it could be some drug that was added. I don't know, Ben; I know Mei's done some questionable things but I can't see her purposefully drugging Laurie, do you?"

"Marcus, I never told you this but it was Mei who gave me my first hit of heroin. She was my drug dealer down in Panama City. Mei is very capable of doing what we suspect. That first time," he started and found himself rubbing the crook of his elbow. "I was just drunk enough not to care what she was doing. All it took was one hit and the pain I had been moaning about went away."

"It's hard to believe but it makes sense, I guess," Marcus ventured. "After the suicide attempt, Mei never came by for a visit and no tea was delivered." A few black birds flew at breakneck speed over them and swooped into the alley below. "Should we tell Laurie?"

"I don't know. I think because of the seriousness of this that maybe it would be better for us to wait."

"I agree," said Marcus.

"I know it sounds odd but I almost hope they do find something and that means Laurie's mind isn't so damaged, I guess."

"I'll call my dad's buddies right now," Marcus said and stood. "The sooner we figure this out the sooner we can help Laurie. Until then, let's just watch her and keep her safe."

Later that afternoon, Ben knocked gently on the door to their apartment. "Laurie? It's Ben." He used the keys from the kitchen and unlocked each dead bolt. The apartment was strangely bright;

the curtains, which had been closed for the last several days, were all pulled open and every window in the place along with the door to the patio was wide open. The day was chilly, barely making it out of the forties with a stiff northwest wind. Even the air conditioner was running on high. It was frigid in the apartment. "Laurie?" he called out. He forgot to check the monitor in the kitchen.

"I'm here," Ben heard her call out in a small voice that came from the corner near the bedroom nook. He found Laurie sitting on the floor in the corner with her knees drawn up. She looked awful with deep circles beneath her eyes. When he came closer to Laurie, the frightened look on her face shook him hard. She was shivering uncontrollably.

"Laurie," he said, trying to keep his voice gentle. "It's too cold to have the windows open like that. And why do you have the air conditioner running? You're freezing," he noted and grabbed the quilt from the bed. Wrapping it around her, he first went and closed the windows and turned the AC off before picking her up and sitting her on the bed. He sat behind her and put his arms around her to try and help warm her up. "Why is it so cold in here?" For a brief moment, he wondered if it was a suicide attempt.

"I was afraid to fall asleep," she said, her teeth chattering. "I thought if the apartment was cold enough, I wouldn't fall asleep. I'm so tired but when I close my eyes I'm afraid I'll see him."

"Him?" Ben asked stupidly.

"The man who hurt me," she said and began to cry. "I'm so tired but I'm so afraid to sleep."

"I'm here now, Laurie," he said and held her tightly. "I'll keep you safe; I always will." Laurie whipped around faster than he had seen her move since his return to Memphis. It was slightly startling, especially with the wild look in her eye.

"Promise me, Ben," she said and grabbed at his shirt with her good hand. "Promise me you'll keep me safe."

"Of course, Laurie; I promise to keep you safe." She broke down again and he pulled her against him. Ben spoke softly to her, stroked her messy hair, and reassured her but in the back of his mind he worried about how she was going to react if those test results came back positive.

Eventually, Laurie lost the fight and for twelve straight hours she slept. He stayed with her the whole time, dozing on and off. When she woke up just past three in the morning, she allowed him to help her take a bath and change into fresh pajamas. After braiding her hair, he fixed grilled cheese sandwiches, Laurie's favorite, using some provisions Jamie dropped off earlier in the evening. She also wanted tea and he was glad to oblige using plain old orange pekoe.

Chapter Forty

Shattered

Laurie kept them prisoners in the apartment the next day; not allowing Ben to leave and relying on Marcus or Jamie to bring them food. Ben hoped that whatever was in that tea would soon work its way out of her system and after three days, she did seem better. There was less paranoia and she could sleep without nightmares. All five deadbolts still needed to be locked twenty-four seven and Laurie startled so easily.

On the fourth day, Marcus knocked on the door. Laurie slept peacefully on the couch and Ben was frankly going a touch batty in the apartment that seemed to grow smaller every day.

"Where's Laurie?" Marcus asked in a quiet and guarded voice.

"On the couch, asleep," Ben replied with an equally quiet and guarded voice. "What's up?"

"Detective Nolan just dropped by," he said and peered past Ben towards Laurie. "They got the test results back."

"And they found something," Ben said, reading the somber look on Marcus's face.

"Yes, they found that the tea was laced with a cousin to belladonna. Less fatal but when steeped, as in tea, it causes confusion and hallucinations."

"Son of a bitch," Ben growled.

"I told him about Mei and he was going to go find her."

Ben looked back at Laurie. She looked so peaceful; he didn't want to tell her about the tea but knew he had to.

"Ben, I also gave Detective Nolan Laurie's chef's knife. I had it locked up in the safe. That night after we found her, Jamie wouldn't come upstairs until I cleaned everything up. I just stuck it in a plastic bag and put it and the rest of her knife set in the safe. I was in such a hurry and I never washed the blood off." Ben thought about what Marcus said and remembered how Laurie insisted that the hallucinations seemed so real. "If they find someone else's blood, then…"

"Then she didn't cut herself," Ben finished the sentence for Marcus. "Someone else did."

"She's been so insistent on that all this time."

"I have to tell her," he said. His stomach was a knot of nerves. He had a feeling that Laurie wasn't going to take the news well even if it did confirm that she wasn't going crazy.

"I'm going to get Jamie, just in case," Marcus said and Ben nodded in agreement. He decided not to stall; the sooner he told her, the better.

"Laurie," he said and sat on the edge of the couch. He gently touched her face and she sleepily opened her eyes.

"Hi," she said with a smile. It was such a delicate smile that he knew would soon disappear.

"I need to tell you something," he started. Laurie's face grew concerned and she clumsily sat up.

"What's up? What's going on?"

"Have you noticed that you're doing a little better the last couple days?"

"Yes, it's been a relief. I'm still a little fuzzy but not like I was," she admitted. Ben let out a big breath and took both of Laurie's hands in his.

"The tea you were drinking…"

"The special blend I like," she clarified. "Are we out? I noticed you've just been using regular tea the last couple days."

"I have been and there's a reason why, Laurie." He paused for a moment and forced himself to look her in the eyes. "Do you remember the last time you drank a lot of that blend?" She cocked her head in confusion.

"What?"

"The last time you had that tea, do you remember when that was?" She shook her head in confusion.

"I think it's been awhile," she stammered. "What does… What's going on?"

"The last time you drank a lot of that blend was in the weeks leading up to your suicide attempt. I asked Marcus about it. Try to remember back, weren't you acting the same way." Laurie's face crinkled in thought and she seemed almost to not understand what was going on.

"The tea… it was making me crazy?"

"It was a theory I had so Marcus called in a favor to one his dad's friends. They tested the tea and found it was laced with something that causes hallucinations and confusion." Ben held his breath waiting for a reaction. It didn't take long. Her breathing began to accelerate and she was shaking.

"Someone did this on purpose?" she asked in a fearful voice.

"It looks that way," he said slowly. Tears dripped down her face and she scrambled to her feet.

"Ben… Ben…" Laurie stammered and she looked around the apartment in a panic.

"Laurie," he said calmly and approached her slowly. "Try and calm down."

"That could mean…" she tried to talk but her rapid breathing was making it difficult. "Ben, I always thought that someone else was in here with me that night. No one believed me."

"I never said I didn't believe you," he replied, trying to be supportive.

"Ben, I thought that person who was in here… who I thought I cut with my knife… I thought that was my rapist." The words sucked the breath out of Ben. *Her rapist?* She was backing herself against the wall and completely losing it.

"Calm down, Laurie," he said, focusing, and again tried to pull her in tight for a hug but she was having none of that.

"He was in here… He was in here…" she said over and over and struggled against him as he tried to hold her. "I need to get out of here." She looked around, scared and confused.

"Where do you want to go?" Ben asked and helped guide her towards the locked door of the apartment.

"Just get me out of here." She was so uncoordinated in her panic that he picked her up after unlocking the door. Jamie and Marcus appeared at the top of the stairs.

"What's going on?" Jamie asked.

"Can we go in your apartment?" he inquired and was opening the door before they even gave their consent.

"Lock the door, lock the door," Laurie begged as Ben put her down. As soon as he turned the deadbolt, Laurie's panic increased tenfold.

"There's only one lock," she cried and limped to the door where she began hitting it with her fist. "One lock! He'll get in!"

"Laurie," Ben placed his hands on her shoulders but she jumped and backed away from him. Her eyes were wild and jumped from Ben to Jamie to Marcus. Sweat rolled off her face and her breathing became more erratic. She bumped into a small table, causing a vase to fall and break. This caused her to jump again and she looked around the room wildly as if trying to find somewhere safe.

246

"Please calm down," Jamie begged and tried to approach her but this only caused Laurie to scramble away. Ben saw an opening for just a moment as she wavered on her unsteady feet and he quickly wrapped his arms around her. She fought him hard and with as much force as he dare, he pulled her into an embrace, pinning her arms to her side. She fought against him but it was what needed to be done. He pulled her down to the floor and began talking to her in soft, calming tones.

"Laurie, you're safe. I'm here; I'll protect you." She continued to struggle despite his attempts to calm her. Finally, Marcus approached with a syringe and within moments of administering what Ben assumed was a sedative, Laurie went limp in his arms. It took him a moment to catch his own breath.

"Oh, my god," Jamie whispered and Marcus gave her a hug. There was a heavy, stunned silence in the room.

*

Despite being over a head taller than him, Marcus struggled. Ben's muscles more than made up for the difference in height. "You can't go in," Marcus tried to reason with Ben. "The rules are different on the psych ward."

"She can't be alone," Ben said in a tortured voice.

"She's too out of it to know she's by herself." Ben managed an elbow to Marcus's gut, stunning him just enough to release Marcus's arms that were holding him back. Ben ran to the door of room 417 and turned the handle. The door did not open. Because this was the psych ward, all patient doors were locked.

"Let me in!" he yelled down the hall towards the nurse's station but no electronic clicking came from the heavy metal door. Marcus and Doc both gave strict instructions not let Ben in the room; he was just too emotional after Laurie's mental break. "Son of a bitch," he growled and his anger came to a head. With considerable force, he punched the chicken-wired window of Laurie's door and then ran off down the hall and out of the ward. Marcus let out the breath he was holding and ran his hand through his hair. The last twelve hours were rivaling some of the worst around Laurie's abduction and suicide attempt.

"Where's Benji goin'?" Doc asked as he came down the hall.

"I don't know," Marcus replied. "He's angry about not being able to stay with Laurie. I've never seen him this angry before."

"We'll need to watch that boy," Doc said in a serious tone. "He's teeterin' on that wagon of his again." Marcus knew Doc was right; seeing Laurie completely flip once was bad enough but when that initial sedative wore off, the reaction was twice as bad and Marcus had no choice but to sedate her again and take her to the hospital.

Jamie sobbed as she signed the commitment papers while Ben begged her not to do it. They verbally raged at each other for the better part of an hour in a storage room as the nurses settled Laurie into the simple room in the psych ward.

Jamie finally rushed out of the storage room in tears and Ben began to pace in front of Laurie's locked door like a caged tiger. Marcus had never seen his close friend so angry and when he tried to talk to him, all he did was shoot glaring glances at him and clench his fists. Marcus stayed with him for three hours in the hall outside of Laurie's door until he knew Ben was at his breaking point. He tried talking to him again but it eventually disintegrated to a point of physical contact. And now Ben had run off in anger and frustration.

"Go after him, Marcus," Doc advised. "I've seen that look before. He's headed straight for a bottle. Laurie's restin', there's nothin' more you or Jamie or Benji can do for her here right now. I talked to Teddy and he's goin' to come by and watch over her."

Marcus was more worried about Ben turning to heroin instead of whiskey and he made several slow drives through the entire neighborhood looking for Ben but saw no sign of him. No need to check the bars; those in the neighborhood were closed that time of the early morning. After another drive through Sunset Park, including a quick trip into the next neighborhood over that was known for its drug problems, Marcus returned home.

"Did you find him?" Jamie asked. Her eyes were red and puffy and Marcus realized that she probably did more crying in the last twelve hours than she logged all her life.

"No," he replied and gave his wife a huge bear hug. She started crying again and he held her until she stopped.

"I'm so scared for them both," she said.

"So am I, Jamie."

Chapter Forty-One

Lost and Found

The next day was Sunday; the best possible scenario for the situation, at least gossip-wise. It was an off Sunday for the café so there wouldn't be the surge of Sunset Parkians wanting to know the latest in the Ben and Laurie saga. Jamie could sit with Laurie at the hospital and Marcus searched for Ben with Teddy joining him after the last Mass. Davy spent the day with his grandma.

Marcus sent a handful of texts to a few people he could trust to be on the lookout for Ben. He didn't say why, but he knew that those he trusted were smart enough to figure it out without broadcasting his troubles all over the neighborhood. By late that Sunday afternoon, there was still no sighting of Ben.

"Maybe we should have let him stay in her room," Jamie suggested.

"I think seeing her all drugged up would have been worse," Marcus countered. "This is different than when she was in the hospital for the fever." Laurie was still heavily sedated; just like with Marcus, each time they allowed her to surface from the sedation, she flipped. As her primary therapist, he tried to talk her down but she was locked into the nightmare of that night she was cut, the night that no one had believed her story.

"How long do you think this is going to last?" Jamie asked and dabbed at her tears.

"I can't say," Marcus replied dully and he decided to take a page out of the honesty book that Ben pushed with Laurie. "There's a chance she may never recover." Jamie looked at him in utter shock.

"No," she whispered and he caught her as her knees buckled. It was time for her own mental break but unlike Laurie's, Jamie's took the form of a really good cry in the same storage room where she and Ben screamed at each other.

They stayed until visiting hours were over, then slowly drove through the neighborhood. Ben wasn't in any of the bars or stumbling drunk through the streets that they could see. Jamie even went to Mei's aunt and uncle's house and asked if they had seen him in case he was finding solace with their niece. They said that they would call Jamie if they spotted Ben and then gave her their promise of prayers. It was about the only thing left to do.

They were crushed on Monday as news spread. Jamie could rely on the business to take her mind off of her troubles, but they were so great this time that she eventually sent Callie to the front of the café while Jamie cried in the kitchen. She was an emotional wreck and worked herself up so much she began vomiting in the bathroom off of the service entrance. It didn't help when Sassy Cassie swung by the café and suggested that maybe Jamie was pregnant again.

"That's not even funny," she sneered at her sister-in-law but eventually relented in allowing Cassie to go buy a pregnancy test. It came back positive. "Son of a bitch," she uttered as she read the stick. She just assumed the missed periods lately were normal but she guessed she was anywhere from six to eight weeks along.

Despite the heaviness of the day, Marcus seemed genuinely happy about the news when Jamie broke it to him that night after he returned from another tour of the neighborhood and bars. He held her tight as she broke down again from all the stress. Eventually, she found a tiny bit of happiness in the baby news.

Tuesday broke with dull April sunshine and a depressed spirit in the café. There was no sign of Ben and Laurie had a bad night. Teddy stayed with her the entire night and reported to Marcus that they needed to increase the amount of sedatives. "She's bad," Teddy warned him. Even the customers coming into the café were somber.

"Do you think he left town, like he did before?" Callie ventured as they sat around the worktable in the kitchen that afternoon. The café was empty; the afternoon lull a welcome period for all.

"No," Jamie replied with confidence and Marcus agreed with her. "Ben worked too hard to get Laurie back; he wouldn't do that."

"Then where is he?"

"I don't know," she eventually said before going to throw up in the bathroom.

The situation seemed to get grimmer as each day passed. Although they were finally able to wean Laurie from the sedatives, she was lost within herself and unresponsive. She was close to catatonic and Ben was nowhere to be found. Marcus filed a missing persons report and Jamie made arrangements for Laurie to be transferred to a private mental hospital just outside the city.

Two weeks passed since Laurie had broken down and Ben had disappeared. Laurie was now settled in the new facility, but she showed no indication of emerging from the world of her own private nightmares. Doctors tried a variety of medications, but nothing helped.

Jamie visited her every day but she didn't know if Laurie even knew that she was there. A little piece of Jamie's soul seemed to die every time she saw the condition her best friend was in.

Even with the missing persons report, no one saw Ben despite all the people from the neighborhood who were actively looking for him. Jamie had no idea where he had gone.

Ben's truck was still parked in the alley. When Jamie went through his things, she found nothing that might offer a hint of his whereabouts. Jamie knew that Ben was scary angry, angrier than that day of the funnel cloud or when they fought in that storage room on the psych ward and she recognized his father in him. This pained Jamie and she worried what he was up to. She could not bear to think her worst nightmare, that Ben might be dead.

She kept the café going, of course, but even there she could find no joy in the place.

"How are you doing?" Marcus asked one night on the patio. Davy was asleep and Jamie needed fresh air. The day was warm but the night was refreshingly chilly.

"I don't know," she replied honestly. "I just can't believe what's happened in just the last two weeks." If she had any more tears left, she would have let them go at that moment but she had none left.

Marcus looked up at her cautiously and said "I spoke with Detective Nolan today. They found a second blood type on Laurie's knife."

"No," Jamie whispered. She was starting to put all the parts of that night together. "So it is true. Someone was in the apartment that night and that person cut her. She didn't try to commit suicide after all. And none of us believed her story!"

"It was probably supposed to look like Laurie tried to kill herself," he said. "And it wasn't a random person. The DNA from that blood matched the DNA taken from Laurie's rape kit. The same man who raped her, tried to kill her again that night."

"And Mei was behind it all," Jamie deduced dully.

"It's looking like that. The police have been searching for her, along with the man who raped Laurie, but she's in the wind too."

"Do you think Mei and Ben are together?"

"You're kidding, right? Not if Ben could help it," Marcus said. "But I worry if she found him while he was drunk. Maybe Mei and her pal kidnapped Ben the same way Laurie was taken."

"Why? How?" Jamie asked, confused and more than a little scared.

"Mei's the one who got Ben hooked on heroin when he was in Panama City Beach and now that her dirty little secret is out, she may be looking to..." Marcus didn't have to finish the sentence because Jamie was thinking the same thing he was. The situation was no longer just sad; the danger level was off the charts.

"Fuck," she replied and felt her anger towards Mei, her former friend, flare. "If I ever see her again, I don't know what I'll do."

"I'm afraid of what Mei will do, Jamie. Detective Nolan reopened Laurie's case and he is stationing a plain clothes policeman in the café for the foreseeable future. He also has someone watching the place when it's closed. Laurie is safe because she's in a secure facility, but I am so scared for Ben. Mei is the one who is insane here and if she has Ben…"

They sat in silence for several minutes. Neither could speak as the horror of the possibilities swirled through their minds.

Suddenly, the silence was broken from the muffled sound of metal trashcans being jiggled in the alley behind the cafe.

Jamie gave a huge sigh. "What now? Raccoons again?" Jamie asked as Marcus looked over the side of the patio.

"Yeah," he said, looking too tired to even care and sitting back down next to Jamie. The volume of the silence began to increase slowly.

Finally, she looked at her husband. "Why, Marcus? Why did Mei do this? Honestly, is it really because Ben chose Laurie over her so many years ago? I just can't believe it's that simple. Is she so insane that she just can't get over that?"

"I don't know, sweetie. We all handle rejection differently."

"I know she had a crappy childhood, but so did Ben and Laurie, but you don't see them trying to murder anyone! It just makes no sense."

Marcus was silent, perhaps consumed by his own fears and said nothing in reply. They continued to sit in the dark, each lost in their own thoughts.

Jamie rubbed her forehead; she wanted to try and make some sort of sense of what was happening. She gave herself up to the silence again.

Marcus's cell phone rang causing Jamie to jump. "Hey, Teddy," he said as he answered the phone quickly to stop the silent night from breaking any more.

Jamie watched carefully, her fright increasing from the look on her husband's face. His words and quick movements scared her even more.

"Are you sure? Okay, I'll be right over."

"Marcus what is it? What's the matter?" Jamie stood up also.

"It's Ben. He's at St. Anthony's and not in good shape. I'm sorry, I don't know much more than that, but I have to get over there as fast as I can." He gave Jamie a hug and a quick kiss. Just before flying out the door, he stopped, turned back and looked worriedly at his wife. "Make sure all the doors are locked after I leave. Lock them and then double check that they're locked. Check the windows, too. I'll call you as soon as I can."

*

St. Anthony's was located in the exact center of Sunset Park. It was the only church in the neighborhood; if you weren't Catholic you had to commute out of the neighborhood to worship. The entire circle of friends was baptized at St. Anthony's and, of course, Teddy had returned to serve there after his ordination.

Ben and Laurie held exact opposite views when it came to their religion. It was simple: Ben believed, Laurie didn't. They still managed to make their life work despite their spiritual beliefs.

Marcus parked the Jeep and ran to the back of the church where Teddy said he found Ben.

"Where is he?" Marcus asked Teddy who looked definitely unpriest-like in his torn jeans and faded Sunset Park High sweatshirt.

"In one of the basement wells," he explained and led Marcus towards one of the brick wells found around the basement windows. Most, but not all, were covered with barred gates. "I was taking the garbage out and heard the sound of breaking glass. I figured it was probably one of our homeless regulars. The last person I expected to find was Ben. He's pretty wasted and well, come see for yourself. He looks like hell."

The recess that was below a stained glass window in the basement wall went approximately three feet below ground and was about five feet wide. Ben was hunkered down in the corner, curled in upon himself like a cornered animal. His belt was wrapped around his upper arm and he was trying to use a hypodermic needle but his hands were shaking so bad, he couldn't do it. Blood dripped from Ben's dirty arm attesting to several missed jabs. Marcus hopped down into the well and knelt next to his best friend.

"Ben," he said gently, putting his hand on the shaking arm. "No more." It was actually easier than he expected to take the needle from Ben's hand. Teddy's description of Ben's condition was spot-on. To say that Ben was very wasted was an understatement. Not only did Marcus's best friend smell, both of booze and filth, Marcus thought his friend was on a quick path towards death.

"Let's get him inside," Teddy told Marcus. "I've already called Doc." Between the two of them, they managed to get Ben out of the well and into Teddy's quarters. Ben was in no condition to put up a fight.

In the light of Teddy's bathroom, Marcus got a better look at his friend. Ben still wore the same t-shirt and jeans that he had been wearing the night that they brought Laurie to the hospital two weeks earlier. They were filthy. He had scratches that were barely visible now that there was a matted beard covering his face and neck. Ben's head was no longer bald and his hair was longer than Marcus had seen in several years. He recognized Ben, but at the same time he didn't appear to be the same man he had known his entire life.

"Marcus…" Ben slurred heavily. "My fault… everything."

"For falling off the wagon, yes," Marcus replied. "For Laurie's break, no," he said kindly.

Marcus and Teddy stripped the filthy clothes from Ben and opted to toss them instead of trying to wash them. Even Teddy had to admit that Ben's clothes were beyond salvation. The two friends spent nearly an hour struggling with Ben but finally, they got him naked and into a hot bath. It was painfully obvious from his physical condition that either Ben had used a lot of drugs over the past two weeks, or someone had used the drugs on him; his arms were covered in fresh track marks. Eventually, the two men were successful at removing the filth and smell. Marcus got Ben into Teddy's bed. Doc came by and pronounced that Ben was high, drunk, and lucky to be alive, a diagnosis that both Teddy and Marcus already knew.

"He'll not be feelin' much for a few hours," the old doctor drawled sadly after taking note of his vitals. "By all accounts, Ben should be dead, and I suspect that's what he wanted."

The trio of men who had seen so much together, gathered around a small table several feet from the bed in Teddy's apartment and stared at their mutual friend, a friend who had already been through so much.

"Marcus," the old man said quietly, as if he didn't want to disturb his patient. "I called in a favor. They're holdin' a bed for him in the rehab wing of the same hospital where Laurie's at. I'm not sayin' he needs the psychological part of the place, but to be honest, I think it wouldn't do him any harm."

Chapter Forty-Two

Disgraced

The curtains were shut tight in Teddy's apartment; any bright light was still bothering Ben even late into the afternoon. Despite his disappearance and fall back into the bottle and needle, Jamie was not angry with him. Marcus had shaved him and Jamie almost wished he left Ben all hairy. He looked awful: thin, gray with a hangover and lack of real sleep, somber. *Sad*. He sat with his head in his hands, trembling. Withdrawal was beginning and they would be leaving soon for the hospital. The washed out blackness of the old long-sleeve tee that Teddy had given him seemed to fit his mood perfectly.

Jamie brought him a cup of coffee and a sandwich from the church kitchen. He barely acknowledged her and didn't touch the food but finally he picked up the mug. His hands were shaking as he sipped the bitter liquid.

When Jamie looked at her friend, she was filled with such sadness that she was at a loss for anything meaningful to say and said the only thing that came to mind. "I'm pregnant again."

The news seemed to get through Ben's fog. He mulled the news and finally looked at her with his bloodshot eyes.

"Congratulations," he said. His voice was thick with so many emotions that she didn't even try to figure out which one led the parade.

"Thank you," she replied and reached across the table for the hand not wrapped around the white mug. "Ben," she said and tried to keep her emotions out of her voice. "We're with you in this. We're not giving up on you."

Ben gave her a surprised look and pulled his hand from hers. His gaze dropped and she recognized the emotion on his face – shame. What she said next she was sure of; it came straight from a conversation she and Laurie had around Christmas.

"Ben, I think of you more like my brother and not my cousin. I don't like to see you in so much pain. You've got to fight now, for both yourself and for Laurie. She would not be ashamed or angry with you for taking another drink or even another hit." Jamie was confident in what she was saying.

"Laurie knew how tough sobriety was for you even as you two fixed your relationship. She told me how you often spoke of the fear you had of the urges you fought, despite the meetings and talking with your sponsor. She expected you to succeed but also, she was prepared if you slipped she would be there to help you heal."

Ben did not acknowledge her words. He listlessly drained the rest of his coffee and asked that they leave for the hospital.

Jamie slipped her arm around his waist as he unsteadily walked out of Teddy's place.

Marcus was already at the facility explaining what had happened to a mute Laurie.

On the half-hour drive to the country hospital, Marcus texted Jamie. *No response. Still bring B by to see her.* Jamie wasn't sure if it was a good idea for the two of them to see each other but it was the only request Ben had when they told him he was going to rehab.

The facility was a peaceful place. The pain of the patients was muted in the healing atmosphere. For the second time in a month, Jamie signed commitment papers for someone she loved. It was decided that Jamie make all medical decisions for Ben until he was in a better frame of mind. He had no disagreement with this. It was not a job that Jamie relished. When he received his patient bracelet, Ben was given a wheelchair and then Marcus pushed him to towards signs with arrows that pointed towards the mental health wing. Marcus already prepared Ben for what to expect. Basically, Marcus told Ben to expect nothing.

*

He stood just inside the door of Laurie's sparse room. With the exception of a bed and nightstand the room was empty. At least the walls weren't padded, although with the way he felt emotionally, he would have felt more comfortable with himself if he was locked in a padded cell.

Laurie was curled up on her side on the bed; her back to him. She was dressed in a pair of pink pajamas and her long, brown hair was loose, startling for Ben to see even after so many years together. Seeing her in this facility, a facility where he was also now a patient, was worse than seeing her in the ICU. At least in the ICU there was a hope that she may get better. Marcus explained that neither he nor her other doctors knew whether or not she would snap out of her silence. It was something Ben couldn't even think about. At that moment, all he wanted to do was see her.

There was a time when a situation as painful as this would have caused him to run, but no longer. He slowly approached the bed and knelt next to the side of it. Reaching a shaky hand out, he smoothed her hair from her face. Laurie's blue eyes were... different, her gaze so totally empty.

"Hi, Laurie," he said in a whisper and moved his head so it was in the line of her gaze. For several minutes he looked at her and she at him but he didn't know if she actually saw him. He leaned over and gave her a kiss on her forehead, then the tip of her nose, and then her lips. When he sat back on his heels, Ben noticed her tears.

Chapter Forty-Three

Healing

By the end of May, everyone was caught up in a new routine. Jamie and Marcus opened the café every Sunday for both brunch and Sunday supper. The extra money earned needed to go to Ben and Laurie's rehab. They brought in Cassie, who wasn't so sassy anymore, to help and as soon as the lunch rush ended, Jamie would head for the hospital every day. She wondered if Doc knew exactly what he was doing when he finagled a bed for Ben in the same facility as Laurie. Slowly, as Ben and Laurie were allowed to spend time together, she began a slow emergence and by the 4th of July, there were times when she would respond, although without voice.

Ben came through detox in one piece and worked hard during his various therapy sessions. Marcus and Jamie attended the family sessions on Saturday afternoons during the lull and returned on Sunday evenings, with Davy, for a family visit. There was hope by the end of July, when Laurie began to speak, that they might both be released by Labor Day. It was a strange setup, even for the facility. Ben and Laurie were being treated as individuals but at the same time, they were being treated as one. The doctors believed that their individual success depended on their combined mental health. Or so Marcus tried to explain to Jamie one night. All Jamie knew was that the sooner they were back under the café's roof, the sooner everyone could move on.

The case against Mei and the one against Laurie's rapist grew cold again. There was no sign of either of them. This came as no shock since both had arrest warrants out on them and would obviously be in hiding.

As long as Ben and Laurie were in the secure hospital, the plain clothes officer was removed from the café along with the night watch of the place. Detective Nolan felt that Mei's beef was strictly with Ben and Laurie and until they returned to the café, there was no need for the added security.

Marcus added more locks to the front and back doors of the café and everyone just became a little bit more vigilant - everybody was a "little" more vigilant except for Marcus, who remained a lot more vigilant. He kept a close watch on his pregnant wife and double-checked that every lock was secure before he retired each night.

The time came to explain to Laurie about everything Mei related. The decision to wait until she showed improvement was made by Marcus. The doctors at the hospital were not surprised when she regressed into silence again after being told the truth. Even with that silence, the explanation was deemed a success since she did not completely revert back to her near-catatonic state. Labor Day arrived but, despite the highest hopes of the doctors, only Ben was deemed well enough to leave the facility.

Ben worked half days in the café and after lunch, drove his truck to the hospital for afternoon visits with Laurie. He always stayed through dinner to share the meal with her. The remainder of his evenings were filled with visits to Teddy and AA and NA meetings. Jamie constantly worried about both Laurie and Ben, but Ben honestly told her that the urgency for a drink or a hit no longer controlled him. His goal in life was to see Laurie back home. It was that goal and that goal alone that made him get through every day. Jamie tried to talk to him about Mei and what she did, but that was one thing that Ben would not talk about.

Marcus told her not to push it and she didn't.

The newest member of their family, Grace Laurie Bailey came into the world on a beautiful November morning and when they sat down in the café for the family Thanksgiving dinner two weeks later, Grace was joined by her godmother, Laurie.

The mental breakdown left a lasting effect on Laurie that everyone understood. Even though she managed to return to helping out in the café kitchen just past New Year's, she no longer ventured outside the doors of the café. She spoke to no one outside the immediate family and she still had those gray days when she felt unable to stray from the safety of the apartment.

Strangers were not allowed in the café kitchen. Even so, if there were too many stragglers after the rushes, when Laurie would come down to help, she would often retreat back upstairs.

When April approached, everyone was on edge. April had become a month to be dreaded, but nothing happened. The month came and went without incident and that spring, Sunset Park was glorious.

Chapter Forty-Four

Suicide

Summer refused to close down but no one minded as the improvements in the neighborhood and café made up for the dog days that stretched into late September. The optimism that pervaded the neighborhood when Ben and Laurie reunited returned and even Laurie spoke more. It seemed to Jamie that she saw hope in people's eyes. Things were changing for the better once again and people, especially those living in the café, slowly allowed their guards down. The result was disastrous.

It was a sweltering late September evening and the café was busy for a Monday night with people looking for somewhere cool to hang out until their own non-air conditioned domiciles cooled down. The eight-ish closing time was moved to ten-ish. Jamie, along with Laurie, who had even moved a bit past her fear of a full café, began experimenting with the restaurant quality ice cream machine that Marcus purchased for the café.

"What's wrong with just chocolate?" Ben asked after taste testing their latest gourmet flavor that sounded more like a main course than just a dessert. "We're not a fancy place, ladies.

Chocolate, vanilla, strawberry will go a whole lot further with our clientele than whatever this is."

"Laurie, I think he's telling us he doesn't like it," Jamie said and laughed. Laurie also laughed and Ben couldn't help but smile at her; she had come through some very dark times and was now actually happy. It made his heart glow. He also had moved beyond his own darkness and happy would be the perfect adjective to describe himself also. Despite everything, there was a sense of serenity with Ben and Laurie.

"That's exactly what I'm saying," he said in all honesty. "Chocolate. That's all I'm asking for. Is that too much?"

"We'll see," Laurie quietly kidded him with a glimmer in her clear blue eyes. "Now, be a good boy and take the trash out."

"Only for a kiss," he countered and was rewarded with a very promising smooch. "The sooner I take the garbage out, the sooner we can go upstairs," he whispered in her ear and although she blushed a deep red, she also gave him a thumbs up.

He slung two bags of garbage over each shoulder and walked into the thick humidity. The alley was ripe; garbage pickup was the next day and all the shopkeepers were playing the dumpster game as they filled up their own and began using their neighbor's. It was actually all in good fun but between the smell, the humidity, and the promise of spending time with Laurie, he wasn't in the mood to find the nearest dumpster with enough space. But he wasn't going to be rude and just dump the bags like some did. He finally found space in the dumpster belonging to the bookstore at the end of the block.

His steps were light as he made his way quickly back towards the café's service entrance. Those steps were halted though, by a voice that he honestly hoped he would never have to hear again.

It was Mei.

"You..." she slurred. Mei looked like hell; hair all mussed, clothes dirty, and a look on her face that would have intimidated the devil. "You had to figure it out, didn't you?" Ben's hand went to his back pocket but his cell phone wasn't there. Too late, he realized that he had left it up in the apartment. It had been a while and he'd grown complacent in Mei's absence. He needed to buy time, try to get to the service entrance, but Mei was between him and the door. "I thought you both would have done what I was hoping to do to you, but no, you both had to go and get better."

Ben's breath was lacking and it took everything he had to make noise with his voice. "Why, Mei? Why did you try to kill Laurie three times? Why couldn't you have moved on from you and me? That was so long ago." Mei laughed; a hardy, guttural laugh. "Don't flatter yourself," she said as she took a swig from her flask. "I got over that a long time ago,"

Ben tried to move towards the café's service door but Mei pulled a gun from her purse. Ben chose wisely to plant his feet where he stood.

"Then why?" he asked. He had to buy time. The longer he stayed in the alley the more likely someone would come looking for him. He knew Laurie. He may have become complacent, but Laurie's vigilance had never waned and he hoped she would send someone to find him. The alley was a place she would not go, a place she feared.

"Because, you two survived," Mei sobbed and took another drink from her flask. It must have been empty because she tossed it aside. Just like that night so long ago, the noise of something hitting his truck, this time a flask, was loud. "We all had shitty lives growing up but you two were the golden children, plucked from hellacious homes and given a second chance while some of us had to scrape our way along. You had each other; you had support. I wanted that; I wanted to feel safe in someone's arms."

"You're crazy, Mei. Laurie and I still had to struggle; we're still struggling to this day."

"Shut up!" she screamed. She was loud which was good. If he could get her to scream some more, maybe someone would hear what was going on. He never had a chance though. Out of the corner of his eye he saw a movement and then an intense pain in his lower back followed by another to his left shoulder and as he tried to turn to defend himself, the third strike of the knife entered to the left of his stomach. The final stab was dead center to his chest. He stumbled backwards and collapsed. His ears rang from the sound of a gun going off twice.

The humid night air began to suffocate him and he tried to hold on to the face of Laurie in his mind. She hovered there and seemed to be so real. He reached out to it but his arm felt heavy. *Hold on, Ben* Laurie's voice said and he felt something on his face. It was soft, like Laurie's hand. Her face came closer as the humidity slowly darkened his vision. Ben could smell peaches and he was certain he felt Laurie kiss him. It had to be a dream. Or death. Laurie didn't go into the alley so she couldn't be there, could she?

Chapter Forty-Five

Faith in a Promise

Laurie was doing her best not to panic in the waiting room. Ben had been in surgery for nearly six hours. Doc was trying to find out any information he could while Jamie and Marcus were hunting up coffee. Teddy sat with Laurie in the small room but she couldn't find her voice to say anything. Instead, she focused on Ben. His eyes, his voice, his laughter, his kiss. She had to focus on them; she had to remind herself of them so she wouldn't forget. He lost a lot of blood; the man who stabbed him, her rapist, knew where to go with the knife and the ER doc already prepared Laurie for the worst.

Please don't die, she silently begged the image of Ben in her mind. *You can't.*

The door to the room opened and it was Doc; his face concerned. "They're still workin' on him, darlin'."

Laurie nodded her understanding and gripped the hem of her blood-stained t-shirt tightly. Jamie and Marcus returned but Laurie wanted nothing to do with the sludge they brought back with them. Another wave of tears came and Jamie rubbed her back reassuringly. Six hours turned into seven and then eight. Both Doc and Teddy left to attend patients in their respective rights but Marcus and Jamie stayed, of course.

The awful scene kept playing over and over in her mind. She heard screaming coming from the alley and recognized Mei's voice. She tried to yell for Marcus and Jamie but couldn't get her voice out and ended up tossing several pots and pans on the floor to get their attention. As soon as she made the cacophony, her heart forced her into that alley just as Ben was stabbed by the man she recognized as her rapist. Mei shot the rapist and then turned the gun on herself. Both died in that alley but all Laurie could see was Ben lying in a pool of his blood. She stumbled to his side, held his hand, kissed him, begged him to hold on. He kept his gaze on her as the sirens closed in but was unable to say anything. Laurie told him she loved him and Marcus had to pull her away from Ben as the paramedics began their work. He was going fast and they scooped and ran with him. Laurie pulled herself up into the back of the ambulance. If Ben was going to die, she had to be there.

But he held on until they got to the ER and they rushed him into surgery. Then the long wait began. Finally, the door opened again and a surgeon entered in sweaty scrubs. His face did not convey a lot of hope. Ben lost a kidney, his left lung was damaged and collapsed; both his liver and stomach were punctured. Although the knife missed his aorta, there were several other blood vessels severed. The worst was the fact that his heart had been nicked. The irony was not lost on Laurie.

"Will he survive?" Jamie dared to ask as if she was reading Laurie's mind. After all, she had been stabbed nineteen times compared to his four. The length in the doctor's pause scared her.

"The damage is serious; he's in critical condition." the doctor said somberly. "We'll get a better picture of things if he makes it through the day." Laurie felt like she was slapped and her knees buckled. Marcus caught her and helped her down onto the plastic couch. She was shaking and her thoughts were so jumbled in her mind she couldn't think straight. Her breath seemed to be lost.

"Laurie, are you okay?" Jamie asked and Laurie felt her best friend start rubbing her back again.

Laurie nodded and took a moment to compose herself. Finally, she found her voice and looked up at the doctor. "Can I see Ben?"

"He's sedated. We'll probably keep him that way until we know more."

"I don't care. I have to be there for him."

The doctor sighed. "Only one visitor at a time," he said and gave her his ICU room number. She hoped the fact that he was in the same room she had been in for the fever was a good sign. Jamie and Marcus accompanied Laurie up to ICU and stood with her as the nurses were taking care of a few last details.

"Do you want me to stay here, Laurie?" Jamie asked.

"No, I'll be okay," she replied although she didn't feel okay. "You have the café to worry about."

"Laurie, we're worried about you and Ben. We'll stay."

"Maybe just for a little while," Laurie acquiesced.

"Of course," both Marcus and Jamie said.

"We'll wait out here," Marcus said and indicated to a few chairs lined up against the wall. Laurie took a deep breath and walked into the room. Her legs still felt like rubber, especially her right one, but she did her best not to collapse.

"Hi, Laurie," the nurse said quietly and Laurie recognized Lurinda. She waited until the nurse left to walk around the curtain and get her first look at Ben.

It was a shock and her feet remained planted on the tile floor. Ben lay flat on the hospital bed, a central collection point for wires and tubes and mechanical noises. A machine breathed for him while a soft whir drew Laurie's attention to his upper right arm as his blood pressure was automatically checked. Soft mechanical heartbeats gave her a tiny amount of hope as they indicated his heart was still beating. He wore no hospital gown; a simple white sheet lay over him. White bandages, covering the long incision to crack his chest, peeked out from the sheet. His arms lay still next to him. A tube emerged from under the sheet near his left chest and a vile-colored liquid meandered down to a container under the bed. Several IV lines snaked into a central line bringing him fluids, medicines, and blood but despite all the mechanics, it was Ben's paleness that caused the lump that caught in her throat the most.

Somewhere deep down, a strength she never felt before burst forth and Laurie managed to force her feet to move. Standing next to the bed, she reached out a shaking hand and gently placed it on his cheek. The lack of color and how chilly he felt conveyed to Laurie how close he was in his dance with the grave.

She took several deep breaths through tears but kept one hand on his cheek and then painfully moved her right hand to carefully grasp his. She squeezed it and leaned as close as she could to his ear. "I'm right here, Ben," she whispered. "You just concentrate on getting better and I'll worry about everything else." A giant sob bubbled up but she fought hard and kept it in. "I love you so much, Ben. You can't die on me. Please, please don't die. You promised to always keep me safe and you can't do that if you die." As carefully as possible so as not to disturb or dislodge any of the tubes and wires helping Ben stay alive, she gave him a gentle kiss on the cheek.

And so Laurie's bedside vigil began. That first week was bad. They had trouble keeping his blood pressure up despite transfusions and he went back under the knife three times for more internal bleeding. The doctors gave Laurie very guarded timelines in hours instead of days. They kept him sedated into the second week when the damage to his liver kept him barely hovering in this world. They even tested Jamie in case Ben would need a partial liver transplant but by the end of that week, his liver was looking up. The third week, though, brought pneumonia and the focus switched away from the knife wounds. It was both Doc and Teddy who sat down with Laurie at sunset on a Thursday, four days after diagnosis, to gently but bluntly talk with her.

"He is not going to die," she said simply.

Ben struggled through the weekend and Laurie refused to be in the ICU when the rest of Ben's family came to see him after being called by Jamie. Laurie was livid with Jamie for doing this, especially after Jamie asked Teddy to performe Last Rites.

"It's like you're telling him it's okay to die!"

"Laurie, no…" Jamie tried to explain but Laurie walked away. Ben wasn't going to die; he couldn't. Not after everything.

She found herself wandering around the hospital until she found a quiet corner with a west facing window. The sun was beginning to set. Laurie couldn't count the number of times she and Ben sat on the rooftop patio and watched the sun sink below the horizon; the blues and oranges reflecting magically off the Mississippi. They had to have another chance at watching a sunset together. It couldn't be the end and Laurie was the only person who believed it.

And it wasn't the end. As that fourth week slowly progressed, the pneumonia receded. The doctors called it a miracle. Laurie didn't believe in miracles; she just knew that Ben wasn't going to die. He was a fighter; had been all his life. They both survived horrific childhoods and even with the severity of both their traumatic attacks, death was just not going to take them yet. They had decades ahead to look forward to, to grow old together and witness many, many more sunsets. And besides, Ben promised her that he would always be by her side to protect her and if he died, he would be reneging on that promise.

Exactly five weeks after the stabbing, the doctors began slowly weaning him off the sedation. The first time his eyes opened, Laurie cried and when he squeezed her hand after she called his name, she cried some more but on the day they brought him home from the hospital, eight weeks after the attack, Laurie was grateful. There was still quite a road ahead for them. Ben, who lost many, many pounds from his already trim body, was weak and it would be a while before he could work any type of job. There was also the mental processing to do from the attack. Just as with Laurie,

Ben's memories of what happened were slow to return and he admitted feeling a terrible heaviness about it all. Both agreed to continue talking with each other and with Marcus. This was just a new hill to climb on their continued journey towards their future together.

Chapter Forty-Six

Sunset

Although it was officially winter, Christmas Day had been warm but eventually that warmth faltered at keeping the evening chill at bay. Ben and Laurie sat on the patio in a new two-seater Adirondack bench that Marcus and Jamie gave them as a Christmas present. The aroma of fresh gingerbread and turkey stuffing still hung on the air and reminded them of the special day. After a pleasing but busy and loud day, it was nice to just sit in the quiet together and have peace. They were both tired, especially Ben, but the day was so worth it.

The café had been full of both immediate family members and close neighborhood friends; a much larger Christmas dinner than Jamie and Marcus usually put on but it was one that was also celebratory in nature. Marcus and Jamie wanted to hold it for those who supported them through everyone's trials and tribulations over the years. They would also be celebrating something no one knew about yet except for Ben, Laurie, Jamie, and Marcus. After everyone left for the day, the quartet was joined in Jamie's apartment by Teddy.

The ceremony was simple and took less than ten minutes from greeting handshake to kiss to signing the paperwork. Ben and Laurie were now married. After years of not thinking they needed those bands of gold they now wore, they decided after everything that they'd been through, it seemed a fitting testament to their survival. Ben asked Laurie a week earlier if she would marry him and she said yes without hesitation. She didn't even object to Teddy performing the ceremony.

They sat together on the patio that night as husband and wife. Laurie leaned against Ben and he tucked the blanket tighter around their legs. His hand found her left one and he absentmindedly began stroking the simple gold band that matched his. Laurie's gaze was towards the nearly sunk sun but it wasn't a focused gaze.

"What are you thinking about?" he asked and slipped his arm around her shoulders.

"Everything and nothing," she replied, her voice rough after a long day of visiting with friends and family. "How 'bout you?"

"What a nice day it was, how the evening was better," he said and kissed her wedding ring. "How I'm looking forward to our days to come." He paused and thought back to his time in the hospital, Laurie's time in the hospital, and the last six and a half years and how close he came to losing it all. "I wasn't sure if we would make it this far."

"But you did, Ben. You made it." He looked down at her. Some bad habits still crept up in both of them but not so much as before and not so much where they needed to call each other out on them. Ben gave Laurie a very long kiss and held her face in his hands as the sun dipped its final rays below the horizon.

"No, Laurie, we both made it."

ABOUT THE AUTHOR

Dana Mansfield was born, raised, and still lives in northwest Iowa. She enjoys the intricacy and problem solving of creating stories and is thankful to have achieved remission from leukemia to have the chance to see her literary dreams come to fruition. She teaches reading to at-risk high school students and spends her time writing, watching cooking and clothing competition shows, and being an overprotective mom to her two cats, Boots and Joey.